SPIRITED AWAY

SPIRITED AWAY

A No Ordinary Women Mystery

by
Barbara Deese

Barbara Deese

North Star Press of St. Cloud, Inc.
St. Cloud, Minnesota

This is for my mother, Daisy, who never missed a chance to get in on a good caper. She kept her sense of humor and her sense of adventure right up to the end.

ISBN: 978-0-87839-656-6

Cover art by Jake Karwoski, Monster of the Midwest, LLC
Author photo by Karen Belk

First Edition: September 2013

Printed in the United States of America

Published by
North Star Press of St. Cloud, Inc.
P.O. Box 451
St. Cloud, Minnesota 56302

www.northstarpress.com

North Star Press – Facebook

North Star Press – Twitter

I am deeply grateful for the encouragement and enthusiasm of friends, family, fellow writers and fans. Without you, writing wouldn't be nearly as much fun.

A special thanks to Richard Schultz, Retired Deputy Chief, Minneapolis Police Department, who was willing to share his wealth of knowledge with me.

1

Bright midday light suffused the room with a cheeriness Robin Bentley did not feel. She longed to be outside, where she imagined slipping her camera out of its case to capture the swirl of maple leaves as they fell, and the gathering at the city park of the Canada geese getting ready for their flight to warmer climates.

Instead, she was sitting in the community room of her mother's apartment building, not in itself an unpleasant place to spend an afternoon, but made so by her mother's current mood.

"Living!" scoffed Vivian Tesdale. "You call this living, shut away in a nursing home?" Her hands fretted in her lap and her steel-gray hair, Robin noted, looked lifeless. Vivian's slender frame was still agile, and except for her arthritis, she was in good health.

Some people would say she "enjoyed good health," but in her present mood, it would not be an appropriate description. Robin had always resembled her mother in stature and facial structure, and it disturbed her to envision her own skin slackening with the years and her eyes turning down at the corners.

Robin shifted her gaze to the quilted wall hanging with its colorful heart motif and sighed. She was not going to waste her breath reminding her mother Meadowpoint Manor was a "senior living community." Vivian's comfortable two-bedroom apartment was in the independent living wing, which housed over seventy percent of the residents, where she was as free to come and go as she'd been in her own house in nearby Minneapolis. Nor did she point out to Vivian that she'd moved there of her own volition after falling on the ice while shoveling her driveway two winters ago, injuring her wrist and tearing ligaments in her knee.

Vivian's own furniture filled her apartment, and her own Honda was parked in the underground garage. In fact, counting the amenities in the building, her living space included not only this community room with game tables and large-screen television, but also a sunroom, a library, a craft room, generous storage space, and a laundry. Each floor had its own dining room, where the chairs were upholstered and the tables were set with placemats and vases. Downstairs was a small convenience store, a hair salon and a coffee shop for the residents. Not only that, but Vivian could, if she chose, avail herself of numerous restaurants and stores, services and entertainment within three miles of the building. A small city park was within easy walking distance. Vivian's only restriction, as far as Robin could tell, was her despondency.

It had been years since her mother had sunk into her last clinical depression, but memories going back to her earliest childhood prodded Robin to say, "When's the last time you took your meds?" When her mother shrugged, she said, "It's time, Mom. Even if you won't do it for yourself, you have to do it for me, okay?"

Vivian glowered over the top of her glasses. She picked at a loose thread on the armchair as her eyes wandered over to the bookshelf, seemingly scanning the titles. Slowly, her head moved up and down and she said, "Fine." But before Robin could savor her victory, her mother added, "But anybody with two brain cells can see this is nothing but a glorified nursing home."

Robin made an effort to smile. Feeling, at that moment, weary enough to move into this facility herself, she rose and gave her mother a heartfelt hug before heading to the apartment to fetch her mother's prescription bottle. As she strode down the hallway, she went over the conversation in her mind, already rehearsing it for the retelling. Cate, her friend of over thirty years, would appreciate the frustrating nature of mother-daughter dynamics, and in the telling, they would both find the nugget of humor in it.

Handrails on both sides of the hallways testified to the fact that not all in this building were as able-bodied as her mother. Robin passed the extra-wide elevator and turned left, startled by the figure chugging toward her, a spry, compact woman with mauve hair. Era Dudley was something of an institution here.

Pointing a bony finger at Robin's chest and peering up into her face, Era said, "You're that junior detective, aren't you?" Her voice was brittle, as if at any moment her words might break into little shards of vowels and consonants. Without waiting for an answer, she stood a little taller and looked over her shoulder to the left, then to the right. Her voice took on a conspiratorial tone. "I have an assignment for you."

Junior detective? Her mother must have regaled the other residents with stories about how Robin and the rest of the No Ordinary Women book club had helped to solve the murder of a young woman in Wisconsin last year. *Maybe I should have kept my Dick Tracy junior detective kit*, Robin thought, remembering her badge, decoder and manual. "Okay, what's my assignment?" Robin smiled sweetly, more amused than concerned by Era's behavior. After all, the woman was ninety-six years and counting, and her general lucidity was dotted with episodes of confusion and quirkiness. She still cooked her own meals, but it was common knowledge that for some time now, she had been setting an extra place at her table for her long dead husband.

Era reached into the sleeve of her cardigan, extracting an embroidered handkerchief, blew her nose in it and stuffed it back up under the ribbing at her wrist. Planting her feet wide, she focused on Robin's face with an unwavering stare. "Something has happened to my son. He doesn't come anymore, and he doesn't answer the phone. I don't drive, so I want you to go and break him out of wherever they're keeping him." The creases in her face deepened and her eyes shone with tears.

Robin might have been amused, had the woman not been so obviously distressed. Time must pass slowly for Era, now that she had sold her home and had curtailed many of the activities of a younger person, Robin reasoned. No wonder she concocted stories like this. With her world getting smaller with each passing year, Era had likely begun fixating on her son's visits.

"How old is Winston now?" Robin asked, picking the name from her memory. She'd met the gaunt silver-haired man here on several occasions, and found Winston's visage and manner austere.

Era tilted her head. Her brows puckered. "Thirty-four, I think." She considered a moment longer. "No, wait. Is it September?"

Even as spry as Era appeared to be, the poor woman must be having problems with her short term memory and couldn't keep track of time. "I'm sure he'll come to visit you soon, Mrs. Dudley." She took Era's soft hand in hers, gave it a gentle squeeze, and hurried down the hall.

Once in her mother's nicely decorated apartment, Robin found that the amber prescription bottle, filled almost two years ago, was virtually untouched. Closing the medicine chest, she caught her reflection. It took her by surprise. Her chin length hair wasn't that different from the style she'd worn for years, but now it looked as if someone had pressed the Photoshop command that changed a color photo into a black-and-white one. The blonde had leached out of her hair, and her washed out complexion made her look as she had during chemotherapy two years ago. She hadn't looked that bad in her own mirror this morning, had she? She made a mental note to change the light bulb on her next visit to something less harsh, maybe one with a warmer tone.

Returning to her mother with a glass of apple juice and her antidepressants, she watched while she popped one in her mouth and washed it down.

A little after four o'clock, she walked with her mother back to her apartment, and left her sitting in front of the TV. Closing the door on her way out, she heard the opening theme song for *Jeopardy*, and imagined, as she walked down the hall, that it was playing simultaneously on most of the televisions in the building.

By the time she got into her car, she'd forgotten all about Era's son, Winston.

Taking the scenic route home, she meandered through Theodore Wirth Park. The birch and maple trees were magnificent in their fall glory. She pulled over to watch a group of crows—for some reason referred to as a "murder of crows," she remembered reading—behaving like a bunch of thugs as they chased smaller birds from their neighborhood of oak trees.

She considered grabbing her camera, usually at the ready on the passenger seat, and decided she had enough pictures of birds. Her most recent book of photography, *Seasons in the Woods*, had shown only modest sales, and she was beginning to think her next project should be a departure from her nature series. She'd contemplated including more artful close-ups or less text, but had yet to settle on something that excited her as much as the first two books had.

Leaving the car running, Robin used the hands-free feature to phone Cate, her old college roommate and fellow member of the No Ordinary Women book club.

Having given themselves such a puffed-up name, the five women of the book club had forged friendships that had sustained them through several years. Besides gathering each month to talk about the books they'd read and loved or not loved, they'd celebrated each other's happiest events and supported each other through more than a few tribulations. They'd also, last spring, been drawn into solving a real life murder, sleuthing about with naïve enthusiasm as if they were characters in a mystery novel. And in the process, at least in Robin's estimation, they'd begun to grow into their name.

When Robin recounted her visit with her mother, Cate listened, more quiet than usual. Robin guessed her reluctance to comment had something to do with the fact that in less than forty-eight hours, Cate's own mother, Wanda, would be arriving from Florida, and would soon become the newest resident of Meadowpoint Manor.

"Mom's not exactly the head of the welcoming committee, the way she's been acting lately. What were we thinking, putting our mothers under one roof?" Robin moaned. She was back on city streets now and traffic had picked up.

Cate's laugh was merry. "It might work out better than you think."

"I hope you're being clairvoyant right now," said Robin, only a little bit mocking her friend's uncanny abilities. "Frankly, all I see in our future is a lot of headaches."

Again Cate laughed. "I'm not seeing that far ahead. In our more immediate future, though, I do see two glasses of wine, accompanied by crostini with tapenade. In fact, if you come early, we can talk some more before the others get here." Tonight was Cate's turn to host the September book club meeting.

"I'd need to go home, feed the cats and get my book," Robin said. She sat a split second too long at a stoplight and the driver behind her, a kid who looked too young to be driving in the first place, honked and gestured with his middle finger when he passed her. So much for Minnesota Nice. "Cate, I'm tempted to pull over right here and get out and walk, just so I can kick some leaves."

"If you can get here before five fifteen, you can walk the dogs with me. We have leaves in Saint Paul, too, you know."

She glanced at the car's clock. "I think I can make it."

And she did, by two minutes. The weather was perfect. Cate had Mitsy, her patchwork dog, on one lead. Robin took Cate's black lab, Carlton, who was older and less energetic. Mitsy kept weaving back and forth in front of them, trying to herd invisible sheep as they made their way east on Summit, past the old mansions to where they could see the cathedral and a beautiful slice of the city skyline. Every now and then, Mitsy circled Cate, wrapping the leash around her knees, like a spider with a fly, and Cate had to stop and untangle herself.

On the return, they were mostly silent. The unmistakable smell of autumn evoked in Robin memories of her father raking leaves into piles for her to jump in, and she remembered how each new school year excited her with new shoes and new possibilities. She thought about those early fall evenings when she and her little friends were allowed to stay out in the gathering dark. They played tag and hopscotch and hide and seek, and chanted *Star Light, Star Bright* until the streetlights came on and they scampered off to their own homes. Often on those evenings someone had a bonfire going, and the neighborhood kids gathered around to tell scary stories. She and the twins next door liked to put the ends of their flashlights in their mouths and pretend they were jack-o-lanterns. Even after washing up for bed on those nights, she would fall asleep with the smell of bonfire in her hair.

Robin was jerked out of her reverie when Carlton caught sight of a squirrel and nearly pulled her arm out of the socket. When she tried to switch the leash to her other hand, the dog sensed his advantage and bolted free, getting no farther than the base of an elm tree, where he was again taken into custody.

Back at her house, Cate taped a note to the front door telling her guests to come through the side gate. She lit a fire in the outdoor fireplace and though the sun wouldn't set for over an hour, she turned on the mushroom-shaped landscape lights.

She and Robin were enjoying a glass of wine on the patio when Louise arrived. She was large-boned with big champagne-colored hair and an air of southern grace. She slid onto the bench across from them. Louise and her partner, Dean, a man she'd lived with for over thirty years, jointly owned Past Tense Antiques, and she often sported accessories from her shop. Tonight it was a lace shawl and a beaded bag in the art deco style. There was a hint of the South in her accent when she spoke about the fabulous weather and thanked the good lord for the early frost which had killed the mosquitoes without damaging the hardier plants.

The other two arrived within minutes. Grace's tailored pantsuit told Robin she'd come directly from her job as a financial advisor, and her harried expression undoubtedly had something to do with rush hour traffic, which had become exponentially awful in the Twin Cities in recent years. At the close of her workday, Grace exchanged her briefcase for the craft basket she now carried.

Foxy sat next to Grace and stretched out her long legs on the patio stones. Her russet hair was twisted in a bun, the way she wore it when she was working on a client. After a long day on her feet, she kicked off her shoes and wiggled her toes. She still had the graceful carriage of a dancer, her profession in a previous life, as she liked to say, before she'd studied to be a massage therapist. "Tapenade, my favorite," Foxy said, slathering the olive spread on her crostini. Somehow, calories had little effect on her figure, although she pointed out to anyone who made that observation that she had, in fact, gone from a size six to an eight in the past three decades.

They sipped wine, Pinot Grigio for Foxy and Shiraz for the other four. Foxy passed around photos of her recent trip to see an old friend in Portland. "The climate is just enough different from ours and they can grow almost anything." The pictures of landscaping showed colors and varieties that were indeed beautiful. There were other pictures displaying sandy beaches and driftwood, some of winding roads and dense pine forests. Tina, Foxy's friend from her dancing days, was in several photos. She was still a pretty woman with a dazzling smile.

Often Robin's inclination was to look at photographs professionally, mentally centering an object or cropping out the distractions, but tonight she studied the images as a friend, appreciating the memories Foxy had wanted to capture. Robin laid out a set of five on the table. "Who took these pictures?"

Foxy suddenly became interested in her wine glass. "I took most of them."

"But how about the ones of you and Tina?"

Was Foxy actually blushing, or was the sunset playing tricks of light? "Well, there, uh, there was someone else there."

A look of bemusement passed around the table. They waited.

"It was Bill," she finally admitted. "He has a brother there and . . ." She never finished the sentence.

They had all been aware Foxy had stayed in touch with Bill Harley, the Wisconsin sheriff who'd ultimately cracked the murder case last summer. With a little help from the No Ordinary Women, of course. But as far as any of them knew, the relationship was pretty much professional, with Sheriff Harley scheduling massage appointments with Foxy, but only if he happened to be driving to the Twin Cities for business or to shop at the Mall of America.

"Sheriff Harley?" Cate's eyebrow shot up. "I did not see that coming."

"Neither did I." Foxy covered her face with her hands. "I would have told you, but . . ." She brought her hands down and shook her head. "I'm so confused. Would you all mind if we just didn't talk about it until I sort things out?"

They exchanged another look.

"Of course," Robin said. "What are you crocheting?" she asked, turning to Grace.

Grace, who'd set her crochet hook down in astonishment, picked it up again and passed her work to Robin. "It's a bonnet for my coworker's baby."

They all leaned over to admire the dainty piece.

Louise put on her glasses to look at the pattern. "Looks like a lot of work," she said, fingering the fine cotton yarn.

"A labor of love," Grace said, "but now I need to figure out a little gift to take to her very jealous three-year-old brother, who's now regressed to wanting to drink out of a baby bottle. Any ideas?"

"How about the book by Mercer Mayer," Robin suggested. "I can't remember the title, but it's that big brother one."

Foxy undid her hair clip and, with a shake of her head, her auburn curls fell around her neck. "The only big brother book I know of is *1984*, and I don't think it would be appropriate for a three-year-old!"

Soon they were talking, not about Foxy's confusing love life or their chosen book for September, *The Children's Book*, by A.S. Byatt, which, at over 600 pages, was anything but a children's book, but about George Orwell's hauntingly prophetic novel.

"I swear you could pick up any newspaper on any day, and there would be something in it that makes you think of *1984*," Louise said. Her lace shawl had slipped off her shoulders and she pulled it back up.

They were trying to remember the protagonist's name, when Grace snapped her fingers and said it: Winston Smith.

Winston. "Oh!" Robin said. It was the first time she had thought of Era Dudley's son since the woman had accosted her in the hallway at Meadowpoint Manor. "I forgot all about her." She began to tell them about the incident, ending lamely with, "She was so distressed, but there was nothing I could do for her."

In the house, the dogs had set to barking. Cate ignored the familiar sound that indicated her husband Erik was home. On book club nights, he either went out to a movie or a game of racquetball with Robin's husband. Sometimes he just grabbed a burger on the way home and hid out in the basement until the ladies went home.

"Have you ever met the son?" Louise asked.

Robin nodded. "I've seen him a few times. There's also a granddaughter, I think. It's been my impression that Era frequently has visitors. Not a lot, though. Some of them have big families and always have people around, and some have fewer visitors, like my mom."

"What did she say exactly?" Grace asked. "That your assignment was to break him out of wherever he's being held?"

Robin could still see the intensity in Era's eyes. "Something like that."

"Where did she think 'they' were keeping him?" Grace asked.

"She didn't say. I really think it's just the ramblings of—"

Foxy interrupted. "But you said she's lucid most of the time. How do you know something didn't happen to him?"

"If she's so worried," Louise drawled, "why hasn't she called the police?"

Foxy wasn't one for unladylike snorts, but she snorted now. "If the five of us are questioning her sanity, how do you suppose the police will respond?"

Cate raised one eyebrow. "Ninety-six, and still sets a place for her dead husband to eat. Hmmm. I'm guessing they'd hesitate all of a minute before packing her off to the loony bin."

"Exactly!" said Robin. "Well, the memory unit, anyway. I think that's exactly why she wouldn't call. That's the bogeyman they all talk about. It's not death they fear, but living too long with aches and pains while slowly losing their minds and their personalities."

They sat in thought.

The breeze had a chill to it now and Cate suggested they go inside. As they carried things into the kitchen one of the crostini slid off the plate Foxy was carrying, and Mitsy was right there to catch it. Carlton whined for equal treatment and Cate tossed him a piece as well.

"I didn't realize how cold it'd gotten." Louise stood close to the oven. "Maybe another glass of wine will warm me up." She tipped the remainder of the bottle into her glass.

"So, this Winston fellow, does he live in the area?" Foxy asked.

"In a western suburb, I think," Robin said. "Minnetonka or Deephaven or Wayzata."

"Are you going to investigate?" Grace asked.

Robin remembered all too well how Grace had taken to snooping about last year. Trying to break free of the identity she had once claimed, that of being the only ordinary woman of the No Ordinary Women book club, Grace had virtually channeled Nancy Drew, complete with trench coat and disguises. Well, Robin thought with a grin, she hadn't been alone on that.

Cate opened the oven to check on the eggplant parmesan, turned the temperature back to 200 degrees and closed the door again. From the refrigerator, Robin took a bowl of salad vegetables. Finding oil, vinegar, dry mustard and herbs on the butcher block table next to a mixing bowl and whisk, Robin got to work on the dressing while Grace set out bread and olive oil.

Frowning, Foxy leaned against the counter and ran a hand through her reddish hair. She seemed deep in thought. "If his mother is ninety-six, this guy has to be ancient," she said, as if to herself.

"Hey," Louise interrupted. "My daddy's ninety-two!"

"My father would have been ninety this year," said Foxy. The math seemed to have stopped all of them. Foxy continued, "What I don't understand is why she . . . what was her name?"

"Era," Robin and Cate said together.

"Why did Era talk about someone holding him against his will? Let's say the guy's in his seventies. That's at least sixteen years older than anyone here. Why would she assume something sinister happened? Wouldn't it be more logical that she'd worry he had a heart attack or something and died at home? I mean, it really does sound paranoid, doesn't it, to say you're supposed to, how did she put it, break him out?" Foxy looked around to see them agreeing with her.

"Maybe he said something on his last visit to her," Cate suggested.

Grace jumped in. "Or maybe she knows he's been leading a life of crime."

With her hands splayed on the butcher block, Louise faced Robin. "Well," she drawled, "we're never going to know the answer to that if we don't check it out, are we?"

"We?" Robin looked at the eager expressions on the faces of her dearest friends, and felt she was being led down the proverbial garden path. And yet, she had to admit, the idea of investigating did excite her, just a little bit.

By morning, Robin had other things on her mind. Her waking thoughts were about going to see her mother again to make sure she was taking her meds, which made her roll over and shut her eyes again. She would have drifted back to sleep had not her two cats, Samson and Delilah, insisted on having breakfast the minute they detected the slightest fluttering of their mistress's eyelids. They could get her out of bed when nothing else could. Samson tromped over her midsection, and Delilah's purr headed into the upper registers, which Robin interpreted as sheer rapture at the thought of food. She threw off the covers and trudged to the bathroom.

Downstairs, as she dished up the cats' food, a particularly stinky fish blend, she glanced at the clock. Almost nine thirty—she really had overslept. She was grinding coffee beans when she heard the garage door open. Brad was already back from golfing. He would, she knew, spend a few minutes in the garage, cleaning the club heads and his golf shoes in his precise, almost compulsive way before coming in.

When he was done, he joined his wife in the sunroom. While they drank coffee, she petted the cats, which flanked her on the overwide chair, and feigned interest in Brad's hole-by-hole account of his golf game. His excitement at how well he'd played, which he smugly compared to the other players, only served to make Robin glad she'd never taken up the game.

"What're you up to today?" Picking up the newspaper, he noisily refolded it. He looked at her over his reading glasses when she sighed. "Going to see your mother again?" he guessed.

She nodded. "I just hope her meds have started to kick in." She got up and refilled their coffee mugs. Samson didn't budge, but Delilah glared at her for the disruption and hauled herself off to a sunspot under the window.

"You know antidepressants don't kick in that fast," Brad said, always the doctor. When he saw the look on her face, he hastily added, "But maybe just taking them will have a placebo effect." He ran the back of his fingers over the stubble on his jaw.

Her irritation at his comment was all out of proportion. "And being an obstetrician teaches you so much about depression?"

He took off his glasses and looked at her with exaggerated incredulity. "Are you at all familiar with the mood swings associated with fluctuating hormones in women?"

Robin laughed, but then, perversely, she felt like arguing the point. "I hope you're not suggesting that women's cycles are an illness that needs to be medicated away." She couldn't decide whether his grin was understanding or patronizing. "Pills aren't the answer to everything," she added.

He set the paper aside and stood. "No," he said, moving behind her chair to give her a neck rub, "but for your mother, since she's had some serious episodes of depression, I think there's an argument for chemical intervention before it gets too bad. I think, at least in her case, it clears her brain of negative static so she can work things out."

It sounded suspiciously like her mother's therapist years ago, who sounded suspiciously like a drug commercial. And yet, she had to agree, when her mother was in the grip of depression, her little pills were the quickest way out. This time, though, Robin knew her mother's mood had a lot to do with the reason for the vacant apartment Cate's mother would soon be moving into. "I think it's because of Doris," she told Brad.

Until three weeks ago, A347 had been occupied by a friend of Vivian's from the old neighborhood, a woman Robin liked to visit as a child because she owned a talking mynah bird. Doris had been experiencing short term memory problems for some time, but when she was found sleeping in the bathtub of someone else's apartment a few weeks ago, she was promptly moved to the wing with twenty-four hour supervision, where coded locks kept residents from wandering off.

Brad's thumbs hit on a particularly sore spot.

"Oh, yeah, right there!" Robin closed her eyes and let him work his magic on her.

* * *

SOMEONE DIED AGAIN LAST NIGHT," Vivian said with no more emotion than if she'd said she bought a new pair of earrings. "We saw the ambulance come with the lights on. Just after midnight. When they left again, it was with no lights and no siren—quiet and slow." She rummaged in her cupboard and pulled out a bag of Hershey's kisses.

Resisting the urge to tell her mother that, in all probability, the person hadn't actually died again, Robin asked, "Who was it?"

Vivian poured the candies into a dish and set them before Robin at the small table in one corner of her living room before sitting down. "I don't know. Somebody from assisted living. Second one this month."

Making an effort to keep her voice calm, Robin asked, "What did they die of?"

Vivian flicked her wrist. "Oh, I'm sure it was nothing serious."

Nothing serious! Oh, she could hardly wait to tell Cate that one!

Vivian picked up a chocolate, unwrapped it and popped it in her mouth. "Help yourself."

"No thanks, not if we're going to Chet's for lunch." Robin weighed her words before she spoke again. "That must be hard on all of you when someone in the building dies. How does that make you feel?" The song sparrow on the wall clock chirped one o'clock.

"Like everyone else. We talked about it at the mailboxes this morning. Sally said, 'Lucky them,' and we all agreed." She shrugged. "Sally always says that."

Robin felt a clutch in her chest. "Is life here so bad?" And immediately she thought, *oh, Lord, now I've gone and opened that floodgate.*

But instead of spewing her list of complaints, Vivian smiled and patted her arm. "I'm not quite ready to die, honey, but when I do, I hope it's fast."

"Ah." Mindlessly, she picked at the foil wrapping of a candy.

"And that I'm in my right mind, right up to the end. There's such a thing as living too long, you know. I mean, really! Who wants to be drooling and lighting their hair on fire?"

Robin stared at her. "Lighting their hair on fire? Mom, what are you talking about?"

Vivian chuckled. "You'd have to see it to believe it. I don't even know her name, but I'm sure you've seen her around. She's the one that dyes her hair—what's left of it anyway—that ridiculous apricot color. She's still got most of her marbles, but when she goes out to the picnic benches to smoke, she leans her head in her hand, the one with the lit cigarette, and pretty soon there's smoke coming out of her hair and somebody has to jump up and slap at her head to put out the dang fire."

Robin burst out laughing and then Vivian's laugh turned into a series of snorts, which made them laugh and snort all the harder.

And just like that, her mother's mood had lifted.

Vivian slipped into the bathroom before they left for lunch, giving Robin a chance to check out her refrigerator. Milk, yogurt, sliced turkey, string cheese and eggs. She was about to lift the lid of a Tupperware container when Vivian came up behind her.

"Checking up on me?" she asked.

Without turning around, Robin said, "I see you have all the white foods covered. You really need to have something green in your diet, you know."

"Ah, my words coming back to haunt me. Go ahead and look in the Tupperware. I'll bet that's turned green by now." Vivian cackled.

Robin tossed the unopened container down the garbage chute on their way out.

The wind had begun to pick up, swirling the leaves against the curb. Their stroll became a brisk walk by the time they'd gone the four blocks to Chet's, a sandwich joint with an old-fashioned soda counter. Even though they could have easily split one order, they got two blue-plate specials: a corned beef sandwich with coleslaw and a chocolate malt. The leftovers would provide two more meals for Vivian.

"So, Mom, you know Wanda's coming in tomorrow." She swiveled on the barstool to see her mother's expression. "How would you feel about the four of us, you, me, Wanda and Cate, having a little dinner to get reacquainted before she actually moves in? Cate and I would bring the food, and we could use paper plates, so you won't need to cook or clean up at all."

Their food came and Vivian moved her kosher pickle spear over to Robin's plate. "It's not that I don't like her, but I do have my own friends."

Robin sighed inwardly. "Mom, you've known Wanda for years."

"Known about her, sweetie. You and Cate being friends doesn't automatically confer friendship on the mothers." She peeked into the sandwich and rearranged the corned beef with her fingers. "Besides, Wanda puts on airs. She'll never fit in here."

This was not new information, nor was it the first time Robin thought the whole elderly bunch had regressed to a herd of junior high school students, with girls shunning other girls at the lunch table because they wore the wrong clothes or got too much praise from the teacher. And boys shunning the ones who joined the Audiovisual Club rather than going out for sports, where some obscure misstep could label someone in an instant.

Carrying Styrofoam boxes with identical half sandwiches and half eaten slaw, they walked back to Meadowpoint, put the leftovers in the refrigerator and, at Robin's suggestion, walked down to the community room for a game of cribbage. Vivian's mood may have improved, but Robin was curious to see just how much her mother actually interacted with the other residents.

Vivian greeted a foursome of women playing bridge. A pile of pennies lay in the center of their table. The four women were dressed similarly in loose-fitting slacks and sweatshirts or sweaters over white collared shirts. Their hair color was scarcely distinguishable, ranging from pewter to silver, and similarly cut, ear length in front, a little longer in the back.

She recognized two of them as Daisy and Iris. On their first meeting, Daisy had introduced herself and Iris, along with their friend Rose. When Robin commented on their flower names, Daisy said, "Oh, we're the original Flower Children, long before the Summer of Love and Woodstock. We're a bunch of characters."

They were a bunch of characters, all right. Looking at them now, an idea started to form in Robin's head.

Vivian grabbed a cribbage board from the shelf and set it down on a small table nearby, motioning for Robin to sit. As Vivian shuffled the cards, Robin again brought up the subject of dinner with Cate and her mother.

"I suppose," Vivian conceded. "But how about that husband of yours? Doesn't Brad resent you gallivanting off all the time? It's already twice in one week."

"He's gone plenty, Mom."

"Maybe he doesn't like to come home to an empty house, dear."

An old anger flared in Robin. Her parents had divorced when she was eight, and her mother had sunk into a depression which rendered her unable to be a parent to her young daughter. And now, here she was giving marital advice. "Brad will be watching some sport or another on TV, anyway. But if you don't want me to come, I won't. I guess it's up to you whether you want to make Wanda feel welcome or not."

"Oh, for Pete's sake, you know I'll be just as sweet as fudge with her. I'm only saying that I don't picture us palling around like you and the No Ordinary Women. Can't you just picture us bumbling about playing detective?"

Despite her annoyance, Robin tried to picture it and found herself grinning. "You might actually enjoy it. And it would certainly keep your mind active."

"Are you saying I have an inactive mind?" Vivian pursed her lips.

Would she ever be able to have a discussion with her mother that didn't feel like walking through a minefield?

She looked up to see a familiar figure shoving his walker in their direction. The poor man's spine curved so he had to look up between his prolific brows to keep Vivian in his sights. "Your boyfriend's headed this way," Robin whispered.

"Don't make eye contact," her mother hissed.

"Afternoon, ladies," Virgil said, raising his hand to doff an imaginary hat. His lip twitched in a smile.

"Hello, Virgil," said Vivian without looking up.

He produced a dry chuckle that turned into a tubercular sounding cough, and then shuffled off in the direction of the coffee dispenser.

"Sweet as fudge, huh?"

With a backward glance, Vivian lowered her voice. "I don't want to encourage him." She cupped her hand over her elbow and rubbed the arthritic joint.

"So, should I keep calling him Virgil, or will you want me to call him Dad?" Robin teased.

"Ha, ha!" Vivian laid her cards on the table. She was still a brutal cribbage player. She counted quickly. "Fifteen two, four, six, and a double run for fourteen." She pegged her points and flipped over the crib hand. "Six kings." She pegged those as well. "Are you ready to concede?"

Robin folded the cards back into the deck to deal again. "Nope. We're playing this to the bitter end."

Vivian tapped Robin's arm and pointed to the corner of the room. "I think Era's trying to get your attention. Why don't you go see what she wants?"

Robin was surprised to see Era sitting off to one side of the gas fireplace, a book in one hand, and motioning to her with the other.

"Okay, you win," Robin got up.

"Well?" Era said as Robin approached, "Did you find out anything?"

Robin tried to remember if she'd made any promises to Era regarding her son. She shook her head. "No, I'm sorry."

Era considered her with watery eyes. "There's definitely something amiss." She pulled something from the sleeve of her cardigan, and handed it to Robin.

Relieved to see it wasn't a used hankie, Robin opened the piece of paper and read the address out loud. "Your son's?" she asked.

Era nodded. "All you need to do is run by and see if anything's afoot, will you? Break a window if you have to."

Amiss. Afoot. What the heck did Era expect her to do? "I'll . . . I'll do what I can," she said, and turned back to where her mother sat.

She saw the Flower Children in deep conversation. Daisy and Iris often traveled together, Robin had noticed, and it likely had something to do with the fact that although Daisy's vision was twenty-twenty, her hearing was, well, creative, and Iris, who traveled in a wheelchair, could hear like a bird of prey. The two women turned to stare at her. "Robin, it's so nice to see you here again," said

Daisy, as Robin walked past. Her facial wrinkles suggested a lot of smiling over the years, and her smile now was genuine.

When Robin stopped, Daisy added in a confidential tone, "Your visits seem to lift your mother's spirits."

"They certainly do," agreed Iris. She paused before saying, "Maybe it's none of our business, but may we ask what Era told you about her son?"

The other two bridge players looked on mutely.

Robin glanced back at Era, who was watching her intently. "She seems to think he's not visiting very much lately."

"At all," Daisy corrected. "He hasn't been here at all. It will be exactly two weeks tomorrow. I know, because we always play on Fridays, and three weeks ago was the day I creamed these three in bridge. I took the whole pot."

Iris said, "Creamed, indeed. What kind of a word is that?"

"Teach junior high for forty years and you learn these things." Daisy turned her alert eyes to Robin and continued. "Era and her son Winston were sitting right in those wing chairs where she's sitting now, and when he heard the commotion at our table, he came right over and told me not to spend all my pennies in one place. That's the last time he came, and he's always been like clockwork. Tuesdays he takes her out to dinner and Fridays they sit in here and he brings her little biscuits from the bakery and they eat those with a cup of tea."

Robin had always been drawn to Daisy. She looked at her now with new respect. "You don't miss a thing, do you?" She imagined that Daisy's sharp mind and sense of humor had made her a strict but popular teacher. Robin's knees crackled when she squatted next to the table to be at face level with Daisy and Iris. "Do you really think something bad has happened to Winston?" she asked.

Iris and Daisy looked at each other, then back at Robin and nodded in unison, looking for all the world like the aunts in *Arsenic and Old Lace*.

Robin reached into the side pocket of her car and pulled out her Hudson map. The address wasn't too far out of her way home, and if she drove straight from Meadowpoint Manor, she could avoid the worst of the traffic. She headed west on 394, past the car dealerships and Ridgedale toward Wayzata, and in less than twenty minutes she was turning onto the frontage road, where she pulled over to look again at Era's shaky, but legible writing. After making a couple more turns, she found herself in a quiet residential area. The houses she passed were not anything as palatial as some on nearby Lake Minnetonka, but they were nice, and the wooded properties were deep and the driveways long.

Once she found the street, she slowed to check numbers on the mailboxes. The one that bore Winston Dudley's house number was set in a sturdy brick column entwined with some kind of ivy. Stepping out of her car, she eased open the mailbox door to find it empty. Robin paused, thinking of the implications, and turned up the drive.

She'd driven several yards before the house came into view. It was brick, similar to the brick which housed the mailbox—two stories with a portico and double garage. The sloping of the yard suggested a walkout lower level. She parked her car well back from the house and looked around before venturing out. A bird called raucously from an oak tree, and Robin looked up into the brown leaves to see a crow cocking his head as he watched her.

She had no idea what to do next, but she was here and wanted to make at least a cursory inspection. The trees were dense on either side, giving no visibility of the neighboring houses, and yet she'd seen the closely spaced driveways from the road, suggesting the neighboring houses must not be too far apart. Here, just a few blocks from the freeway, she heard no traffic sounds.

Despite the afternoon sunshine, the breeze was chilly. She wrapped her scarf around her neck, buttoned up her windbreaker and walked slowly toward the front door, a heavy oak door that tapered to a peak at the top, like a church window.

In front of the anchoring shrubs and spreading junipers were pots of yellow mums, lime green sweet potato vines and purple kale—three pots on either side of the portico. The light frost had damaged some of the foliage, and one pot of plants was crunched down on one side, but the mums and kale still bore most of their original color.

The lawn, she noticed, was neither overgrown nor had it recently been mown. No newspapers had piled up in front of the door. Walking up the three steps to the front door, she examined the doorknob and around the lock for signs of forced entry, but all seemed to be in order. The door offered no window to peep through and all the blinds were drawn.

Robin held her breath, rang the bell and waited. She rang again, giving ample time for someone to answer before she turned away. On second thought, she pounded on the door with the side of her fist and called his name. Only silence inside. What if he was lying there hurt, unable to respond? she wondered. But if it had already been three weeks . . .

Then again, there was the empty mailbox. How was she to interpret that? Was he coming and going daily, and happened not to be home at the moment? But then, why hadn't he visited his mother?

She traipsed across the driveway and down the slope at the side of the garage. The single window on the side had some kind of covering. Perhaps it had been boarded up from the inside. She considered going around to the back of the house and looking in the windows there, but the isolation of this place had begun to feel ominous, and she was uneasy about trespassing any further.

Trudging back up, she stood on the driveway and perused the scene once more. Nothing struck her as odd, so why, she wondered, did it all feel a little bit off?

Ever since childhood, she'd been easily spooked when she was alone, and knew her imagination could turn the most innocent things into nightmare scenarios. She forced herself to think of logical explanations. If he was on an extended trip, perhaps he had asked a neighbor to take in his mail and newspaper while he was gone, or had stopped delivery of both. It was entirely possible, given Era's elusive recall, that he'd told her about an upcoming vacation, and Era had simply forgotten. Surely that was possible, even probable.

She wrapped her scarf more tightly and strode back to her car, pleased that she'd solved this little mystery so handily.

The crow jeered once more, bobbing up and down as if laughing at her.

* * *

WHEN CATE AND HER MOTHER walked into Vivian's apartment the next day, Wanda was dressed mostly in brown, from her turtleneck sweater to her cropped pants and knee-high boots. Her shawl was brown and lime green, echoing the colors in her feather earrings. Her hair was an unnatural shade of copper.

Vivian took one look and muttered, "Good Lord!" accompanied by an exaggerated roll of her eyes.

Robin hoped she was the only one who heard.

Wanda angled her hand near her mouth to say something privately to her daughter, and Cate's lips tightened. They locked eyes for a split second and then Cate set a green salad on the kitchen counter next to the casserole Robin had brought.

After an initial awkwardness, the two mothers apparently decided to behave themselves. Vivian had set the table with a linen cloth and her good china, and insisted on leaving the paper plates Cate had brought in the grocery bag. While the casserole heated, they sat, Cate and her mother on one loveseat and Robin and her mother facing them on the matching loveseat. Vivian passed bowls of butter mints and mixed nuts, and they talked about Wanda's upcoming move.

The chicken and artichoke dish was a hit, and Vivian actually had seconds of the salad. Robin figured it was more green food than her mother had ingested in months. They finished up with key lime pie, which Cate knew was her mother's favorite. Wanda said it was almost as good as the key lime pie she bought in Florida.

During the meal, Vivian had become more and more lively, and at meal's end, the two mothers kicked their daughters out of the kitchen while they did the dishes. Cate winked at Robin and they dutifully left the room.

"The current events group will be meeting down in the library in a few minutes," Vivian called out over the sounds of running water and clinking dishes. "I'm going to take Wanda down and introduce her to everyone."

Wanda thought it was a splendid idea and off they went, leaving Robin and Cate alone and very pleased with themselves. The subject of their mothers could be touchy. When Cate had first urged her mother to move up from Florida and suggested renewing her acquaintance with Robin's mother, Wanda had responded, "She's bourgeois, and a fusspot fuddy duddy to boot," a comment Cate had laughingly repeated to Robin, verbatim. Robin had restrained herself from swapping insults by repeating how her mother had described Wanda with words like *shallow* and *stuck-up* and *pretentious*. Instead, she'd said her mother had a full life that didn't leave much room for new friends.

But all that seemed to be forgotten, at least for now. After a few minutes, Cate suggested they wander past the library, to "make sure no fist fights have broken out." Enough people attended these discussions that the staff brought in folding chairs each evening to accommodate them all. As they strolled by, Robin guessed there were at least fifteen, many of whom she recognized. Era was there by the door, and all three Flower Children were in attendance. Frannie sat off by herself, knitting, as she always did. There were two wheelchairs besides Iris's, and a gaggle of walkers. Virgil and three other men were huddled in one corner, apparently cowed by the sheer number of females.

On many occasions, Vivian had reported, the conversation was dominated by Marva, who considered these nightly meetings her platform to convince them all of her political and religious views and to brag about the extensive traveling she had done with her husband over the years. Tonight, Robin noted the bully, Marva, was subdued, sitting at one end of the room, and it was Wanda and Vivian who were holding court.

"Keep moving," Robin urged when Cate lingered too long in the doorway. So they moved on to the community room, where Robin opened the game cupboard, located the Sequence box and set it up on one of the tables.

No sooner had they started to play the board game when Era chugged past, her forward momentum taking her past the doorway. After making a U-turn, she made a beeline for their table.

"Mrs. Dudley," Robin greeted her. "I'm so glad you came in."

Era stood over their table, her face almost at the same level as Cate's, who was seated. She regarded Cate. "Are you a junior detective too?" She smelled strongly of gardenias and her mauve curls were disheveled.

Cate kept a straight face. "I am."

Although Era continued to stare at Cate, her words were directed at Robin. "Do you have anything to report?" She held her head high. The only indication of emotion was a tremor at the corners of her mouth.

Robin jumped up and dragged a third chair to their table. "Please." She eased the chair under Era as she sat.

Era set her hands on the table, prayer-like. "Well?" she said in her cracked voice.

As Robin told about her visit to Winston's home, Cate, who had already gotten a full report, nodded, as if she'd been there as well. "Is it possible your son is on vacation?" Robin asked.

Era shook her head. "Oh no, dear. He only travels in the autumn."

Cate and Robin exchanged a glance. "Ah," Robin said. "Where does he go?"

"Here and there."

"Does he have a cabin?" Cate asked.

"Oh, yes. When Diana was little, they had a place up near the Gunflint Trail, but he lost that too." She pursed her lips.

"Lost it?" Cate and Robin said together.

"That wife of his took everything. She even got Diana. I never did understand what Winston saw in that Josephine. All she cared about was money."

Robin wanted to fix these people in her mind. "Your son Winston was married to Josephine, and they had one daughter named Diana. Did I get it right?"

"Yes you did, dear," said Era. "Of course the courts couldn't see through Jo's veneer and the mothers always get custody, you know. So after the divorce she set about to poison Diana's mind against her own father. Di was a willful child to begin with, and with her mother filling her head with ideas, she never did forgive her father for the divorce, even though it was her mother who started it." She nodded, apparently concurring with her own memory. "Diana wasn't even out of high school when she took to drinking. Then she ran off with some ne'er-do-well and broke poor Winston's heart." Era's lower lip began to quiver and she looked over Robin's shoulder, trying to compose herself. "I shouldn't say this, but I find myself wondering if she had something to do with Winston's disappearance." She pulled out her hankie to dab at a tear.

"Where does Diana live now?" asked Cate.

"I don't know." Era's expression was one of disgust when she talked about her only granddaughter. "The last I heard, she was in Arizona, in one of those places people go when they can't be trusted not to drink themselves to death."

"A halfway house?" Cate suggested.

"Yes, that's the word. Of course, she may have moved back in with her mother by now. I think Jo is living in Arizona with her new husband. He's number three or four."

Except for the comment about her son traveling only in the autumn—and here it was September—Era seemed remarkably lucid about the details. Robin had the urge to take notes, but didn't want to interrupt the flow.

"I can see Diana doing something vindictive, but not Josephine," Era said. "She's on dialysis now, anyway."

Remembering one of Era's visitors a couple of months ago, Robin asked, "Does Winston have a granddaughter?"

"Just one. Kiki. She's nothing like Lady Di."

It took a second for Robin to realize she was referring not to British royalty but to Winston's daughter, who would be Kiki's mother.

"Kiki is a lost little lamb, even though she wears too much makeup," Era said.

Robin made a mental list: a missing son, a money-grubbing ex-daughter-in-law, an alcoholic granddaughter, and a great-granddaughter who Robin now pictured as a lamb with Tammy Faye eyelashes.

"Has Kiki been here recently?" Cate asked.

Era's face brightened. "Oh, yes, she was here . . ." She broke off and sat, thinking. "She was here just last week. She brought me the sweetest Easter bouquet of daffodils and purple tulips."

Again, her confusion was one of time, Robin noted. To Era, she posed the question once more. "Do you think Winston is on vacation?"

Era looked bewildered. "He's a good son."

They waited for her to say more, but when she did not, Cate said, "You look tired, Mrs. Dudley. Do you want to get back to your apartment?

Era nodded and stood unsteadily. Refusing assistance, she headed down the hall, muttering to herself.

Watching her, Robin knew she would have to act on the idea which had been percolating in her mind ever since she'd encountered the Flower Children in the community room.

Robin poured herself a large mug of herbal tea and settled herself next to Delilah in the sunroom. As soon as she picked up the phone, Samson jumped onto her lap, nuzzling his head under her chin. Apparently the telephone was a distraction from his owner's main job of petting him.

Dialing her publisher, she felt a surge of excitement as she pitched the idea. Her publisher immediately saw its appeal. This book, they decided after some conversation, would be a deviation from Robin's coffee table books of nature photography. This one would have only black and white or sepia photographs, and because of its smaller size and absence of color prints, it would have a lower cover price, an appealing idea in these tougher economic times. Not limiting themselves to the major booksellers, they could also market to independent and Christian bookstores and gift shops, with a special blitz for Mother's Day, Father's Day and Christmas. The target readers, Robin suggested, could encompass three generations, since it would appeal to seniors, their children and their grandchildren.

They discussed the proportion of photo to text. "I was an English major. Writing was my first love," Robin reminded her.

When Samson slipped off her lap, Robin rolled a lint brush over her pants leg where he had deposited enough hair to make an entire new cat. "The photography came later, so I look forward to doing more writing." Thinking of the characters she would interview, she said, "They all have something to say, so all I have to do is let them talk and they'll practically write the book for me."

There were some open questions. Should she, for instance, photograph and interview only the residents of Meadowpoint Manor and would she include those in assisted living and the memory wing as well? What would the overall tone be—uplifting, nostalgic, bittersweet? Not depressing, they both concluded. Ultimately, Robin knew, the people themselves would shape their own stories and joy and melancholy would coexist, because that would be the only honest way to handle it. She just needed to be careful with balance. They agreed she should start with the people she already had some level of trust with, and revisit the final form as she went along.

As soon as they hung up, Robin made a list, starting with Era, Daisy, Iris, Rose and Virgil. She was intrigued by Frannie, who never talked, and added her to the list. Marva was a possibility, although she blathered on every night and really didn't need another chance to be heard. There was Margaret, not much younger than Era, who attended every funeral she could still drive to, and it was said she never had to buy her own food because she never failed to bring doggie bags home from the funeral luncheons. As an afterthought, Robin added, "Apricot hair, smoker, sets own hair on fire."

Then, eager to talk about her newest project, she called Cate, who answered, her breathing audible. Robin could hear the whine of the treadmill in the background.

Cate listened and then said, puffing from the exertion, "How about my mom? You could start with her."

It was not the response Robin expected and it caught her off guard. "But she hasn't even moved in yet," she said lamely. Her attention turned to Samson, hunkered down on his perch with his tail swishing back and forth as he watched a sparrow. During the ensuing silence, Robin realized that the very thing she proposed to do—underscore the value of senior citizens through photography and stories—could also be divisive. The order in which she interviewed them, the number of words devoted to each, the slant, real or perceived, of their stories, the photos themselves, whether or not they were flattering, and the editorial choices she would make as a photographer—each of these areas was rife with opportunity to offend or to favor. "I want to save our moms until last," she said to Cate. "But I think I need to interview Era first. Who knows how long she'll be around?"

More heavy breathing. "Of course," Cate said.

* * *

ROBIN SPENT THE REST OF THE AFTERNOON making calls, the first one being to the assistant housing director for permission to contact the residents. That person, in turn, referred her to the housing director, who needed to check with the parent company and would get back to her. She spent some time on the Internet, looking for "permission to photograph" forms, and wound up combining a couple of templates to come up with her own. She figured anyone in the memory wing would be considered a "vulnerable adult," and that would require the signature of a relative, probably whoever held power of attorney for that person. This was all new to her, as she'd never gotten permission from the wild turkeys or moccasin flowers she'd featured in previous books, and she'd never considered asking a doe for permission to photograph her fawns resting under an apple tree among the windfalls.

When the phone rang again, it was her younger daughter, Maya, calling from college to say her text books were more expensive than she'd estimated, and asking if Dad could please deposit another three-hundred dollars into her account. Her voice carried a tone that indicated to Robin it wasn't just about money—something else was on her mind. When Robin asked the open question, "What else is going on in your life?" Maya reported her roommate was currently under the care of student health services because of bulimia. "She says if you don't have an eating disorder, you're not a serious student. I think she's a cutter, too," Maya said. "She always wears long sleeves and never undresses when I'm in the room."

Robin's heart constricted. "I'm so sorry, honey. Maybe you could request another roommate."

"Mom, I'm not going to do that." There was a hint of scorn in her answer.

"Are things going okay, otherwise?"

Maya's words were clipped. "Sure . . . I love the sounds and smells of someone puking up their guts five times a day. It's friggin' bliss."

Robin took a deep breath. "I'm sorry this is happening." She had learned the hard way that Maya was not asking for advice. She was blowing off steam, and, having put her unhappiness into words, she would, in all likelihood, go on to have a perfectly lovely day, leaving her mother with a heavy heart about her living conditions and her state of mind. But worry, Robin reminded herself, was a choice. Her new mantra.

"I need to go," Maya said.

The next call was from the director, who gave Robin permission to take photos and conduct interviews with those who lived independently. As for those in assisted living, she gave a resounding "maybe." Well, it was a start.

She bundled up against the sharp wind and set out to walk around Lake Harriet. The three-mile walk usually served to clear her head, and always improved her mood. A pair of rollerbladers swooped past on a parallel trail, wearing less clothing than the fall weather demanded. She remembered that effortless glide of ice skates at the neighborhood rink and the rhythmic thrust of cross-country skis. Two winters ago, surgery and chemotherapy had rendered her too weak for such activities, and last winter, after having her other breast removed as a precaution, she had undergone reconstruction. She longed to get out on her skis again this winter, like any other healthy fifty-two-year-old.

A flock of geese landed on the water, honking. Reflexively, her hand cupped the camera she often wore around her neck. But she had taken so many photos of geese on Lake Harriet that she practically knew them by name. Besides, her eagerness to get started on her new project made everything else pale in comparison.

By the time she had passed the Lake Harriet band shell, she figured out it would cross a boundary of privacy to use her mother's Meadowpoint phone directory to contact people. She would have to go to the community room or library and ask them in person. She veered off the path that circled the lake, and turned up the short street toward her house. Would the residents of Meadowpoint Manor be eager to talk to her, she wondered, as she stepped into her kitchen, or would she have to butter them up?

Yes, that was it. Before she took off her jacket, she pulled two sticks of butter from the refrigerator and a bag of chocolate chips from the pantry. Nothing like a fresh batch of cookies to draw people to her, and put them at ease.

* * *

THE NEXT MORNING ROBIN called Cate on her way to Meadowpoint. Even though Cate was neither a photographer nor a writer, her creativity in thinking was usually helpful, and it almost always stimulated new ways to look at things. Today, though, Cate was preoccupied. She and her mother were just getting ready to leave for the Mall of America. Her mother needed a whole new wardrobe, since parkas, boiled wool sweaters and mukluks were not among her possessions, and she'd been walking around the house, Cate reported, in capri pants, a twin sweater set, Cate's wool socks and beaded sandals. Robin's shutter finger itched to get a picture of that.

Robin had timed her visit to coincide with her mother's beauty shop appointment. In addition to having her hair cut and colored, Vivian had also signed up to see the "foot lady" who came every three weeks to Meadowpoint Manor. Getting their toenails trimmed was not a luxury for many of the residents, but rather an issue of health. The task of bending over and cutting thickened nails was difficult for the senior residents with arthritis or diabetes. Besides, the foot lady massaged her clients' feet and legs to increase circulation, which helped to avert a number of medical problems.

Foxy, she remembered, had talked about volunteering as a massage therapist, as long as it wasn't full-body, deep-tissue work. Working on seniors might be just what she was looking for. Thinking about Foxy made her curious, all over again, about her relationship with the sheriff. Maybe she could work that into the conversation when she called.

Grateful for the chance to talk to the residents without her mother's presence, Robin set up in the community room with a notebook, pen, tape recorder and a plastic tub of chocolate chip cookies. The only two there were a man and woman whose names she did not know. They sat several feet apart from each other and had to holler when they spoke. He had a newspaper in his hands, and she was trying to read a book. They were not, her mother had said, husband and wife, but they often sat together and bickered like a couple married for a lifetime.

"What?" the woman said, not looking up from her book. She was a tiny woman in a shirtwaist dress. "Speak up."

He crumpled the newspaper in exasperation. "I said, blue is not a natural color for hair," he yelled back. He looked at Robin and winked.

"At least I have hair. And it's on my head, and not like those wooly bears you call eyebrows." She looked smug.

They both went back to their reading. After a few minutes, he pulled out a large handkerchief and blew his nose loudly. The woman watched him refold the hanky and put it back in his pocket. "Don't you ever wash that thing?" she said.

"Well, unless you're offering to do my laundry, I don't know who else would wash it."

The corners of her mouth tightened in a grimace. "I suppose you clean your glasses with that filthy thing."

"The better to see you with, my dear." He leered at her over the top of his glasses and she swiped at the air as if to erase him.

Normally, this kind of nastiness would have sent Robin out of the room, but she watched and listened, surreptitiously writing down the words. After a few volleys, she realized they were actually enjoying their banter. *Well, if that's what it takes to keep the blood running through their veins, the more power to them,* she thought. She took the lid off the cookies and was about to offer the non-couple couple some, thinking a little sweetness couldn't hurt. Just then Era rounded the corner. Her face was radiant as she headed directly to Robin.

"Mrs. Dudley, I was hoping to see you today. Sit down. Have a cookie."

Era did just that. She took one dainty bite and brushed a crumb off her chest. "Delicious." She took another, larger bite. Robin noticed her teeth were perfectly shaped, most likely dentures.

"How are you today?" Robin asked, picking up on the woman's upbeat demeanor.

Era clasped her hands together. "I may not need your services after all." She stuffed the rest of the cookie in her mouth. When she was done chewing, she said, "I saw my son. He came, and he told me I shouldn't worry about him. Everything is going to be just fine."

"Oh, I'm so happy. You must be very relieved." Robin felt a little foolish now, thinking about how she'd skulked about on Winston's property, her heart pounding. But, she had to admit, being embroiled in a real murder mystery last year had given her an appetite for sleuthing, and she realized she was a tiny bit disappointed that this story was over before it began. "Had he been on a trip?" she asked.

For a moment, Era looked confused. "Yes, I believe he said he went somewhere. It must have been a wonderful place. He looked years younger. He was always such a handsome boy." She sat in thought for a while, then pushed herself up from the chair with shaking arms. "I need to get ready now," she said enigmatically. "May I have another?" Her fingers dipped back into the plastic tub and she headed down the hall with a cookie in her hand.

Daisy came in next, greeting Robin by name. She carried a large sweetgrass basket, and told Robin she was going to make a presentation shortly about how to knit little dolls for the children's home. "These are usually children who have been abused or neglected for some time before they're taken by Child Protection, and are brought to the children's home with nothing but the clothes on their backs. Now, when they're brought in, they can at least be given a little something that can be their very own, something that reminds them there is still kindness in their lives." She reached into the basket and took out a menagerie of dolls which she lined up on the table.

"They're adorable," Robin said, meaning it. The stuffed dolls were just the right size for a small child to cuddle. Daisy showed them to her, one at a time: a dog, a cat, a lion, a little girl with pigtails, a baby doll, a koala bear, a monkey, a rabbit and a mouse, each with its own distinct personality in its embroidered eyes and mouth. Robin examined them with appreciation. When she'd been only ten-years old, Robin's newly divorced father had taken her from her mother's custody, along with a suitcase of clothing and two toys, a hard plastic doll which had never been her favorite, and a tattered teddy bear. She'd left the doll in a motel in Ohio, and the bear had lost an ear and an eye along the way. Months later when she was returned to her own home in Minneapolis, Teddy's one remaining button eye was hanging by a thread.

Now she picked up the dolls, one by one, turning them over to see the details and squeezing each one, imagining the comfort they would bring the children. "What a beautiful thing to do," she said, tears stinging her eyes.

Not directly addressing Robin's reaction, Daisy's words told her she was a kindred spirit. "Remembering the hardness in our own lives is what motivates us. Elie Weisel said, 'Just as despair can come to one only from other human beings, hope, too, can be given to one only by other human beings.'" She delivered this with ease.

Robin was impressed. Daisy had not really retired from teaching, she realized. She'd merely changed classrooms.

Daisy picked up the little girl doll and fussed with its yarn hair. "I had a beautiful doll when I was little. I named her Sissy. She came with her own little steamer trunk full of the most beautiful clothes—puffy-sleeved dresses and lacy pantaloons and petticoats and the most exquisite leather boots with tiny little buttons. When our house burned down, I wasn't allowed to go back and get her. I cried for a week, and then my father brought me a pillar of wood he'd salvaged from our porch, and he helped me carve a new doll out of it. She wasn't very pretty or very cuddly. I made her clothes from some torn clothing from the charity box someone gave to us after the fire." Her tone was matter-of-fact. "Do you knit?" she asked Robin.

"I do."

Daisy reached into the basket and pulled out a folder with patterns and photos of the completed dolls. "I have an extra set if you'd like to join us. Today is just the presentation, but I'm going to propose our first class to start on Sunday afternoon." Her smile was infectious, and Robin found she wanted to prolong her time with Daisy.

Robin stroked the mane of the lion, a combination of yarn and embroidery floss. "But are you sure your friends want—" She groped for the right word. "Wouldn't they resent an outsider here?"

Daisy laughed. "And miss a chance to tell you all about their lives before they came to live here? No way."

How had that happened? Robin had wrestled with how to approach various residents about writing their stories, and without even knowing it, Daisy had provided the perfect opportunity. "I'd love to," she replied, holding up her tub of cookies. "I even brought the treats."

Daisy's eyes twinkled as she peered into the container. "Chocolate is my favorite food group."

6

During the night, an ambulance came once again to Meadowpoint Manor. Since ambulances were rarely called for those in the independent living wing, it was the general assumption that someone in assisted living or the memory unit had taken ill—or worse. But around mid-afternoon, when people began to gather in the second floor vestibule to check their mailboxes, Daisy commented to Iris she had not seen Era all day. Normally, they agreed, Era would have been out at least twice by now, getting her exercise in short, vigorous strides up and down the hallways.

The vestibule served as a gathering place, since, in addition to the mailboxes, it held a large bulletin board on which was posted the daily movie and upcoming events and classes, along with the week's menu. There were sign-up sheets for various activities and places to drop cereal box tops and soup labels for education fundraisers. Today, there was a bright yellow flyer announcing a new program, Companion Animal Day, which was to be offered monthly. There was excited chatter from those who'd had to leave their beloved animals with friends or relatives when they'd moved from house to apartment. The facility allowed one cat per apartment, but no dogs.

Standing in front of the bank of locked mail slots, Daisy and Iris tried to keep their voices low, not wanting to cause alarm. It was not easy to have a quiet conversation, considering one of them sat two feet lower in her wheelchair, and the other had a significant hearing deficit.

Frannie silently sidled up beside the two women and slipped her hand into her mail slot. "It was her ticker," she said so quietly that Daisy didn't hear her at all.

Iris, whose hearing was usually quite good, looked up from her wheelchair. She peered at Frannie, perplexed. "Did you say whiskers? What on earth are you talking about, Frannie?"

Frannie took a deep breath. "I said it was her ticker," she said as loudly as she could.

"Whose?" Daisy and Iris asked.

"Era Dudley's. She was unconscious when they found her. They did CPR and got her awake, but she doesn't remember a thing."

"How on earth would you know that?" Iris asked. Frannie so rarely spoke, many assumed she lived in her own little world.

"Iris, let her talk," Daisy said.

Frannie's mouth pulled together as if it had a drawstring, and her watery eyes showed her indignation. "I see things." She tucked her mail into her knitting bag and turned away.

"Hmmm." Daisy and Iris exchanged a look.

* * *

AS SHE DID THE DINNER DISHES at home, Robin turned her head at the clattering of the ice dispenser. Brad hummed as he filled his monogrammed glass with ice and poured Cutty Sark over it. Turning the television on to ESPN and setting a bowl of almonds on the table next to his recliner, he grabbed the latest issue of the *American Journal of Obstetrics and Gynecology* to read during commercials. Soon the sounds of some game or another were blaring. He was not on call this weekend, and so Robin knew he wouldn't be budging for the duration of the game.

When she was a young mother who longed for adult conversation at the end of the day, she used to feel guilty leaving Brad when he had a chunk of time available. But she'd come to realize that at the end of his demanding workday, he wanted to spend the evening in mindless activity, and her presence in the room would not alter that. Besides, there was a rescheduled choir practice tonight—unusual on a Saturday night. Robin had been in the church choir since she'd come back from college a married woman, and had sung in the youth choir long before that. It was part of the rhythm that formed her life. She put on her lined windbreaker, grabbed her purse and walked over to rumple her husband's hair as he sat staring at the television. "Don't wait up for me."

Brad grunted, not taking his eyes from the screen.

The brick building, with its bell tower and steeple that lifted your eyes heavenward, had been the church of her youth, and was among Robin's earliest memories. After her father was gone, she and her mother continued to worship there, surrounded by people who had prayed for the whole family during her absence, and continued to pray for her mother to overcome her "sorrowful time," as Pastor Berg had put it.

Robin arrived at the church a few minutes early tonight, and she took the stairs down to the basement room where the church choir practiced. Tonight, the basement felt cool and dank, so she left her jacket on.

Grace was already there, plunking out the notes of their newest score on the piano as she tried to demonstrate something to the director. "This is a little ambitious for the altos, don't you think?" Grace asked, jabbing a finger at a line of the sheet music. "I know at least three of us that will have to stand on a ladder if we're ever going to hit that note."

It was this attention to musicality combined with a sense of humor that had first caught Robin's admiration, when, in pre-book club days, Grace joined the choir and immediately became a thorn in the choir director's side. Although Millie, the director, knew music, her sense of humor was nonexistent as far as Robin could tell. Standing next to Robin in the middle row during her first rehearsal, Grace had made a comment which had them giggling through endless repetitions of the introit. Millie had stopped the choir and demanded to know what was so funny. "I said the tempo's too slow. We sound like a bunch of Oompa-Loompas," Grace had said. A few tittered, and then several eyes followed Robin's to gaze upon the rack where their white choir robes hung, draped with pointed brown stoles, and the image of Oompa-Loompas was complete. While Millie waited for their laughter to stop, Robin had already decided she and Grace would be friends.

Tonight, Grace greeted her with a grin, but then returned to her power struggle with the director. In the years Grace had been there, she had often voiced out loud to Millie, the only person who could really do anything about it, what the others merely grumbled about: scores that were out of range for an aging choir, inadequate practice for those hymns sung in foreign languages, dirge-like tempos, the overpowering soprano section, and the entitlement attitude of some of the longtime members that drove away the newest members.

Millie stepped over to the piano and played three chords, signaling the beginning of their practice time. When they were all assembled in their sections, the man on Grace's left asked if anyone had seen Paul, one of the tenors. Nobody had, although a couple of the men had just seen him at the men's prayer breakfast the day before. "Well, we can't do 'Take My Life' without him," Millie said, as if no one else in the choir could sing that solo part. "If he's missing for another rehearsal, we'll just have to scrap the song." She looked over the choir, one section at a time. "Anyone else missing?"

Winston. The answer came to Robin's mind, unbidden.

As if reading her thoughts, Grace put her sheet music in front of her face and said to Robin in a low voice, "Did you ever find out about that Dudley woman's missing son? Marlboro, was it?"

Robin snorted and covered her mouth. "Winston," she said, behind her music. "Yesterday Era said he came for a visit. But she was a little rocky."

"I remember his name popping up. He was some kind of financial consultant and I think he had quite an impressive client list at one time."

Millie cleared her voice loudly and fixed them with a piercing stare. "Would you two care to conduct your private conversation elsewhere so we can begin?"

"Sorry," they said in unison, but as soon as Millie looked away, Robin said, "Troublemaker!" under her breath, and Grace elbowed her in the ribs.

* * *

IT WASN'T UNTIL THE FOLLOWING morning, when Robin was at her mother's apartment after church, that she learned Era was in the hospital. Evidently, in the early morning hours, Era had tugged on the emergency call cord over her bed and then lapsed into unconsciousness. Now, in the hospital, she was conscious, but confused and weak. An EKG showed a mild heart attack. At least that's what everybody was saying.

Vivian reported all this with the air of a dispassionate newscaster, as if she had barely known Era Dudley, much less lived down the hall from her. This flatness of emotion, Robin had come to recognize over the years, was not a result of her mother's antidepressants, but rather her staunch refusal to get attached to people who were destined to leave her eventually. And Era, as the most senior resident, was on the short list of people who would leave soon.

After church, Vivian and her daughter, armed with notebook, camera and recording device, walked down to the community room. Robin wasn't sure what to do now that Era would not be available for an interview.

Daisy was already sitting at the large table by the fireplace. Knitting needles and several sets of instructions lay on the table next to a basket of embroidery floss and yarn of different colors rolled into small balls. Daisy's broad smile warmed Robin. "I took a page from your book of hospitality," Daisy said, reaching for a tin and opening the lid to reveal pale rectangles encrusted in sugar and slivered almonds. "Try one."

Robin and Vivian each took a cookie and Daisy watched the expressions on their faces turn to bliss. "These are amazing!" Robin said, and Vivian echoed her praise.

"We Swedes know a million things to do with butter and sugar, but this is still my favorite," said Daisy, helping herself to one.

Iris glided into the room in her hand-powered wheelchair and rolled herself into the space beside Robin. Her sweatshirt today bore the words, OLDER THAN DIRT. "I'm here for the knitting class and story hour," she announced. When Robin gave her a curious look, Iris said, "Daisy told us you wanted to get our stories down for posterity, and I figured, Why not? Everyone around here has already heard our tired old tales, but if you put them in a book, why, we'll have a whole new audience." She widened her eyes coyly.

Daisy nodded. "Fresh meat."

Robin laughed out loud. *Oh, I'm going to enjoy this*, she thought.

Rose came next, bearing the unmistakable smell of a new permanent. After sampling and then re-sampling the cookies, they all got down to business.

By agreement, the knitting lesson came first. "This pattern is for a little girl. We're going to start with the shoes and then the legs, so let's start by choosing a skin color. Do you know Crayola now has a set of multicultural flesh-colored crayons?" Daisy said as she set out several yarns ranging from pinkish beige to a rich cocoa brown. After the others had chosen their palette, Rose selected hers, announcing her doll would have one purple leg and one green, and mismatched shoes, one aqua and one pink. "Well, I am a flower child, after all. This one is going to be psychedelic," she said in explanation.

Daisy was a proficient teacher and soon they were all making dolls, starting with one miniature leg, then another, and then joining them to knit the trunk.

The more adept they became with their knitting, the more they began to talk about things other than casting on stitches or getting an even gauge or whether they were on a knit or a purl row. Robin considered the best way to get them started telling their stories. It didn't seem the best setting with them all together, competing for airtime, and she wondered if she should make individual appointments with them.

But without prompting, Iris sat back in her wheelchair and began to talk about the accident that had killed her tyrannical husband and rendered her legs useless. "That One," she said, refusing to give her husband a name, "gave lawyers a bad rap. He was under investigation for bilking clients out of their savings when it happened. He'd become conservator for half a dozen elderly people and, being the way he was, he thought nothing of using their bank accounts as his own piggy bank."

The women shook their heads.

Vivian chewed on a hangnail, and Robin sensed the reason for her discomfort. How, after all, could her mother comment on another husband's transgressions, when her own had served several months in prison?

Iris continued. "When it all came out, I guess he was afraid I'd testify against him, but I knew nothing about what he'd been doing all those years. He always treated me like I didn't have a brain in my head. Everything was in his name and he took care of everything. He paid the bills, did the taxes, never talked to me about our finances, and if I asked him, he'd tell me to leave it to the experts."

"My husband paid all the bills," Rose said.

Daisy reached over to help Edie with a dropped stitch. "You're going to unknit that row until you get to your dropped stitch," she instructed, "so just do each stitch backwards." She demonstrated on her own needles. Edie fumbled for a moment, but then her eyes lit up and she said, "I get it!"

"So you had no idea your husband was embezzling?" Rose prompted Iris.

"Not until he was served papers. We were at home having our usual before dinner cocktail when the doorbell rang. That One was on his third old fashioned, and he told me to see who was at the door. It was a young man with some kind of papers. He asked for my husband, who wouldn't come to the door, so I took the papers and started reading them. Just then the telephone rang and it was a reporter."

Robin looked around the table, and from the expressions on their faces, she figured most, if not all of them, had heard the story. But it was all new to her, and she was hooked. "And that's the first you knew of it?"

"It was. But when the news stories came out, I began to piece things together, a little clue here, a little clue there, and it all fit. I started thinking how I could help the prosecution. I saw a clear pattern. That One had been helping himself all along. It was a real low point for me when I found out my engagement ring was the very ring his grandmother had 'lost.'"

Robin noticed Iris's bare fingers and wondered what had become of the ring.

"But we kept on, at least publicly, as if nothing had happened. They put a picture of us in the newspaper along with the story. It was our official engagement picture, with me standing next to him like the sap I was, completely in the dark about the man I was marrying.

"How awful," Robin breathed.

"Yes, it was. We waited for the trial to commence, and every week, it seemed, some new ugliness was revealed. We went on this way for six months. Then one night we were coming back from a fancy dinner put on by the law firm, and That One had had a few highballs. He was steaming mad because he thought his partners were shunning him. I made the mistake of saying he was lucky they didn't tar and feather him, and he slammed on the brakes. He turned to look me in the eye and said he'd done it all for me, to give me the lifestyle I loved. I told him I'd rather be penniless.

"I thought he was going to hit me and as I turned my face away, I saw we were stopped on the railroad tracks. I started to scramble out of the car, but he grabbed my arm and held on. His grip tightened when the train whistle sounded. Even in the dark I could see the hatred in his eyes. I gave one last tug, but then—" She gestured to her useless limbs. "I don't remember anything after that, not until I woke up in the hospital."

"How horrible," Robin said. "How did you get through it all?"

"Horrible was everything that preceded the accident. The accident itself was my deliverance." Iris smiled. "Oh, I have some aches and pains, and of course I miss the use of my legs, but I wake up each morning knowing that the day is mine to spend however I see fit. That One used to tell me I couldn't find my way out of a phone booth," Iris said, almost cheerily. "But he's been dead for thirty-six years now, and I seem to be getting along just fine." She picked up her knitting again, finishing the doll legs that were about as useful as her own.

Robin had been so engrossed in the tale, she'd forgotten to ask permission to record her words. Just as she was about to do so, Frannie walked over to admire their handiwork. When Daisy tried to interest her in the project, Frannie held up her bag to indicate she had work of her own.

"What have you heard about Era?" Iris asked her.

"Just what I told you yesterday." Frannie eyed the open tin.

"Have one, please," Daisy offered, and Frannie snatched up a cookie and dropped it into the pocket of her sweater.

"You were certainly right about Era," Daisy said. "But how about her son? Did Winston ever show up?"

When Frannie shook her head, her chins wobbled. "They tried to notify him, but they couldn't find him."

Robin chimed in then. "But I thought he came to visit her just this week."

"Hogwash!" said Frannie. "She's a bit daft. Did you know she talks to a picture of her husband as if he's sitting right there in the flesh?" She hovered over the table as she spoke. "She doesn't know one day from the next."

"She has other relatives," Robin said. "Her great-granddaughter comes around, doesn't she?"

Daisy turned to Iris, who repeated the question, and then she addressed Robin. "I remember Era saying that every generation in her family had just one child. Era and her husband were both only children. So there's Era, who had one son, Winston, who had one daughter, who had an only child whose name is Dee Dee or Ceci or something. She'd be Era's great-granddaughter."

"Kiki," Robin said, remembering her discussion with Era. She was tempted to say something about Era's suspicions regarding Winston's daughter, Diana. "It sounds like Winston's ex-wife and daughter are difficult people," she said.

"Well, by the looks of it, that great-granddaughter isn't much better," said Rose.

Daisy cocked her head. "She's no different from some of the students I had. From the looks of it, she's very considerate of Era." Daisy's smile broadened. "And she still has light in her eyes. I wouldn't be too quick to give up on her."

Frannie harrumphed and bustled off to her usual place on the bench. Soon her needles were clicking away.

"I think she's a bit daft." Rose tossed her head in Frannie's direction.

After Iris repeated the comment to Daisy, they smiled at each other. "Actually," Iris said, "she picks up on plenty around here."

"Who knows?" Daisy said, "There might be advantages to people thinking you're daft."

"You have to admit Frannie's a sourpuss," Rose said. "She's been here for at least a year and hasn't made a single friend."

"She is quiet," Daisy conceded.

"I think it's more than that. She just doesn't like people."

Daisy leaned in conspiratorially. "Maybe Frannie is a modern-day Madame Defarge, and is recording everything that goes on here by knitting secret codes into her afghan."

Vivian snickered and Rose guffawed.

"I remember her, the woman in *A Tale of Two Cities*," Iris said. "But I can't remember what codes Madame Defarge was knitting."

There was a wicked sparkle in Daisy's eyes. "Why, the names of everyone she wanted killed, of course," she said.

It was unbearably hot. Having kicked the covers off in her sleep, Cate now woke with a strangled scream to see that there were no flames licking around her as she lay on a . . . why had she believed she was lying on a shelf? The smoke of her dream became dust motes in the morning light pouring through her bedroom window. She took in the familiar surroundings: her reading glasses sitting on top of a book on her nightstand, the dreamcatcher hanging like a spider web in the window and the plush cushions on the window seat.

Her pajamas were damp with her sweat, an all too familiar occurrence since she'd hit the stage of life referred to as perimenopause a few years ago, which had now given way to full blown menopause. She swiped wet tendrils of hair from her forehead. Rolling over, she gazed into the concerned eyes of her aging black lab, sprawled next to her on the bed. On the mornings Erik rose in the early morning hours to go to the hospital where he worked as an anesthesiologist, Carlton would wag his tail, watching from under the bed as his master padded into the bathroom. Then Carlton would bound up onto the bed as if he were still a pup and burrow under the covers before Erik's warmth had dissipated. This morning the dog whined until she calmed him by patting his flank and talking to him in the fatuous tones usually reserved for babies.

The other critters were waiting for her in the kitchen, and she filled their dishes. As the two dogs and three cats crunched and slurped and lapped at their breakfast, Cate filled Prickly's dish with the hedgehog's special low-fat food, and hand-fed him a strawberry, his favorite treat. He looked as happy as a caged animal could be.

Coming from the guest bedroom, her mother's snoring sounded remarkably like the growling of a bear. Tossing her pajamas down the chute, Cate stepped into the shower, still thinking about her dream. She'd had dreams—nightmares, actually—about fire, ever since the conflagration at Spirit Falls which had almost claimed the life of her dearest friend. She fervently hoped she was not destined to have that dream every time she had a hot flash during the night. If so, she'd just as soon not sleep. In this dream, she had actually smelled burning wood.

She dressed in worn jeans, a turtleneck and a quilted down vest, then fingered her thick hair, plaiting a loose braid she draped over her shoulder. While she made breakfast and set two places at the table with her pottery plates, she felt lighter, knowing that by tomorrow her mother would be in her apartment, and life here would resume a familiar pattern. She heard her mother's footsteps on the stairs as she arranged two baked tomato halves and a sticky bun on each plate and poured the orange juice into stem glasses.

But her mother had no appetite this morning, even though Cate had fixed her favorite breakfast. Cate tore off a hunk of the warm caramel roll and put it in her mouth, savoring the buttery sweetness. Her mother cut the tomato into bite-sized pieces, but instead of eating them, she merely pushed them around on her plate.

Cate slid her turquoise amulet back and forth on its chain around her neck, something she did when she was worried or deep in thought. "Is something wrong with the food?" she asked.

Clearly preoccupied, Wanda shook her head. "It's very nice."

"It's okay if you're nervous about the move, Mom. You've made a lot of changes lately." Cate took a sip of coffee.

"I never should have given up cigarettes," Wanda muttered.

Cate tilted her head back and closed her eyes, counting to ten before opening them again. Her mother was still there.

"Honey," Wanda began, staring in the general direction of the refrigerator as she fiddled with the rings on her fingers. In the past decade, Wanda had begun to wear several rings on each hand. "There's something—" She sighed heavily and began again. "You know how you always said you hated being an only child?"

Cate stared at her, then started to giggle. "Oh, my God, Mom, you're pregnant?"

Wanda slammed her hand on the table. "Look, this is hard enough for me without you saying stupid stuff like that. You don't have to make a joke of everything." Her nostrils flared as she spoke. Still, she would not meet Cate's gaze.

Cate propped her forearms on the table and, lacing her fingers together, she said. "Okay, I'm listening."

Wanda took in a shuddering breath. "My dear Catherine, this is not easy."

Cate sucked in her breath and waited for the blow.

By the time Wanda's revelation was complete—at least Cate hoped to God there was nothing more to tell—they had accumulated a pile of soggy Kleenex between them. Cate blotted her hot and swollen eyelids. Her legs were wobbly and her breath shallow. She watched her mother ascend the stairs, her steps lighter now that she'd unloaded her burden onto her daughter.

As soon as she heard the door of Wanda's bedroom click shut, Cate dialed Robin's number, one hand to her chest to calm her heart. "You are not going to flippin' believe this!" She practically spat the words into the phone.

"Cate?" Robin said. "What's going on?"

Her heart still pounded wildly and her mouth was dry. "She has never said a word about it before, but today my mother decided to inform me that I have a brother." She waited for Robin to respond, but there was only what she assumed to be stunned silence on the other end. "They've been corresponding for a while now, and she decided to tell me because he wants to meet her now, after all these years. And me too, I guess."

She stared at the photo her mother had left on the table. The man's face did not look much like hers, but like her, he was lanky and tall, at least in comparison to the woman he had his arm around. It was a typical vacation photo, with palm trees and ocean in the background. The middle-aged woman was plump and cute. The man—her mother called him Ricky—had thinning hair and glasses. They both squinted into the sun. In all the years she had wished for a brother to walk to school with her and boost her over the fence to steal the neighbor's apples and teach her how to drive a stick shift, she had not pictured this aging man.

"Cate, are you okay?" Robin said.

Cate realized she'd asked the question more than once. "He's fifty-eight. I've had a half-brother all this time." Just saying the words stunned her. "Mom was seventeen when she gave him up, and she's known for years where he lived. He was adopted by someone from South Dakota and then they moved to a couple places out east, and now he's back in South Dakota. Do you know how many times I've driven through there and I could've—I just—I don't even know what to say!"

"Do you want me to come over?"

Of course she did. "No. Mom's upstairs packing the last of her things. We're headed over to the place this afternoon and I have to pull myself together. God, Robin, I feel . . ." She groped for words. "You know how it feels when your foot falls asleep and you try to stand on it and it's numb and painful at the same time? Well that's how my brain feels."

Robin chuckled at the imagery. "Really, Cate, I could be there in half an hour."

"No. But thanks anyway. Mom obviously feels awful, and I feel awful and everything feels awful, and I just need to absorb it all." She breathed deeply and her pitch came down to her normal register, "I know she's hurting too. It must have been agony keeping the secret all those years, and I don't want to make this move any harder for her than it already is, but I just want to scream, 'Liar, liar, pants on fire.'"

Robin snorted, and this time Cate laughed too, in big hiccupping gulps that verged on hysteria.

"Are you all right?" Wanda called down the stairs.

"Getting there, Mom," she called back. Into the phone, she said, "I needed to process this with you, and God knows I needed to laugh with you. Now I know I'm going to be okay."

* * *

ERA SAT UP IN BED, certain she had heard Winston calling her name. She'd been having the nicest dream about a picnic by the creek with her old friend who'd been dead for years. She blinked in the dim light until the room came into focus. Gone were the puffy down comforter and the carved rosewood dresser that had been her mother's. Instead of the sleigh bed she'd shared with her dear husband, she saw the plain brown footboard and, lifting her hand, she felt the cool metal railing of an institutional bed. Even before she saw the contraption stuck in the back of her hand, she understood she was in the hospital, but she was darned if she could remember how she got here.

Winston stood at her bedside, just off to the side where she had to turn her head a little to see him. He was looking down at her with such compassion she wanted to stroke the worry lines from his face as she had when he was a boy. He was wearing a nice tennis sweater that showed off his tan. He kept his hands folded in front of him as he told her, "You've had a heart attack, Mom."

She looked to the other side of her bed where a machine with several panels like television screens showed a series of squiggly lines. The machine beeped and glowed and made her afraid. A heart attack, he'd said. Of course. She smiled at her son so he wouldn't worry, and he smiled back.

When her husband—he was such a dear man—had his heart attack, they'd put him in a bed in a room with glass walls. He had no privacy there—it was like living in a terrarium. Intensive care, that's what they called it. He didn't get out of there alive. These walls were not glass, she saw, but like any ordinary hospital room. She closed her eyes and started to drift back to sleep.

A tapping sound made her open her eyes again. She sensed Winston was still there in the shadows. A dark-skinned man in a white coat stepped into the room. "How are you feeling, Mrs. Dudley?" he asked, a little too jovially for her taste.

The first answer that came into her head was a phrase her granddaughter used to say: I feel like I've been French kissed by a Mack truck. But that would not be appropriate. "I've felt better," she croaked.

He introduced himself. His name was Indian, maybe, or Pakistani. His accent and the way he emphasized the wrong syllables, combined with medical jargon, made him almost impossible to understand. It took time to process each phrase, and by then he'd moved on to something else she had trouble making sense of. The only thing she clearly understood was, "I think you're stable for now, but I can't guarantee you won't have other episodes."

Well, of course I'll have other episodes, you fool! How long did he think they could keep this dilapidated old body going, anyway? After ninety-six years in this old thing, she was ready for something new.

"We're still trying to locate your family. Mrs. Gumm over at the nursing home has been calling the numbers she has on file."

"I do not live in a nursing home, young man. I have my own apartment." Her voice was stronger now.

He glanced at the clipboard in his hands. "Yes, of course. But do you possibly have another phone number for your son? You have Winston Dudley listed as your next of kin and your agent, and I'm sure you want him to know you're here."

Era could not believe this man's idiocy. Couldn't he see? "My son is standing right there in front of you, plain as day!" She turned to her left. She blinked and blinked, her eyes beginning to fill with tears.

Where Winston had been standing, there was only an IV stand.

From her vantage point on a bench at the nexus of two hallways, Frannie could see all the way down to the garbage chute at the end of one hall and to the emergency exit at the end of the other. Two men in black jackets and backward baseball caps had propped open the elevator doors just after ten in the morning, and Frannie had watched them wheel a bunch of furniture down to the apartment which had been Doris's and then come back for another load.

Frannie knew who the new tenant was—it was that woman Vivian had brought to the evening discussion a few nights ago. She'd introduced her as Wanda, and Frannie thought she'd looked ridiculous with all that jewelry, just like a gypsy woman.

There were those other two women, too, the younger ones. The dishwater blond with pale skin was Vivian's daughter, and she figured the taller one was Wanda's daughter. She was long-legged and dark haired, and her coloring and the long nose made Frannie think of a gypsy too. Or maybe part Indian, the teepee kind. The two daughters seemed to be pretty buddy-buddy. Well, didn't some people have all the luck, with kids that actually visited them!

It was one of Frannie's favorite ways to spend an afternoon, sitting where she could knit and keep an eye out for action. The knitting was mindless, but it gave her hands something to do while she watched and listened. She had already knit three bags full of afghans to give to the homeless shelter. "Yes sir, yes sir, three bags full," she chanted as she knit. If one of her middle-aged kids didn't come pretty soon to collect them, maybe she'd talk to Daisy about giving all of her afghans to that children's home she was talking about.

As long as Frannie could remember, she had hated being the center of attention. When teachers called on her, she'd duck her head, even when she knew the answer. When her two friends got roles in the high school play, she had helped them with their lines, glad she wouldn't have to get up on the stage herself, and when her husband's company used to throw parties, she'd feel sick for days, knowing she'd have to make small talk all evening.

She knew some people assumed she wasn't in her right mind, and other people looked right through her like she wasn't even there, but being invisible was just how she liked it. She'd found that knitting was as good an excuse as any to avoid conversation. If she didn't feel like talking, all she had to do was dip her head and focus on counting the stitches on her needle.

While the movers still had the elevator tied up, Wanda and her daughter came up the stairs and stopped only a few feet away from Frannie to catch their breath. Wanda's shoes were open backed with a pointy heel, perfect for breaking your neck on the stairs. They stood for a minute, trying to decide whether or not to go down the hall and tell the movers where to put things.

Frannie noticed right away that both mother and daughter had red-rimmed eyes and pink noses like they'd been crying. Maybe they were overcome with emotions about moving into an apartment. God knows she hadn't wanted to move herself, but Frannie thought it was something more with those two, something about the oh, so careful way they talked to each other. They walked right past her down to the apartment without even noticing her.

After a while the movers came back, one of them hauling a furniture dolly behind him and the other one stuffing a check into the big billfold he had chained to his pants. They got into the elevator and the door closed. She heard the car descend.

Several minutes later the door opened again, and Mary Gumm, the resident services director of Meadowpoint, stepped out, along with a skinny kid Frannie recognized as Era's great-granddaughter. Except for that skimpy skirt and a top that looked like underwear, she could have passed for a boy. The things girls did to themselves these days! Why, that slip of a girl had a tattoo on her arm like a sailor and some kind of metal rod poked through her eyebrow. That had to hurt. Mary led the girl in the direction of Era's room.

She saw movement down the other hall. Daisy was coming from the laundry room. When she saw who it was, Frannie took a new interest in her knitting, sliding the stitches on her needle and counting out loud. "Eight, ten, twelve, fourteen," she counted until Daisy was out of sight. The director came back by herself and scooted through the fire door to take the stairway.

Frannie knit almost seven rows before the girl came back. She had some clothes on hangers draped over her skinny arm, and was trying to juggle an armload of other things on top of it all. Something fell from the load. It looked like one of those little zipper bags people used for toiletries, and when the girl bent to pick it up, a glasses case and a big old bra slid out of her grasp. The girl gave a big, dramatic sigh, threw her head back, and opened her arms up, letting the whole mess fall in a big pile. Then she just stood there staring at it for a long time. Maybe she expected it to jump back up into her arms.

"Let me give you a hand," Daisy said, coming back down the hall just when the girl started to cry. She was carrying her little coin pouch, like they all did, with quarters for the washer and dryer. "There's a shopping cart down by the office on the first floor. You're free to use it as long as you put it back."

The girl brushed a tear away and got that tough look people get when they don't want anyone to know they're human. "Yeah, I could do that, I guess." She nudged the pile with her boot. "Can I leave this here until I get the cart?"

Daisy bent at the waist and picked up the bra and a cotton nightie. "You go right ahead. I'll watch this until you get back." That was the thing about Daisy. She'd spent her life teaching teenagers, and she must have learned how to keep everything on an even keel with them. Piercings, tattoos, bad manners, nothing seemed to faze her. Daisy's own kids and grandkids visited her all the time, too, so maybe not reacting was the secret.

When the girl went down in the elevator, Daisy turned to look directly at Frannie. She could narrow her big blue eyes and stick you with a look.

Frannie disconnected from the piercing eyes and spun some yarn off the skein.

"Is that girl the only one who's been to the apartment since Era went into the hospital?" Daisy asked.

So much for blending into the background. "Do you expect me to know who comes and goes around here?"

Daisy didn't say anything right away, forcing Frannie to look up again. Then she smiled at her and said, "Actually, Frannie, I do." She didn't sound mean. More like they were sharing a joke.

Frannie felt a warm flutter in her chest. "Yes, she's the only one. She's the great-granddaughter, you know. She always came with her grandfather before. This is the first time she came alone."

"See?" Daisy said, "I was right to count on you."

Frannie had to duck her head to hide her smile.

When the girl returned with the cart, Daisy said to her, "We've been thinking about your great-grandmother. How is she doing, Kiki?" She picked up the slippers and underwear from the floor and put them in the cart.

"She's gonna be okay, I guess. But she's, like, all worried about my grampa, 'cause he—" She stopped abruptly. After pulling at her short hair and sniffling, she said, "I mean, nobody knows where he is."

Daisy cupped a hand behind her right ear. "You'll have to say that again, and slowly this time. My hearing isn't the greatest."

So Kiki repeated a slower version, ending with the same tug on her hair.

"I see," Daisy said as she rearranged things in the cart. "That would be worrisome. When did you last see him?"

The girl wrinkled up her nose and a tear rolled down her cheek, leaving a streak in her makeup. "Not for a while," she mumbled.

Once more Daisy cupped her ear. "Again, please?"

"I haven't seen him for a while. We kind of had a fight and he, like, got all judgmental and I'm like, 'You don't have to be such an asshole.'" Her furtive glance at Daisy showed she knew that wasn't a nice word. When she didn't get a reaction, she kept talking. "And he's like, 'Maybe you don't need my help anymore, either. Maybe you think I've been an asshole to give you a car and a respectable place to live.'" Her lips pulled down at the corners like she was trying not to cry, and she said, "I went and stayed with my friend for a few days. But then when I did call Grampa, he never picked up." She wiped her nose on the back of her hand.

Daisy studied her. "And you think that had something to do with your last conversation?"

Kiki nodded her head.

"There's probably another explanation. People say things they don't mean sometimes." Daisy touched her shoulder and the girl leaned against her for a second before breaking away. Daisy gestured to the loaded cart. "Do you expect your great-grandma to be in the hospital long?"

The girl looked dismayed. "I dunno. That's a lot of stuff, huh?"

"Let's think for a minute," Daisy said. "I'm guessing she'll want the robe and slippers and underwear, but she'll probably need just one outfit for coming home. Do you know if she has a pair of shoes there?"

Kiki shrugged.

Daisy nodded in thought. "Okay, let's bring shoes and a light coat, and I know how much she loves her crossword puzzles. Did you see any of her puzzle books sitting around?"

Kiki nodded. Her black mascara was smudged, and when she looked at Daisy with those smeary eyes, she wasn't a rebellious teenager anymore, but a little kid who just wanted to crawl up in someone's lap and bawl her head off.

* * *

IT WAS TWO DAYS LATER when Robin and Cate met at Cuppa Java. Robin ordered chai tea and Cate ordered a glass of cabernet. They'd both been so engaged, in their separate ways, in the goings on at Meadowpoint Manor that they decided to meet so they could catch up on the other parts of their lives. And yet the discussion quickly returned to the senior apartment complex.

"The move went smoothly, all things considered," said Cate. She described the items brought by the movers and how surprised she was that everything fit so well into the small space. "Mom has a knack for arranging furniture and decorating. I wish I'd gotten that gene."

"Your place always looks good," Robin said, thinking of the clean lines of Erik and Cate's mission style house. She sipped the aromatic tea, holding the cup in both hands to warm them.

"Oh sure, the house has good bones, and as long as I keep it simple, it looks fine. But she has a real eye for it. Anyway, I was going to hang a couple paintings for her, but she said the custodian has to put things up so they don't ruin the walls."

"That's Benny. It's not a rule, really, but he'll do it for free. Actually, they encourage people to hang pictures and other things to make it feel like home."

"Home!" Cate snorted. "It might take mom a while to adjust. She's still dressing like she's in Florida." She picked up her wooly scarf that had slipped onto the floor and draped it over her neck. "Who else would wear slingbacks with a kitten heel on moving day? And those giant hoop earrings of hers kept catching on the rhinestoned collar of her denim jacket!"

Robin had to laugh at the mental image. She looked down at her own Finn Comforts and wool socks. "Maybe she doesn't want to fit in. Do you really want her to wear sweatshirts and elastic waist pants all the time?"

"No." Cate sighed and downed the last of her wine. "You want a refill?"

Robin handed her the cup and soon Cate returned with their drinks and an order of artichoke dip and bread. Usually when they got together, they talked nonstop, but now they sipped mostly in silence, commenting only on the tasty food. Soon Cate's wine glass was empty again.

Noticing how Cate crossed her legs and bounced her foot up and down a little too vigorously, Robin asked, "Have you thought any more about meeting your brother?"

She gave Robin a look of disgust and curled her fingers around the stem of her glass. "What would be the point? It's not like we're ever going to be one big happy family."

"The point is I think you want to talk about this even more than you don't want to talk about it. Am I right?" When Cate looked away, Robin plunged forward. "It's a lot to absorb. Part of your identity is being an only child."

Cate grudgingly conceded.

"You don't have to start by actually seeing him in person. Maybe start with an e-mail, and then talk to him on the phone after you've established some kind of relationship."

Cate tapped her nails against the wine glass. Finally she nodded. "Damn it all, Rob, I'm so mad at her. How could she keep it from me all these years? Dad's gone. I don't have kids. I thought my entire family consisted of exactly two people. Frankly, I'd still like to strangle her." Her fingernails clicked on glass again. "But then it would be just me."

"Uh huh."

"I'm excited, though. Scared too." She stared out the window and shook her head. "I've been wondering what I would have done if I'd been pregnant at seventeen."

"I can't imagine." Robin hadn't even dated until her senior year of high school, and when she and Brad met, she was almost twenty, and he'd been her only long-term relationship. Cate, on the other hand, had dated young and often, and not usually with great results.

When they were in college, while Robin and Brad dated steadily, Cate had gone through a series of relationships which ended badly. For Cate, the comment about unwanted pregnancy was not a purely academic one. Nobody used the term "date rape" in those days. It was considered by many to simply be poor judgment if a girl found herself overpowered by a boy she'd agreed to go out with, and so girls rarely reported it. Cate and Robin were roommates when such a date caused Cate three very anxious weeks before she ruled out pregnancy. During those weeks, they'd discussed her options. Abortion was illegal back then, but many of the girls on campus had a vague idea where it could be done.

"Things are different now," Robin said, "Some people think nothing of having children with people they don't plan on marrying. But back then . . ."

"You're right, being an unwed mother back then would have been pretty awful."

The first thing Robin noticed when she entered the community room was a peculiar agitation among the residents. Rose and Iris and Daisy sat at a table strewn with half-finished dolls, but instead of working on their projects, they had their heads together in deep conversation. Frannie, sitting by herself by the fireplace, kept looking up from her knitting, scanning the room as if expecting something out of the ordinary to occur. Mary Jo stood by the bookcase, taking out one hardcover book after another, reading the dust jacket and putting it back. She kept glancing up toward the office of the director.

Setting her camera bag on the floor by the table, Robin opened the box of Victorian Brittle she'd picked up at Byerly's on the way, and offered it to the three ladies. Even as they munched the treats, they seemed distracted. Daisy's trademark smile seemed forced.

Wondering if she'd somehow offended them, Robin finally asked if something was wrong.

Daisy pointed to her right ear. "You'll have to talk into my good ear, or at least my not-so-bad one."

"She's wondering why everyone's upset," Iris said, as Daisy watched her lips move.

Daisy nodded, then tilted her head toward Robin. "The plot thickens. We were told that Era would be able to come home today, but instead, they're keeping her at the hospital until they can figure out what to do next." She tented her fingers together in front of her.

Rose looked grim. "She's had a little setback."

The other two nodded, and Daisy continued. "The police were just here talking to the director, Mary Gumm. Evidently poor Era is all confused, and why wouldn't she be? They've changed her medications and even had her on morphine for a while. It takes time to bounce back from that."

"I can attest to that," said Iris. "When the doctor talked to her, she wasn't making total sense, so now they're questioning her ability to stay in her own apartment. They were discussing possibly moving her into assisted living as soon as there's an opening." She jutted out her chin. "I figure she's managed on her own for ninety-six years, and if she wants to come back here and live alone, what's the worst that can happen?"

Daisy nodded emphatically.

Robin glanced around the room and saw that all eyes were on their table, even Frannie's. "But why the police? If it's just an issue of her health, why send the police?"

They all started to answer at once, but Rose prevailed. "They've been unable to locate Era's son and now they don't think she's competent to make her own decisions. When I had my heart attack, they gave me morphine and I talked goofy for days. But I was only seventy-two then."

Vivian sat back, shaking her head in disgust. "What's the big rush? What would it hurt to give her another day in the hospital before making such a huge decision?"

Rose said, "Exactly! They're railroading her. When she told the doctor her son was right there in the room, they decided she's senile. They won't even consider other explanations. Winston wasn't there, of course. Not in the sense you'd normally say something like that."

Robin pondered that riddle.

"Even though Era has her little dinner ritual, setting an extra place at the table and talking to a picture of her late husband," Daisy said, "it's never interfered with her ability to take care of herself."

The others nodded solemnly.

"And who's to say he doesn't come to visit her?" Daisy added.

Robin thought she understood the point Daisy was making. "But still, why is it a police matter? And how do you know—?"

"Ah," said Daisy, flipping her hands toward Iris in a gesture that reminded Robin of a magician's assistant.

Beaming, Iris sat back in her wheelchair and picked up the story. "When I saw the policewoman go into Mary's office, I scooted myself over there, and just as I was going past the office door, I dropped my keys, wouldn't you know. Well, I couldn't pick them up with these clumsy old fingers, and I couldn't really leave my keys on the floor, now could I?" She widened her eyes coquettishly. "Frannie rushed right over—to help me, naturally—and she heard it too. Era's son Winston has gone missing. That's what the police said. They talked about Era and her great-granddaughter filing a missing persons report."

"Oh!" Robin said, wondering if she'd misunderstood her last conversation with Era.

Iris continued. "They talked about what to do since Winston is Era's emergency contact, and then the policewoman asked about other family members. Mary told her there was a granddaughter who lived out of state but had nothing to do with Era. Then Mary told the policewoman she had let Era's great-granddaughter into her apartment a couple of days ago, and that sparked a lot of new questions, like where she lived and whether their relationship was friendly and did Era seem to trust her with decisions."

Robin was beginning to understand their agitation now as she listened to this tag-team telling of Era's woes. A family member was missing, creating a set of circumstances that tapped into their own insecurities and vulnerability. Era's confusion could be temporary, and yet now that she'd landed in the hospital, she was no longer trusted to make decisions about her own life.

It could happen to any of them. They'd all named emergency contacts, and perhaps some had already signed over power of attorney to a trusted relative. But what if you didn't have someone you could trust? Or what if the person you trusted couldn't do it? Robin wondered if that young girl would now be in charge of Era's life.

Daisy broke into her thoughts. "The police seemed quite interested in contacting Kiki. Too interested."

"We're worried about the girl." Rose looked over her shoulder before leaning forward to speak in a whisper. "We're worried they might think Kiki did something."

"And by something, you mean . . . ?" Robin asked.

Daisy looked at her friends before answering. "We've talked it over, and we've all come to the conclusion that Winston is dead. And not of natural causes." The others nodded, and she continued. "We all know that in the case of murder, they always look at the family first. Now Kiki is the kind of child that attracts negative attention. She thinks she's making a fashion statement with her combat boots and purple hair, but to the police, she's only signaling to them that she has problems with authority. She'll be a lightning rod for their suspicions."

Robin could see her point.

"She's not a bad kid, just a little lost," Daisy explained. "When she was here the other day, I could see under all that bluster that she's actually quite sweet. I invited her to my apartment to show her my dolls and I offered to teach her how to knit."

Robin grinned. "Of course you did."

Daisy grinned back. "You might not think it to look at her, but she is quite avid to learn. I had students like that every year who looked as hard as tempered steel but were just looking for a safe place to explore who they really wanted to be. Some people just experiment more." She sighed and shook her head. "But now, who knows what will happen?"

Who knows, indeed, Robin thought. Chagrined, she remembered her first reaction when Era Dudley had approached her about her missing son. She hadn't exactly dismissed Era's concerns, but neither had she taken them seriously. The woman, after all, was just shy of a century old. She'd been active and alert, yet few things could be said about Era that wouldn't end with the stated or implied phrase, "for her age."

Daisy stood and gathered her things into her basket. "I have to get ready for my hot date tonight. My daughter and granddaughter are taking me out for a seafood dinner and a movie."

Robin checked her watch and realized another day had gone by, and once more she'd gotten so caught up in listening to these senior citizens she'd forgotten to take photos or turn on her digital recorder. She made her apologies and headed to her mother's apartment for a quick visit before going home.

"I hope you weren't offended that I didn't join you," said Vivian.

"No problem, Mom. I know I can't compete with *Jeopardy*."

"Keeps the mind young. I even knew the new name for The Republic of Upper Volta."

Robin strained her brain to think if she'd even heard of the old name.

"Burkina Faso. It's just north of Ghana and Togo and the Ivory Coast." She drew a map of Africa in the air and pointed to the rounded west coast.

"I'm impressed."

A few minutes later, Robin gathered up her things and headed for home. As she drove, the weight of Era's predicament lay heavily on her conscience. Had her dealings with the woman been just as callous as the doctors? She considered whether it could have changed anything if she'd only believed her from the beginning.

But, Robin thought in self-defense, she had at least gone so far as to make a reconnaissance trip to Winston's house. And thinking about that, she began to wonder if she had missed something.

* * *

VIVIAN CONSIDERED WANDA'S WORRISOME BEHAVIOR. If anyone knew the signs of depression, it was Vivian Tesdale. Despite invitations from Vivian and at least two of the Flower Children, Wanda hadn't ventured out of her apartment since she'd moved in, other than to check her mailbox.

This morning, when Vivian knocked on her door, Wanda didn't answer, so she kept on knocking until she finally came to the door. In her robe. At eleven thirty in the morning. Vivian could see into the living room, its carpeted floor strewn with papers and opened packing boxes. There was a blanket on the couch and a red-flecked wine glass on the coffee table.

Wanda languidly shoved a tangled hunk of hair behind her ear. "Good morning," she said without warmth. Her face was creased from sleep and her shoulders slumped forward.

Vivian pulled two tea bags from her pants pocket. "I'll put on some water for tea while you get dressed. Then I'll help you empty one of those boxes."

Wanda shrugged and stepped aside. "Be my guest." Her shuffling walk made her appear to have aged ten years in a week.

Vivian washed the wine glass with hand soap since she couldn't find the dish soap, tossed an empty potato chip bag into the garbage and made tea. The apartment was overly warm and stuffy, so she turned on the ceiling fan and cracked open the window that overlooked the front patio.

All the time she tidied up, she wondered how often her own young daughter had cared for her in a similar fashion. Poor Robin had suffered mightily from her parents' decisions: her mother's refusal to get help for depression which led to divorce, and her father's ill-advised decision to take Robin out of that environment against custody orders.

When Wanda came out again, she was dressed in a silky jogging suit that Vivian guessed had never been used for jogging. Her hair was still a fright and she moved as if in pain. If she noticed Vivian had cleaned up a few things, she made no comment. Dropping herself onto the couch, she took the cup of tea from Vivian and blew on it before sipping. "Nothing's right," she said, sagging back into the cushions and closing her eyes.

Vivian didn't ask her to explain. She knew the feeling well enough. Luckily, she also knew that sometimes you just had to put one foot in front of the other, and one action would lead to another and then another, and pretty soon the fog would begin to lift. Leaving home and friends was no small adjustment for any of them, and Wanda had the added loss of leaving the Sunshine State for Minnesota, the land of subzero wind chills.

When they'd drunk their tea, Vivian dragged one of the opened boxes close to her chair and peered inside. She removed a pair of hand towels, handing them to Wanda along with a bottle of dish soap and a box of Band-Aids. "Here, you know where you want these."

Wanda looked at them dubiously.

"I keep my towels in the little hall closet along with my sheets and cleaning supplies, and my Band-Aids in a kitchen drawer, near the knives."

Wanda nodded dully and shuffled off. Handful by handful, she followed orders and soon there were two empty boxes Vivian set in the hallway. Wanda had arranged her toiletries on the glass shelves in the bathroom, just as Vivian had done with her own. Set precariously on the edge of the bathtub was a pill organizer, identical to her own, with four compartments for each day. Vivian picked it up to see that only the Sunday morning compartment was empty. "When did you last take your pills, dear?" she asked.

Wanda leaned into the mirror and poked at the fleshy part of her jowls. "Oh, I don't know. I might have missed a day."

Or five. Vivian popped open the Friday morning compartment and recognized the calcium pills and the brown ibuprofen tablets. Well, no wonder she was achy. She took Wanda's hand and dumped the pills into it. "I'll get you some water."

Wanda dutifully swallowed them one by one, grimacing as she took the large fish oil capsule. She accepted Vivian's offer of lunch and followed her to her apartment. Sitting at the small table of Vivian's sunlit room, Wanda stared at her own hands and picked at the age spots while Vivian heated tomato soup from a can and grilled two cheese sandwiches in lots of butter.

"I've made a mess of things," Wanda said when Vivian set the food in front of her.

"You're in good company, then," said Vivian. "I've made some colossal mistakes."

Wanda's eyes flicked up to meet hers. She tore a small corner off her sandwich and looked at it as if it were something distasteful before setting it back on her plate. "I'm afraid I've hurt my daughter terribly."

Vivian waited for her to say more, but she didn't. "Haven't we all!"

Wanda went back to fretting with her age spots.

"Whatever you've done, Catherine is not going anywhere." She watched Wanda press her lips together in an attempt to hold herself together. "She's a loving daughter."

"But what if she doesn't get over it?"

"Well, then I guess she'll die mad."

Wanda almost laughed at that.

Vivian polished off half her sandwich and was digging into her soup when she saw that although Wanda had torn her sandwich into pieces, none of it had wound up in her mouth. "It's okay if you don't want to tell me—"

Wanda cut her off. "I don't."

Vivian nodded and Wanda took a spoonful of soup.

"Now, listen," Vivian said, smoothing the paper napkin over her knees. "There's something going on here at Meadowpoint that I wanted to talk to you about. Our oldest resident, Era, is in the hospital, and some of us think they're not taking her seriously because she's old."

"You mean the one with lavender hair? She is old."

"Well, so am I. And you're only two years behind me, but that's beside the point. Anyway, I told Daisy I'd drive her to the hospital this afternoon for a visit. We want to see for ourselves if she's as bad as they say, and let her know we still care about her." As one of the residents who still had a driver's license and a car, Vivian was often asked to drive, and people usually offered her gas money in exchange. "Do you want to come with us to the hospital?"

Wanda looked up. "Thanks anyway, but I don't even know the woman. No, I think I'll stay here and get those papers organized now that you got me started."

* * *

WHEN THEY WALKED INTO HER ROOM, Era was propped up in bed doing a crossword puzzle in her jumbo book. Her hair was flatter than usual but she'd run a comb through it. She greeted them by name. "Daisy and Rose, and . . . is that Vivian? Are you one of the Flower Children now?" Her dry laugh turned into a cough.

Vivian grinned. "Besides wanting to see you, I'm the chauffeur today. If I drove a bus, half the floor would have come to see you."

"Only half?" Era smiled at the compliment and set her pencil and puzzle book on the table. Taking their hands one by one, she formally thanked them for the visit. Nothing in her manner indicated that her condition had taken a dire turn. Rose handed her their gift, a bouquet of yellow calla lilies along with a card they'd picked up in the hospital gift shop.

"My favorite flowers!" Era said with delight. "They're called—wait, don't tell me the name." She frowned in concentration. "Oh, what is that flower called? It has a beautiful scent and thorns . . ."

Vivian shook her head. "They are not roses."

Era snapped her fingers. "Rose! That's right. Rose, what the heck do you call these calla lilies?"

Daisy was the first to pick up on the joke, and soon they were all laughing and cackling out loud. A nurse popped her head in and they repeated the joke. When Era began coughing again, the nurse pulled out her stethoscope and placed it on her chest and then her back. "Do you feel up to a little walk down to the visitors' lounge, Era?" she asked, more loudly than necessary.

Era nodded her head vigorously. "They want me to keep my lungs clear," she explained to her friends as she swung her legs over the edge of the bed. "I'm not used to all this lying about, having people wait on me." Her robe was draped over the foot of her bed and she slipped it on. Gripping the nurse's arm, she took a couple of careful steps in her hospital booties. "I'll take it from here," she announced, letting go and heading out the door on her own.

"She seems to have all her marbles," Rose commented to the nurse on the way out.

"Make sure they put that on her chart." Daisy emphasized her words by thumping her cane on the floor. Today Daisy was leaning heavily on the brass handle shaped like an eagle's head.

Era was moving down the hall at a good clip now. "When are they going to spring you from this joint?" Daisy asked Era when she caught up to her.

"If they don't do it tomorrow, I believe I will have to spring myself."

In the lounge, the four women settled into a grouping of brocade chairs. Era's legs didn't quite reach the floor and they dangled in the air like a little girl's. Rose brought them Styrofoam cups of bad decaf coffee from the kitchenette and Era talked about the night she had come here on a stretcher. She'd been frightened, she had to admit, not about dying, but about a heart attack or a stroke leaving her helpless to care for herself.

She described waking up in the emergency room and having blurry vision. She knew now, of course, that the people in the room that night had been strangers, medical people, but without her glasses she had mistaken them for people she knew. When she'd called them by name—Horace and Diana and Sally—they'd talked about her confusion, right in front of her, as if she had no mind at all!

"In the middle of the night some doctor who couldn't have even graduated from high school came in and asked me how many fingers he had. I can be a bit of a smart aleck sometimes, and so I said, 'I assume you have eight.' Because you don't count the thumbs, you know, but he didn't laugh. Then he asked me who the president was and I said 'Osama bin Laden.' Of course I knew it was wrong as soon as I said it, but before I could correct myself, he was already writing on his little chart."

How awful, thought Vivian, to have so much riding on a few questions. Not to mention she'd been in a strange place with strange people, and that she'd been scared and without her glasses. And on morphine to boot. "It must have been terribly disorienting."

Era sighed. "That's the word for it."

"I think every doctor should be required to be hospitalized before dealing with patients," Daisy said. They were all in agreement about that. Era suggested that just walking around in a hospital gown would teach them all a lesson in humility.

Vivian thought there had been a movie about that, but no one could remember the name of the movie, or the actor who played the doctor.

Rose rested a hand on Era's knee. "You seem like your old self."

"I think so too. As soon as Kiki brought me my glasses and a few other things, my world started to make sense again. But now that I've flunked their little tests, they say they need to make sure I'm not still loopy before they let me go home."

"Was it a full-blown heart attack?" Rose asked.

"Quite mild, actually." Era tapped her chest. "They won't be able to read the expiration date on this old ticker until they open me up, and then . . . well, it should be obvious by then." She coughed and spat something into a tissue she had in her bathrobe pocket.

Vivian excused herself to use the bathroom. When she returned, talk had turned to what had been happening at the Manor in Era's absence. Virgil had broken his partial plate and was walking around all gap-toothed, still doffing his imaginary hat to all the ladies. The woman who kept setting her hair on fire now had a bald spot on her right temple, and it looked like she'd lost half an eyebrow too. The man and woman who always quarreled, the ones who were not married to each other, were seen kissing in the laundry room, and not just a little peck on the lips, either.

Era clapped her hands in delight.

Nobody mentioned the police visit.

After a bit, Era began to sag and her eyelids were at half-mast. For a while, she seemed lost in thought, and then she said, "I just let myself get too worked up over my son, but there's not much I can do about that now."

Daisy and Rose exchanged a look.

Setting her jaw, Era said, "He came to me, you know, but he's no longer here." She looked at their expressions and said, "Oh, I know what you're thinking. I get things tangled up in my brain sometimes, or at least by the time I say it, it sounds tangled, but I've done what I can. I already talked to that girl, the junior detective. She'll figure it out." Era's hands fluttered like bird's wings as she talked.

Vivian glanced at Daisy, who was frowning, as if trying to follow the thread.

"What girl?" Daisy asked.

Era's head was tilted to one side and she was staring at the empty chair.

"What girl, Era?" Daisy repeated.

Startled, her eyes snapped to her visitors. "What?"

Daisy leaned forward and took her hand. "What girl are you talking about? Who do you call a junior detective?"

"Oh, yes." She nodded, searching their faces until she settled on Vivian's. Crooking her index finger at her she said, "Your daughter. She's already on the case."

Vivian gave a little laugh and looked nervously at the others. "I . . . I don't know what you mean."

Era chuckled. "That's because you don't need to. But she knows." She leaned her head back against the chair and closed her eyes. Her lips parted and almost immediately she began to snore.

10

Sitting near the window at Chet's, Cate gripped the plastic tumbler of water with both hands and waited for her mother to make eye contact. "Did the father know?" she asked.

There was an awkward pause as Wanda sat openmouthed. A croak emerged from her lips.

"You never told him?"

Her mother's headshake was a slight tremor.

"Why not?" she asked more gently. Today the smell of fried onions, usually a favorite of hers, had a nauseating effect.

Wanda held herself erect with her hands clasped demurely in her lap as if she were on a witness stand. "If I'd told him, he would have offered to marry me and if I'd told my father who it was, he would have insisted on confronting him and forcing him to make an honest woman of me."

Cate nodded, although understanding had not yet occurred. Her mind was playing contortionist, taking the things she'd always thought to be true about her parents and grandparents, and bending them into unrecognizable shapes.

Wanda's jaw was set. "I did not want to marry him."

Cate imagined any number of reasons. He may have been married or physically abusive or incapable of being faithful. "What was wrong with him?" she asked, prepared for almost anything her mother might say.

Wanda sighed and got a faraway look. "He was the worst thing I could imagine at that age."

Cate waited for a heartbeat, bracing herself.

Wanda let out a sigh. "He was boring."

Cate stared at her mother as the young waiter brought their food. That was one answer she had not expected. Before she could form a response, she got a clear mental picture of herself at seventeen. Life was so full of exciting and exotic possibilities back then. Stability was of little value to her in those days, and boredom, she had to admit, had not been a choice she would have willingly made. "What did you do?"

"Your grandparents arranged for me to go to a home in Missouri where I stayed until he was born. He was a cute little thing with a thatch of brown hair and long fingers. I had less than an hour with him . . . and then he was gone." Though her lips quivered, she continued, "Rather than raise embarrassing questions by coming home after the 'little problem,' as my father called it—" She stopped, her eyes drifting off. "You know, to this day, I do not know if he was referring to the baby or to me as the little problem."

Cate bit her lip. She could see the weight of that question on her mother.

"So, rather than come home, it was arranged for me to finish my senior year in St. Louis a year after I would have graduated at home. And then I decided to stay on there. Even before I graduated, I got myself a job in a department store and rented a room above a tavern."

Their food sat untouched.

Cate knew the rest of the story, or at least she thought she did. Her mother had worked only a few months in the small store, waiting on customers, stocking merchandise and occasionally answering the telephone. One fall day, a striking young man with his long hair in a glossy braid had come into the store and had taken her mother's breath away. Tall and lean, with a sharp nose and twinkling eyes, George Running's resemblance to his Cherokee grandmother had made him exotic in Wanda's eyes, and she had known in that moment he was the one she had come to Missouri for.

"I didn't tell your father for months. Not until we were driving back to Illinois so he could meet my parents, and I told him everything, even who the baby's father was. I didn't expect him to be happy about me having had a baby, and he wasn't. I could see it in his eyes. He asked only a few questions, and then he said, 'It was in the past. We don't need to bring it up again.'"

Cate pictured her father's inscrutable stare. "You never talked about it again?"

"He never brought it up. He never threw it in my face."

"But didn't you wonder what had happened to him? To my brother?"

Wanda met her eyes. "Of course I did. I used to search for his face whenever I saw children." She wiped a sticky spot on the table with her napkin. "But then you came along and it all felt so right, just the three of us, and I really believed you were the child I was meant to have for my very own. And if I ever wondered what happened to my firstborn, your father would assure me that I'd done the right thing, that he was growing up with the right family. And it turns out he was. He's had a pretty good life. It wasn't until his mother died last year that he decided to find me."

"But you're his mother."

"No, his mother raised him, just like I raised you. I can hardly come in at this late date and claim that title." She shook her head emphatically. "No," she said again. "She was his mother."

Cate looked at her mother in wonderment. There was nothing maudlin in the retelling. No self-pity, no drama, no evidence of revisionist history. For the first time since hearing of her half-brother, she considered her mother's story without blame. Wanda had made a hard decision and had not looked back. It was so typical of her generation, Cate thought, wondering if she could measure up to that kind of grace under pressure.

The place was filling up. Three older men sat down at the table right next to theirs, talking loudly. Cate noticed two of them wore hearing aids. Wanda thought they lived at Meadowpoint and were in a golf league together.

Signaling the end of the discussion, Wanda picked up her pastrami sandwich and took a bite, gesturing to Cate to do the same. Cate was suddenly ravenous.

As they tied into their meal, the conversation at the table next to theirs caught Cate's attention. The men were complaining about the cancellation of Animal Day at Meadowpoint Manor.

Cate did not doubt for a minute that she was meant not only to overhear these words, but to resolve the problem. Immediately her mind spun off on how she could offer the services of her own pets. Mitsy, her patchwork dog, was way too bouncy for the senior crowd, but Carlton had mellowed nicely and had even gone through training to be a therapy dog. She could also bring Mercy, the spotted three-year-old cat she'd recently taken in. As far as Cate was concerned, Mercy's story was as compelling as anyone's at the Manor.

On their short walk back to Meadowpoint, Wanda looked tired and agreed to Cate's suggestion of a nap. Cate slipped down to the office of Mary Gumm to ask if she might be allowed to bring her own pets for Animal Day. Mary met the offer with questions reflecting her guarded enthusiasm. Were the pets well behaved? Were they calm around a lot of people, especially those that traveled on wheels? Did they know not to leap on people?

Cate assured her that Carlton and Mercy were unsurpassed on all counts. As she left the office, Cate saw Robin stepping off the elevator and got an instant, and somewhat disquieting, glimpse into their own future at Meadowpoint Manor or someplace like it. Their hair would be greyer, the gait slower, but—please, God!—their minds would still be sharp. Maybe, she thought, all five of the No Ordinary Women should reserve their rooms now, so they could spend their twilight years together. Life could be worse.

* * *

KIKI WALKED DOWN THE HALLWAY, carrying a paper cone of flowers. She wanted to do a few things before the medi-van brought her great-gran back. Letting herself into the apartment with the key, she found a vase in the cupboard above the refrigerator. She couldn't understand why anyone would put a cupboard up there where some old, breakable person would have to stand on a chair to get anything out. After setting the vase with the flowers on the nightstand, she stripped the sheets off the bed, gathering them up with the bathroom towels and taking them down to the laundry. The sheets smelled like her great-gran, flowery like that powder puff she had in her bathroom. It gave Kiki a cozy feeling.

Dropping the last quarter into the machine, she closed the lid and turned down the hall towards the apartment of Daisy, the nice lady with the dolls, who had said to let her know when she came back. Lifting her fist to knock on the door, she thought her friends would never believe it if they saw her hanging out with these old people, looking forward to it, actually. But they were just like other people, really, just older.

Daisy had her usual big grin. "Perfect timing! Have you had lunch yet?" she said.

Kiki felt her stomach rumble and realized she'd forgotten to eat again. There was something on the stove that smelled really good. A lady sat on the loveseat by the window, petting a fat gray cat.

"Kiki, come and meet Robin and Jane."

Which was which, Kiki wondered. But then Daisy said, "Jane's full name is Nurse Jane Fuzzy Wuzzy."

"Whoa, that's some name," Kiki said.

"She was Uncle Wiggley's housekeeper in one of my favorite books when I was a child. I used to go to the library twice a week."

"Oh." Kiki patted Nurse Jane on the head and the cat rolled her yellow slanted eyes up to look at her.

The lady named Robin smiled at her and said it was proper to greet cats before people. She'd never heard that one before! Robin was kind of medium tall, medium weight and was maybe the same age as her mom, but didn't have leather skin like her mom did from sun tanning. She didn't gush all over her like some people did, but she didn't ignore her or look at her in that suspicious way either.

Robin started telling her all about how she was going to be talking to her great-gran and taking some pictures of her so she could make a book about her. There would be other old people, too, but Kiki felt proud that someone would think Great-Gran was interesting enough to put her in a book.

She figured out Robin was going to eat with them when Daisy showed Kiki the silverware drawer and handed her three blue placemats and three paper napkins that had daisies on them, and just expected her to set the table like she was family or something. Robin helped, and pretty soon they were all sitting together like they did this every day. The food, which was kind of a cheesy goulash, was really good too. "M.O.," Derek would have said, which was short for "mouth orgasm." But she would never say that to these ladies.

Everything was going great. She let her mind play a game, pretending that Robin was a classy version of her mom and Daisy was her gramma and they all lived in this little cottage with the fat gray cat.

And then Daisy asked her the question: "Why aren't you in school?" she said.

"I graduated early," she mumbled. She reached up and tugged at her hair.

"You don't have to tell me," Daisy said, like she didn't believe what she'd just said.

Kiki had to stare at her plate to get the words out. "Okay, after the fight with Grampa I, um, never went back to school. My friends are letting me couch surf until we figure out what's going on with my grampa. I work two jobs, so I'm not at their apartment much." She looked up, expecting the women to be mad at her for dropping out. Or worse, they could feel sorry for her, but instead they were looking at each other like they already knew that, and more.

"Actually, before you came, we were talking about how we can help you figure out the situation with your grandpa," Robin said.

She felt her whole body tense. "What do you mean?"

Daisy calmed her with a smile. "You said you want to stay with your friends until you get more information about your grandfather. Is that a safe arrangement?"

Kiki started pulling on her hair as she considered her current living situation. "Living with them? Yeah, they're okay. Ashley, that's my girlfriend who works at the same coffee shop as me . . . she and her boyfriend are letting me stay at their apartment. He's kind of a geek, but they're not charging me rent as long as I clean up and pitch in on food."

Both of the ladies nodded. Then Robin said, "We want to help you find your grandfather, but first we need to know a little bit more. Can you tell us about him?"

"The police lady already asked me a bunch of stuff at the hospital." Her stomach squeezed tight thinking about it. "I need to use your bathroom." The apartment was just like her great-gran's, so she knew where it was. She didn't feel so good, and after she'd done her business, she sat there rocking and hugging herself. She splashed cold water on her face, and when she swiped the towel over her face, the edge of her eyebrow zinged with pain. She stared at her pasty reflection. As if she'd meant to all along, she unscrewed the jeweled ball at the end of the eyebrow ring and slipped it out, dropping it in the wastebasket next to the john.

When she came out, Robin and Daisy had cleaned up the dishes and were sitting in the living room. The fat cat was sleeping on top of the TV.

"Okay," Kiki said, "fire away." When Daisy cupped her hand behind her ear, Kiki said, a little louder this time, "What do you want to know about my grampa?"

Answering their questions wasn't as awful as she'd thought, but it wasn't fun, either. They asked pretty much the same things the police lady did, but they didn't treat her like she was some kind of spoiled brat. They wanted to know what her grampa did for a living before he retired (some kind of business consultant). They asked about his friends (didn't have many) and enemies (none that she knew of) and why she left Arizona (because of her loser mother.)

When they wanted her to go over the fight she had with her grampa, her stomach started acting up again, but she managed to sit there without running to the john. It was like her body was going to get rid of something one way or another, if not through her gut, then words were just going to pour out of her mouth instead. She answered all their questions.

Her grandfather could be nice or strict, she told them, and sometimes it was hard to know which way it was going to go. Sometimes he was generous with her and she figured it was because he felt guilty that he'd raised such a loser daughter. Then other times he wanted to teach her some kind of lesson. That's just how he was.

But that last time he'd freaked. He yelled, which he'd never done before, and said he needed to know where she'd been all night.

"He was already upset about my boyfriend, even if he never actually met him. He figured out I was going out with somebody, but I never told him Derek's name. When he got super mad because I didn't come home, he said it was because he was so worried. But then he acted like I was sleeping with, like, the whole state of Minnesota." A tear slipped down her cheek and she brushed it away. "He said I was just like my mother." That part really hurt. It still did.

"Was Derek ever at the house?" Daisy asked casually.

"No," she said, shaking her head.

She told them that right after she'd had the fight with her grampa, Derek split. More like he called her a spoiled brat and then he laughed at her when she cried and called her other names she didn't feel like repeating.

The whole time she talked, she stared at her lap, not wanting to see the look she was sure was on their faces. Maybe they weren't looking any way at all, but she wasn't taking any chances.

Daisy was pretty cool about it though, and dropped the whole Derek thing. Her next question was about what happened after she and her grandfather "had words," as she put it. "Did you try calling him afterwards?"

Kiki looked out the window, feeling jumpy. "Not right away." She slid her eyes over and saw their faces were empty, at least empty of judging.

Robin asked her what made her think something was wrong with her grampa. She didn't use the word "dead," but Kiki knew that's what she meant.

The cat jumped down from the TV. It sounded like she said, "Oomph," then she stretched and waddled off to her food dish.

Kiki had no trouble remembering how she'd felt abandoned, but couldn't quite think when the other worry started, the worry that he'd actually gone away. Or later, when she started thinking something bad had happened to him and it was her fault. "I didn't call right away, but a couple days after I decided Derek was a loser, I went back to the house."

Daisy nodded at her to keep talking. She wasn't smiling, but the wrinkles her smile made were still there.

"I had it all planned what I was gonna say. Not an apology, exactly, but like, 'Chill, it's over anyway with Derek. I hope you're happy.' But he wouldn't answer the door." She rubbed her wrist across her nose and sniffled. "I could hear the doorbell, so I knew it wasn't broken."

Daisy tilted her head and patted her lap for the cat to jump up, which it did with the same *oomph* as before. "Do you know if he was even home?"

"Well, I thought he was. He usually is in the afternoon. See, every morning he has this little ritual. He goes to his post office box, buys coffee and goes to the library to read the newspaper and *The Wall Street Journal*. Every day!"

"Ah" Robin said, and sat there like she was thinking about something.

"What about his car?" Daisy asked her. She leaned forward.

"He's got a big old Caddy." Then she figured out why she asked. "I didn't know it was gone at first. Not until I went around and looked through the garage window."

"But the windows were covered," Robin said.

Kiki started to say something, but then it hit her. Robin had gone to the house! Maybe she was just another cop after all. Kiki squinted up her eyes to let her know she didn't trust her. "When were you at my grandpa's?"

"Oh!" Robin looked surprised. "Your great-grandmother asked me to go over to the house when she started worrying about him."

"So that's what Era meant!" Daisy said, her eyes dancing with excitement.

"What?" They both said at the same time.

Daisy turned to Robin. "Era said that 'the girl' was on the case and when we asked what she meant, she said something about the 'junior detective' taking care of things. I should have known who she meant. After all, your mother told us all about how you and your friends helped solve that murder last year."

Robin laughed. "Yup, I'm the junior detective."

Kiki really wanted to know more about that, but Robin started talking again before she had a chance to ask.

"But how could you see whether or not the car was there? The window on the side had something over it."

Kiki gave Robin a look. "You'd better be telling the truth, 'cause I'll ask Great-Gran."

"It's true, and by all means, ask her."

Kiki relaxed. "Grampa didn't want people looking in, so he leaned a hunk of plasterboard up against the garage window, and then he could take it down if he wanted light in there. But it was leaning just enough to make a skinny crack I could see through if I stood in the right place." She gave Daisy a quick look and saw she was trying not to smile.

"But wasn't it dark in there with the window covered?" Robin asked.

Kiki thought back. Slapping her hands on her thighs she said, "Nope, there was just enough light coming through that high up window, the circle one."

Robin grinned at her. "Well, aren't you the little detective!"

"I can be pretty resourceful. That's what my grampa says."

"What else did you notice?"

Kiki's face fell, thinking about that day. "I just felt bad, thinking he was home all the time and maybe I should just break in." She wasn't just sad, she'd been really mad at him. But they would totally freak if she said that.

Robin got a funny look on her face and for a second, Kiki wondered if she could read her mind, but then she said, "It certainly changes things, that his car is missing. When he travels, does he take road trips?"

Kiki shrugged. "Yeah, I guess. A couple years ago, I had a big fight with my mom and called him to see if I could come live with him. He didn't answer for, like, a couple weeks, and when he did call, he said he was in Florida. Or maybe it was Texas. Someplace warm, anyway, 'cause I remember thinking if he wanted warm, he could've just as well come to Arizona."

Daisy said, "Do you know anyone who wanted to harm your grandfather?"

Whoa! "Yeah, my mom hated his guts. She thought Grampa was selfish because she lived in a trailer and he had all this money. She didn't even call him her dad. When she talked about him, she called him the 'old man.'"

Daisy frowned. The two ladies looked at each other.

"Does your mother ever visit him?"

"Uh-uh. Not for years. When I came here from Arizona, she sent me on a bus."

"Is she still in Arizona?"

"Yeah, I guess . . ."

Nobody said anything for a while, and then Robin started again, asking about the day she went back to the house. "Why didn't you just go in?"

When she said she lost her key, Robin tilted her head and looked at her from an angle until she said something more.

"Before I saw his Caddy was gone, I was thinking maybe I'd just pound on the front door and yell until he came, and then I saw that he even took away the fu— the flipping welcome mat. That's when I just, like, gave up. I didn't think he could be so mean." She tried really hard not to cry, but when a tear slipped out, she just broke down and cried.

All of a sudden, the cat bounced off Daisy's lap and onto Kiki's. She stretched up on her chest and put a paw on her chin.

"That's a good little Nurse Jane," Daisy said to the cat.

It niggled at Robin all the way home. When she'd gone to Winston's house she'd had a camera in her car, as she usually did, so why hadn't she taken pictures? She visualized the front door, heavy and churchlike, but couldn't recall whether or not there had been a welcome mat in front of it that day. If one had recently been removed, she reasoned, it might have left its outline on the wide front step. Surely she would have noticed that.

At the stop sign near her house, Robin absent-mindedly rolled to a stop, then surged forward, robot-like, not even noticing the silver SUV approaching the intersection from her right. Both drivers slammed on their brakes just inches before contact. The other driver, a young woman with two children strapped in the back seat, looked scared. She held one hand up in a "what the hell?" gesture before driving off. With adrenaline still prickling through her, Robin gripped the wheel and set her mind on her driving for the last eight blocks.

Coming into the kitchen through the garage door, she held out her hands for the cats to smell and told them all about her dalliance with Nurse Jane Fuzzy Wuzzy. She had their full attention as she opened the little crock and gave them each a pinch of dried catnip. Samson licked it up daintily, but Delilah, the voluptuary, rolled in it with feline decadence.

Robin saw the potted basil was wilting, and as she wandered from kitchen to sunroom to dining room watering plants, she tried to make sense of what Kiki had told her. Had Winston been so petty to remove the welcome mat symbolically just to hurt his granddaughter? It was an odd reaction, to say the least.

Their relationship had been convoluted, that much was clear. Winston had given Kiki a home, fed her and enrolled her in school. And just today Robin discovered he'd also bought her an old Buick and paid her car insurance. By the looks of it, he'd cared for his granddaughter deeply, though he scorned his own daughter.

And that was another thing she'd like to know. What had happened between Winston and his daughter? According to Kiki, if she had related the story accurately, their last fight had to do with his suspicion his seventeen-year-old granddaughter was engaging in sex. He'd accused her of being like her mother. Had that caused the original rift with his own daughter—having sex at an early age?

Robin remembered all too well the ugly scene she'd had with her own daughter, Cass, over that subject. It was hard to see your little girl become a sexually active young woman, knowing how ephemeral relationships can be. Her job for so long had been to protect her daughters from harm, and even though she knew intellectually that they had to make their own mistakes, she'd always felt negligent when they came home with a skinned knee, a bounced check or a broken heart. She could only imagine how Winston had spent years trying to prevent his own daughter from taking unacceptable risks, and, after giving up on her, had then turned his attention to her only child, trying to keep her from the same fate.

She broke off several spent blooms and yellowed leaves from the hibiscus she'd brought in from the front walk only last week. This would be the third year she'd overwintered the hibiscus. The mums last year hadn't been so lucky. They'd languished until she'd put them out of their misery.

Like the photo she had neglected to take, the yellow mums at Winston's house clicked into her mind. One of the pots of mums and kale and sweet potato vine had shown only the withering of cooler fall nights, but the other had been crunched down. She heard the shutter click in her mind now, her mental camera focusing on the front step. What if someone—Winston, for instance—had fallen in front of the door, collapsing onto the planter? It would have caused the foliage to have been flattened and broken, exactly as it had been.

She closed her eyes. The mental picture shifted. What if there had been blood, for instance, on the welcome mat, so that it had to be discarded?

She got Era's number from her mother, who told her Era had just come back from the hospital. She would have to give the poor woman some time to settle in, but it wouldn't be an easy wait.

Era sounded befuddled when she answered the phone two hours later. She said she'd been taking a little catnap in her chair. "I'm all in. The ride home took the stuffing right out of me," she said with a dry laugh. "My eyes closed the minute Kiki left."

Robin figured the worry about her son had been as exhausting as her heart attack. Era's bleariness cleared up, though, as she talked about Winston, and Robin realized she wasn't in denial at all about the likely fate of her son. Actually, she talked about him almost matter-of-factly. "There's nothing to be done for him now," said Era. "He's gone on ahead of me, and I'll be seeing him soon enough. It's our little Kiki we're worried about."

It certainly sounded as if she believed he was dead. "What is it that worries you about Kiki?"

There was a long enough pause so Robin asked again. Then Era said, "I don't know for certain. Winston has been maddeningly quiet lately."

Robin wished her comments were not so enigmatic. She took a deep breath and launched into her reason for calling.

When she'd finished, Era said, "I see." She coughed dryly. When she spoke again, her voice cracked. "Listen, dear, if you think

I should call the police about this welcome mat business, I'd better do it this minute before it gets too late."

Or maybe she said, "before it's too late," but before Robin could ask for clarification, Era had hung up.

* * *

THE NEXT MORNING ROBIN picked Cate up to drive to Stillwater, a charming town on the St. Croix River, which separated Minnesota from Wisconsin. Originally named Dacotah, Stillwater was rich in history, beginning as a fur-trading hub before Minnesota became a state, then growing into a thriving mill town. It was Minnesota's first city, and in its heyday it had boasted some of the grandest homes of lumber barons, an impressive opera house and several breweries. Over time, some of the homes had been adapted to serve as bed and breakfasts for the tourists who now flocked to Stillwater's eateries, shops, antique stores and antiquarian bookstores, art studios and galleries, all with a scenic backdrop.

For Cate and Robin, who both pursued their own artistic endeavors, this trip was a mix of business and pleasure. Cate needed to replenish her handcrafted precious metal jewelry on display at a gallery in Stillwater, as well as her newest line of copper rings and bracelets at a local gift shop. The same gift shop carried Robin's books of nature photography, as did the small independent bookstore in town. Another gallery carried several of her framed photographs and unframed prints. Today she brought new autumn-themed prints for the gallery's upcoming show.

In less than forty minutes, they arrived in Stillwater, where Robin found a parking spot near the gift shop. Cate hoisted a large leatherette tote out of the trunk and popped into the shop, while Robin walked the short distance to the bookstore with a canvas bag of her books. The wind had a little bite to it today, and she was glad she had worn her boiled wool jacket.

They met up later at the art gallery that carried Cate's jewelry, and Cate spent some time arranging her display in the glass case, using smooth stones on which to rest her newest triple-metal bracelets, wide silver bands with accents in gold and copper. The adjacent case held an elegantly whimsical collection of woodland fairy creatures made of wood, clay and fiber.

From there, they drove to the second gallery. The owner, Jillian, eagerly leafed through Robin's prints and unwrapped the framed photos as Robin and Cate hauled them in. She was pretty, with dark hair and freckles. "Yes!" she said, setting the largest one, over four feet wide, framed, against the wall and backing off to assess it.

Robin was delighted when Jillian removed a painting in the front window and hung her photograph there instead. It was one of Robin's favorites, taken one morning last fall at a northern resort, showing two little tow-headed girls sitting on a log. Their faces were turned to stare in wonderment at a brown rabbit in the grass just inches from where their feet dangled. Behind them, a fire in a stone ring smoldered, obscuring the background and lending the scene an aura of mystery.

Cate commented on how another of Robin's new photographs, the one of a three-legged fox and her kits frolicking in an open field, picked up the exact muted green and rusty hues of the collection of pottery on one of the shelves.

"Do you like the pottery? He's new here," said Jillian, holding out a globe-shaped vase.

Cate took it in her hands. "Beautiful. Is it Raku?" She let her fingers slide over the pot, imagining the potter's fingers making the subtle grooves in the clay.

"Not all of them are Raku, but this one is. He does exclusively wood firing. Anagama."

"That's his name?" Cate asked.

Jillian's laugh was like a wind chime. "Oh, no, his name is Jon Nord. Anagama is the oldest type of Japanese kiln. Some of the early anagamas were made by tunneling into natural banks of clay to make a single-chambered kiln. Now they're made out of bricks, but they still have the tunnel shape of the old kilns."

While Jillian talked, Robin picked up the artist's statement. For her own bio in the store, she had chosen to avoid the pompous style so many artists gave in to. Reading this one reminded her why she'd chosen simplicity. Jon Nord's statement began, "The amalgamation of earth and fire; the marriage of functionality and artistry; the honest labor of cutting and splitting wood; the hallucinogenic nights stoking a ravenous fire; the transcendent synergy of clay, ash and flame. These are my masters, and my masters insist that I create!"

Jillian placed a second pot in Robin's hands. The cylindrical piece had rough and smooth patches, and the colors—earth tones with flashes of reddish-orange and khaki green—indeed matched the colors in her fox photograph.

"With wood firing, the colors come out in unpredictable and exciting ways. He does interesting combinations of glazed and unglazed. Like this one. Only the top edge is glazed." Jillian showed them a goblet with a smooth glazed lip in robin's egg blue.

Cate set her pot on the shelf and picked up a tea bowl, rolling it between her fingers. The outer surface was earthy, and the inside was smooth with a ruby glaze. "Didn't one of *The Cat Who* books have something to do with pottery?" she asked Robin.

This was a mystery series they both liked, beginning with *The Cat Who Could Read Backwards* and ending, many, many books later, with *The Cat Who Had 60 Whiskers.* The prolific author's books had spanned Robin's and Cate's entire reading life and they had eagerly read them all. But for the life of her, Robin couldn't recall one with pottery.

Cate set the tea bowl down and picked up the rest of the five-piece set, caressing each piece in turn. "They feel right in the hands," she commented. She tested the lid of the stubby teapot to ensure it would stay in place while pouring. A crease deepened between her brows. "There's something about this set that speaks to me," Cate said. "I think I have to buy it."

"Excellent." Jillian nodded and bustled into the back room to get a box and wrapping paper.

Robin turned to Cate. "What's going on in your little brain?" She'd seen the look on her friend's face before, and it usually meant Cate was seeing or hearing something most people did not see or hear. Most of her hunches came to nothing at all, but there had been times—significant times—when her intuitions or hunches or whatever they were, had been eerily accurate. At least one premonition, Robin believed, had saved her life.

"It's just so tactile. I can imagine the process, being spun and shaped, and then the intensity of that wood fire . . . Her words trailed off and she glanced back to the shelf where her newly purchased tea set had sat only minutes earlier.

"Whatever you're thinking, is it—?" Robin searched for the right word.

"E.S.P? Second sight? Hocus pocus?" Cate offered.

"I was going to ask if it's something important."

"Aren't all my thoughts important?" Cate joked, but her right hand snaked out of her pocket and her fingers curled around her turquoise amulet, sliding the pendant slowly back and forth on the chain. "I'm not sure."

12

Kiki parked her Oldsmobile in Winston's driveway, several yards back from the house. Opening the rear car door, Robin looked up, half expecting to see the crow at his sentinel post high up in the oak tree. Autumn was on hold this week, with temperatures rising into the low seventies, and an early morning shower had greened up the grass under the fallen maple leaves.

Kiki jumped out and opened the door for Daisy, who ignored offers of assistance. Daisy's gait was careful but steady as she crossed the lawn, using her cane to probe the uneven surface. The other two flanked her, just in case she should lose her footing.

"Even if the police said I can keep living here, I don't think I could ever sleep here again. It's just too creepy," Kiki said, chewing on her lip.

Daisy poked a soft spot in the earth and made a small course correction. "As long as it's not a big problem, you might as well stay with your friends while this sorts itself out."

Robin thought the phrase misleading, since they had set out on this little jaunt precisely because things were not sorting themselves out on their own. The three of them had discussed it and decided coming to the house might elicit a memory that would shed some light on the inexplicable disappearance of Kiki's grandfather.

Standing together on the lawn, they were quiet for the moment as they perused the scene. Nothing on the property appeared to be out of place. Trees obscured their view of other houses in the neighborhood. In Robin's estimation, nothing had changed since she was last here.

Kiki had filled Daisy and Robin in yesterday after she had talked to Officer Lester. Having received missing persons reports from Kiki and Era, and interviewing both of them, the police planned to talk to neighbors on either side to see when they had last seen Winston and to inquire about any unusual activity at the house.

From Kiki's description, it was obvious Officer Lester was the one talking to Mary Gumm at Meadowpoint Manor. According to Kiki, the detective said they were listing Winston Dudley as "missing," but not "endangered." For now, officially, they had no reason to believe he had not left of his own accord. As for Kiki's situation, because she was over sixteen and had a place to live, child welfare had no reason to get involved.

Robin was surprised to learn they had no plans to talk to Winston's ex-wife Josephine and her husband in Glendale, Arizona to see if Winston had been in contact. As far as Kiki knew, Jo—she said she never thought of her as her grandmother—had not been in contact with him in years anyway. Even more surprising, the police evidently saw no merit in tracking down Winston's daughter Diana, who, according to Kiki, hated her father.

On the drive over today, Kiki told them something new. She said she'd tried calling her mother a few days ago when she got really worried about Winston, but her mother hadn't answered. "She's probably back at Restart," she'd said, explaining that her mother had gone to the halfway house in Arizona once before. She had no idea if her mom had been in touch with Winston since May when she'd made arrangements to send Kiki to Minneapolis by bus.

"There's not much else we can do," Officer Lester had told her. "There's nothing in this report to indicate foul play." She'd gone on to explain they were a small department, and as a detective, she was involved in a number of investigations, some of them more urgent than this one, which she said didn't "rise to the level of concern" that merited a big expense of funds or personnel. It certainly wasn't a case that justified sending a detective to another state.

The officer had time enough, though, to "grill" Kiki, as she'd put it, about her taste in companions. Kiki seemed to be quite destroyed by the fact that as soon as she said something about her "loser" mother probably being in treatment again, the detective treated her differently. She was defensive at any suggestion she might have inherited terrible judgment from her mother. After that, Robin doubted Kiki was forthcoming about any of her relationships, including the one with the young man.

Robin looked across the lawn and tried to calculate how long it had been since Winston had gone missing. According to Daisy, he had last visited his mother two weeks before Era had cornered Robin, deputizing her to find her missing son. That had been over a week ago, so about three and a half weeks, altogether. Would the grass be longer by now, she wondered?

Kiki frowned and pulled on her hair as she stared up at the second floor windows. "It really feels empty, doesn't it?" she said.

Robin noticed the concentration on her face and asked, "Are you remembering something?"

"Yeah. No, not about my grampa anyway. I was just thinking how me and my friends used to snoop at this old house in Colorado, near where me and my mom were living. We thought the house was haunted 'cause it was old and falling apart. We used to bike over there and get ourselves all freaked out, and excited too 'cause we thought we might see a ghost. This one day we climbed a tree to look in the upstairs window, and we were almost up to the branch where we were gonna sit, and I look up and there's some old lady looking right back at us." She bit her lip. "I wet my pants."

Daisy covered her mouth with her hand. "Scared it right out of you, did it? I think I might have had the same reaction." She took a few steps to look more closely at the planter next to the front steps and, using her cane to hold the shrubbery back, she scoped out the area underneath, bending at the waist to peer into the shadows.

"What is it?" Robin asked.

"It's hard to tell. The soil seems to be depressed here."

Kiki snickered.

"I suppose you think we should give it a Valium?" she said to Kiki, who giggled and nodded.

The girl got down on all fours. "Yeah, I see what you mean. It's like maybe somebody fell down here. Or stood here." She lowered herself to her belly and poked around with her fingers. Her search produced nothing more exciting than a pale rock that crumbled in her hand and two acorns. Clearly disappointed, she sat back on her heels. "I thought maybe I'd find Grampa's watch—his dress watch, not the one he wore all the time. He couldn't find it and he asked me if I'd done something with it. Like I'd wear a watch. He didn't exactly accuse me of stealing it, but he gave me a look like he didn't trust me anymore. He said it cost a lot." She bit her lower lip. "It was a couple days later we had that awful fight, so I think he didn't believe me."

Kiki stood and brushed her hands against her black jeans. "I'm going to check the back of the house."

"I'll go with you." Robin fell in behind her. Leaving Daisy to her own devices, Kiki and Robin circled down the hill and around the back, looking for signs of forced entry or other evidence of mayhem, but the house was closed up, just as Winston would have left it if he'd chosen to take a long trip. They circled around a second time in the opposite direction, this time walking closer to the perimeter of the lot.

When they rejoined Daisy, she put a hand on Kiki's shoulder. "Didn't you come here earlier to get your things?"

"Yeah."

Several small birds were noisily chasing a crow from the treetop in a neighboring yard. High above them a plane passed, it's distant roar the only sound.

"Hmm. And you went inside?"

"Yeah."

"How did you get in if you lost your key?"

Kiki's eyes lit up. "I did lose it, but a few days later I found it on the floor of my car. It must've come off my key ring."

"Show me," said Daisy, and Kiki went to the car and extracted her key ring from the ignition. It was a simple split ring which held five keys and a purple peace symbol. Two of the keys were for the apartment, she explained, plus one each for the coffee shop, her car and this house.

"The police put no restrictions on your staying in the house then?" Robin asked.

"Yeah, they don't care. I just don't want to." She wrapped her arms around her waist.

"Let's check it out, then." Daisy moved toward the door. Robin helped her up the step and over the threshold while Kiki unlocked the door.

Inside the air was stale. Turning on the lights, they glanced about at the simple, tastefully decorated living room with its brown leather and pale wood. The kitchen was clean, utilitarian, obviously a house never subjected to a woman's touch. Kiki put a hand on the leather armchair, caressing the indentation made by her grandfather's head.

While Daisy looked around on the main level, Robin and Kiki went upstairs. Here too the atmosphere was one of simplicity, efficiency and order. There was a faint smell of cleanser and aftershave. Bathroom towels were hung with fastidious perfection. The medicine cabinet held a bottle of Old Spice and other toiletries, some low-dose aspirin and a sinus spray, all lined up with military precision.

An almost full bottle of Lipitor was the only prescription medicine. Robin didn't voice her observation that a man doesn't leave behind his prescriptions when he takes a trip.

Kiki touched the slats of the wooden blinds, which were exactly horizontal. "Grampa always said a cluttered house is the sign of a cluttered mind."

Winston's double bed was made and his small walk-in closet was loosely filled with dress shirts and suits, a rotating tie rack, creased pants and freshly polished shoes. "Yup," Kiki said, looking it over, "that's the way he always keeps it." She put her face into the blue terry robe that hung on a hook inside the closet door. "It still smells like Old Spice," she said, breathing into the robe, and then the sobs came, loud and shuddering.

Robin stood at a distance, letting Kiki grieve. Though it had happened decades ago, memories of her own father's death were still painful, not the sharp twist in her chest that it had been at first, but a heavy weight settled on her heart each time Robin remembered the phone call, and the rush to the hospital only to find her father in a coma.

He had been released from prison after serving only ten months because the doctors had found a heart abnormality. At her young age, Robin's understanding was that her father had a broken heart. Even though he had lived four more years after his release, he was never again the robust and openly demonstrative father she had so loved.

Standing in Winston's bedroom watching Kiki cry, Robin had no doubt this man loved his granddaughter, just as Robin's father had loved her before his broken heart had stopped for good. Only as an adult did she come to understand how easily a parent might be tempted to make the mistake he'd made, removing his only child from an environment he deemed unsafe. But for all three of them, the price had been way too costly. So much time had been wasted.

She reached out to touch the girl's thin shoulders, turning her away from the robe and into her arms.

When she'd pulled herself together, Kiki swung open the door to the pale lavender room which had been hers. Robin observed that while it was neat, it felt quite different from the rest of the house that reeked of masculinity. The simple white blinds were draped in gauzy fabric. The pink and lavender bedspread was for a younger girl. Two oversized purple pillows bore the peace symbol that had been so prevalent in Robin's youth and was echoed on Kiki's key ring. Against one wall was a plain birch computer desk with a goose-necked lamp and swivel chair. Above it, a padded paisley bulletin board was empty except for a handful of decorative pins. The fake fur area rug was bright pink. One thing was certain—thought and love and expectation had gone into preparing this room for Kiki's arrival.

Robin noticed a bare nail on the wall. "What was here?"

"A picture of me and my grampa in a fishing boat when I was little. Going fishing with him is one of my best memories." Kiki swallowed hard. "I took it with me."

"Nothing can take those memories from you," Robin said softly.

Kiki told her how, when they'd still lived in Minnesota, her mother would sometimes drop her at Winston's house and not be heard from for days. She said her grandfather openly disapproved of Diana's careless parenting, but had never let it affect his feelings for her. In fact, she admitted, "I think it made him even nicer, just to make up for the way she treated me. When she dumped me here, he always tried to distract me, like taking me fishing or to Valleyfair. He even went on the rides with me. Even after he threw up on the big roller coaster."

For all his compulsive neatness and austere visage, Winston obviously had a tender spot for his granddaughter. It hurt Robin to think that this one solid, loving presence in her life might be gone for good.

In the upstairs hallway, they passed the laundry chute and Kiki stopped to open it, looking down the dark chute into the dark basement laundry room.

"You know what I told her?" Kiki said.

It took Robin a moment to realize she was back to telling about her conversation with Officer Lester.

"I said if you don't think anything happened to Grampa here, and there isn't any evidence of foul play, then where the hell is he?'"

"Valid question."

"The police woman said she'd like to know the answer to that question, too."

Downstairs they found Daisy in the paneled office, sitting in the swivel chair behind a maple credenza. She shook her head at them to indicate she'd found nothing of interest. "Where does your grandfather keep his files?" She opened the desk's file drawer to show only a few legal-sized folders suspended from the metal frame. "It's just tax stuff," she said.

Kiki answered immediately. "He keeps everything on his computer." She scanned the room. "It was a laptop. He must've taken it with him."

Robin slid open the leftmost drawer of the credenza. It held only pens and stapler, a pair of folding reading glasses in a leather tube, a calculator and a silver case that held his business cards: Winston Dudley, Investment Strategies.

Kiki picked up the Mont Blanc pen from its wooden holder and doodled a butterfly on her left wrist. "I have my own laptop, so I never used his. Besides, he's got like a million passwords on everything."

"I'm concerned about this house sitting empty for too long," Daisy said. "Some decisions will have to be made sooner or later.

What happens, for instance, when the utilities aren't paid? Winter's coming and if there's no heat, the water pipes will burst."

Kiki replaced the pen in its holder. "Grampa paid everything online. A lot of guys his age don't want to mess with computers, like they're scared of them or something, but not my grampa. He even pays his bills online, so if he wants to go on a trip or something, the house will take care of itself. That's how he put it."

Daisy planted her cane and stood. "I've always said good old-fashioned paper has served me all my life and I don't want to change now. I want proof in my hands." She turned to look about the room, as if she may have missed something.

"Same with my mother," Robin said.

"But I do understand going paperless for the sake of ecology." She turned to Kiki. "So the utilities are taken care of by automatic payments?"

"Exactly."

"I'd be afraid other people could hack into my account," Daisy said.

Robin was impressed she knew the term.

They were jolted by the sound of the front door opening.

"Hello?" called a man's voice.

Kiki's hands flew to her mouth. Her eyes were huge. Her one word was whispered behind her hands, but audible to Robin. "Grampa."

Daisy's mouth formed a near perfect circle and Robin leaned with one hand at her chest, the other against the credenza.

"Hello? Who's there?"

Kiki pushed past them. From her expression, two things were clear: that she had not expected to be seeing her grandfather again, and that she was overjoyed to do so.

Robin and Daisy followed close behind.

"Oh!" said Kiki when she saw the figure in the doorway. She covered her mouth again.

Robin could see his well-developed chest and arms. She thought he was in his fifties. It was not the way she remembered Era's son.

"Who are you?" said the man as he widened his stance. He wore jeans and polo shirt. A pair of sunglasses was propped atop his thinning hair.

"I'm Kiki. Who are you?"

"Uh!" the man grunted. The features on his tanned face softened. "Where's Winston?"

"I don't know!" Kiki's voice rose to a squeak. Then, as the two women came to stand closely behind her, she straightened her shoulders and said, "I think you should tell me who you are, and why you just walked in here."

"You're his daughter's kid, right?"

She nodded.

"I live next door. Conrad Bauer." He stepped forward. "Miss, ma'am, ma'am," he said as he shook their hands in turn.

He explained that since both he and Winston were retired and living alone, they looked after each other's property when one of them was on a trip.

Kiki's eyes brightened. "Do you know where he went?"

"He said nothing to me about any plans to be away."

Kiki's disappointment was palpable.

"The police came by the other day and told me they were checking with the neighbors because someone reported him missing. Was that you?"

She nodded.

He harrumphed. "Tough deal."

When Robin looked at her, Kiki's eyes had become flat and impenetrable.

Daisy suggested to Mr. Bauer that since the house would be empty for a while longer, he should continue to keep an eye on the place.

He chuckled. "Not a problem. If I sit around I'll get flabby. If you need anything, I'm right next door."

Kiki, staring at the floor, said nothing.

"Well then, since I already have a key, I'll just let myself out and let you get back to what you were doing." He backed out, pulling the door shut.

"So what happens next?" Daisy was making her way to the kitchen.

Kiki came out of her stupor enough to follow her. "I don't know. I was going to ask Great-Gran what I should do, but then she had that heart attack."

Robin wondered what Brad would say if she were to offer Kiki a place to stay. Trying to imagine his response, she knew that was not the best plan. Kiki had a place to stay. What she needed most was moral support.

Daisy pointed with her cane to several items on the kitchen counter. "I found some things in the refrigerator that should be thrown out."

Kiki opened the milk carton, sniffed and recoiled. After pouring the sour milk in the sink, she dumped baking soda down the drain and flushed it with water. Opening the lower cupboard door, she found a plastic trash bag and tossed in the empty milk carton, along with some furry cottage cheese, a few slices of less than fresh bread and a couple of foil-wrapped items. Automatically, she headed for the garage with the bag when Daisy stopped her. "Unless your neighbor is taking the garbage can out to the street, we shouldn't put it there," she said.

Kiki's shoulders slumped. "Oh, yeah."

"Let's just take this bag to the dumpsters at your great-grandma's apartment," Robin suggested.

Before they left, Robin opened the door to Winston's two-car garage, flipping the light switch.

The floor was cleaner than her garage had ever been. With no car in it, it looked spacious. There was a single workbench toward the back, and mounted behind that was a white-painted pegboard, its wrenches and hammers and screwdrivers hanging in order of largest to smallest. Opening the lid of the large plastic garbage container, she found it empty. Her curiosity was piqued. Had Winston taken out the garbage, waited for pickup and then brought the can back in just before going missing? It was looking more and more likely that he had left of his own volition.

"Should we call it a day?" It was clear that Daisy's energy was flagging. Her arm shook as she leaned on her cane.

But on the ride home she perked up and chatted with them, letting the conversation slide back to Kiki's erstwhile boyfriend, Derek.

Kiki was much less guarded, less emotionally shutdown than she'd been in the house. On the drive back, she answered questions in a straightforward manner. As for what Derek did for a living, she said he'd done "drywall and stuff," adding that with the slowdown in new housing, he had taken side jobs, like laying tile and mud jacking. "He hates what he does. He says it kills creativity. I heard him talking to some guy, and they were both saying if we lived in a civilized country, the artists wouldn't have to do anything but create art. They both said it was bullshit for anyone to be a starving artist, like the government was supposed to pay them." Checking her rearview mirror, she merged onto the freeway.

When Daisy asked how she and Derek had met, Kiki said, "At a party. It was right after I got here. We just started talking and I really thought he was my age 'cause he acts kind of immature. Loser." The last part she said under her breath.

"What?" said Daisy.

"Derek's immature," she said again. "He does stupid stuff like the flaming dog poop thing."

Robin was pretty sure she knew the stunt, but listened while Kiki explained it to Daisy. "One night I thought we were going to hang out, just the two of us, but that day some guy stiffed him for the tile he put in, so he says we're going to teach him a lesson. We drive over to the guy's house and I sit there in the truck while he runs up and puts a big old pile of dog poop in a lunch bag on the front step and lights it on fire. Then he rings the bell and runs back to the truck so we can watch."

In the front seat, Daisy turned to her. "Watch what?"

"The guy hears the doorbell and comes out, sees something burning and stomps on it. Derek thought it was the funniest thing ever, but I was totally embarrassed. The guy was old, like your age," she said, looking at Robin in the rear view mirror. She pulled into the visitor's row in Meadowpoint's ground level garage and shut off the ignition.

"The things people think of," said Daisy.

Retrieving the plastic bag from the trunk, Robin wondered if there was some rule about nonresidents throwing garbage in the dumpster. Scoping out the area for security cameras, she saw only one, and it was directed toward the back door and the elevators. The alcove that held the dumpster was not subject to the same security. She heaved the bag in.

Cate marveled at the transformation Carlton had on the residents. The black lab made his rounds of the room, spending a minute or so with each of the twenty-two senior citizens who had shown up for Animal Day. The dog's demeanor varied slightly with each person. He did his version of a smile at one man, for instance, with his tongue lolling out. With Iris, he nudged her hand to indicate she should stroke his ears. And for Daisy, he wagged his tail against the floor hard enough to drive nails. When he came to Era, he put his head against her knee, leaning into her and closing his eyes as they communed silently.

Mercy, the spotted cat, wound herself around Era's ankles and then hopped onto Iris's lap to nuzzle into her hands before checking out a ball of yarn in Frannie's bag. Two years ago, the cat had been hit by a car and managed to drag herself to the bushes in front of Cate's house where Cate found her, dehydrated and in shock. Pronouncing her odds grim, and sure that if the cat should survive she would never walk, the vet nevertheless agreed to operate. When bone and muscle miraculously healed, the cat got up and walked, awkwardly at first, exploring the veterinary hospital and demanding to visit the other four-legged patients. It was noticed by many on staff that the animals she was allowed to visit were calmer. Eventually Cate brought her home, naming her Mercy. One day Cate let Mercy out in the fenced patio area of her backyard while she gardened. Within minutes she looked up to see that Mercy had a pair of bunnies dangling from her mouth. She wouldn't let Cate take them away and Cate resigned herself to an ugly predator/prey episode of Animal Planet. But apparently Mercy's compassion toward the two abandoned bunnies overrode her carnivorous instincts. For days the spotted cat carried them around by the scruffs of their necks and let them sleep on her back until they were old enough to be released back to nature, where they promptly nibbled away the entire patch of leaf lettuce Cate had planted.

When the hour was over, the residents were reluctant to leave, but Era stood, saying she was "all in" and in need of a nap. The others shuffled off and soon the meeting rooms and hallways were uncharacteristically quiet. Cate, with Carlton on his leash and Mercy back in her carrier, stopped in for a quick visit with her mother. Carlton looked like he was ready for a nap too.

Wanda was talking to someone on the phone and waved Cate in while she took the wireless phone into her bedroom to finish the call. Cate assumed she'd been talking to her newly discovered half-brother.

When Wanda came back, she confirmed it had been Ricky on the other end, but didn't elaborate. Cate had, after all, explicitly told her mother she needed time to absorb the idea of having family after all these years, and Wanda was probably just honoring her request. Cate was curious all the same.

"I thought you were going to come down to the lounge with everyone else," Cate said, offering treats to Mercy and Carlton.

"Why would I do that when I can get a private showing?" Wanda countered. She picked up Mercy with two hands and hauled her over to a sunny spot by the window. The dog settled at her feet.

"Help! Help!"

Carlton roused, ears perked.

At first Cate wasn't sure she'd heard it. Finger to her lips, she hushed her mother.

"Help!" The tinny voice called again.

Cate threw the door open. Twenty yards away down the hall a disheveled Era Dudley stood. Her glasses were askew and her hands fluttered in front of her chest. Cate rushed forward, catching her as she began to collapse. "I'll call the doctor. You wait right here." She tried to release her, but Era dug her bony fingers into Cate's forearm.

"Not my heart," said Era breathlessly. She planted her feet wide.

"I'll go get help."

Era hung onto her. "Wait, I'll go with you."

"What's happening?" Wanda called from the doorway. Carlton whined, straining to get away from Wanda's firm grip on his collar.

As she held the old woman, Cate could feel her heart, rhythmic if not strong, beating against her chest. Keeping one arm around her, she turned her toward Wanda's apartment.

"Wait, my cane."

Cate stopped to retrieve the shiny black cane lying on the hallway floor and together they made their way through the open door. "Do you want to lie down?"

"I most certainly do not." Instead she sat in the straight-backed, upholstered chair and, hand to heart, she caught her breath. Mercy immediately sat under her chair.

"Put that thing away," said Era, eyeing the cell phone in Cate's hand. "I do not want to give anyone an excuse to declare me incompetent. And for the record, this is not about my health." Her hands wavered as she composed herself.

Wanda brought her a glass of water.

Era took two sips. "He tried to kidnap me." Her jaws tightened with outrage and a tear slipped down her cheek.

Kneeling beside her, Cate took her wrist and felt her pulse. It was rapid. "Are you hurt? I really think we should get you to a doctor."

"No." Era pulled her hand back and massaged her forearms. Cate peeled back the sleeves of her sweater to reveal a red mark on her left wrist and a deepening bruise just below her left elbow. "That's nothing compared to what I did to him." Era smiled thinly.

"You said someone kidnapped you," Wanda prompted.

"I don't know what this world is coming to when young men abduct old ladies in broad daylight."

"Who was it?" Wanda and Cate asked together.

"I have no idea. He knocked on my door, and like a fool, I opened it."

"Didn't you look through the peephole?" asked Wanda.

Era shook her head. "It's too high up for me."

Cate got up from her crouching position. "Don't you want to call the police and report it?"

"No. Please let me tell you what happened first."

Cate sat next to her mother on the loveseat. "Okay. What did he look like?"

Era's lips quivered. "He was big. His hair was brownish, or maybe blond."

"How old?"

"Twenty or thirty, I expect, not much younger than my Winston."

Cate and her mother exchanged a worried look.

"He pushed his way in and held me while he went through my pocketbook. Then he said we were going for a little ride, so I said I needed my cane. Winston bought it for me even though I told him I didn't need one. I keep it in my front closet," Era said as if lost in thought. She rubbed her arm and winced.

"Let's get some ice on that." Cate got a bag of peas from Wanda's freezer, wrapped it in a dishtowel and placed it over the developing bruise. "I think we need to call the police," she said again.

"Absolutely not! They would take one look at me and figure there is no way in heaven I could have overpowered that man."

"How did you overpower him?" Wanda asked.

Era allowed herself a toothy smile. She tapped her forehead. "I used my noggin."

They waited for her to say more, but again she seemed to have retreated into her thoughts.

"How did he manage to get you out of your apartment?" said Cate.

"He hauled me out by my arm. I'm sorry to say I didn't put up much of a fight, even though I don't think he had a weapon. I suppose he figured it wouldn't take much to subdue a little old lady."

They waited for her to continue.

"He was practically dragging me down the hall and telling me to hurry up. He called me a very bad name. He had no manners at all. There was nobody in sight, so I used my cane and pointed high up on the wall and said, 'Smile for the camera.'"

"I didn't know there was a security camera there," Wanda said.

Era sat up a little taller. "That's because there isn't. But he didn't know that. He let go of my arm and ducked down, just as I had hoped. That's when I hit him on the back of his nasty little head with my cane. It wasn't a very hard blow, but it took him by surprise. He tried to grab me again, and that's when I jabbed him hard, right where it would hurt the most, and started yelling at the top of my lungs."

Cate and Wanda were transfixed.

"Then what happened?"

"He ran off. No, actually he hobbled off holding himself. He took the stairs. Unfortunately, he also took my pocketbook."

"We really have to report this," said Cate, pounding her fist into her other palm.

"Yes, dear, we do. I will take care of it. I have to get back to my apartment, though, so I have the numbers when I call the bank.

Oh! My keys were in the—No wait, I left them in the bowl on the kitchen counter."

Cate addressed her mother. "I'm going to take Era back to take care of those calls, but you need to call Mary Gumm immediately."

"No, no," Era protested when Cate said the name of the resident services director.

Cate was undeterred. Again addressing her mother, she said, "We need to warn others of this stranger. Tell her that you and I," she stressed the pronouns, "tell her you and I saw a young man with brown or blond hair acting suspiciously. Tell her we saw him knocking on Era's door, and that he ran off when he saw us."

Wanda understood immediately.

Slowly Era nodded. "Yes, of course. We can't have other people opening their doors to the likes of him."

"And then call Vivian and tell her what really happened."

Wanda locked her door behind them and Cate led Era by the elbow as they walked down the hall.

Era's small file cabinet was organized. Though the file folders were not labeled, they were color-coded and well thought out. Era pulled out the financial file that held papers for her savings and checking accounts and contact information for her Visa card. She set aside a fat bundle of papers, saying they were this year's statements from her investments.

By the time Era was done reporting her "lost" pocketbook to the bank and credit card company, she sat back to close her eyes. Cate was wondering if she should leave the woman alone for a nap when seven sharp taps on the door played the familiar "Shave and a haircut" code. She looked through the peephole, which was indeed at the wrong height for the diminutive Era. It was Vivian, Robin's mother, and she had brought along the troops. Wanda, Vivian, Daisy and Iris spilled through the door, filling the room with anxious excitement.

On Iris's lap rested a pen and a spiral-top notebook, the kind Cate associated with police. She twirled her wheelchair to face an overwhelmed Era, and as Era told them the real story of the attempted abduction, Iris took notes.

Cate noted that Era's recounting varied somewhat from the original. This time the man wasn't big, but tall and wiry. He had dusty shoes and now his hair was very light. She added a detail. Once inside her apartment, the man had taken some interest in her small grouping of photos on the end table. As she spoke, they all glanced at the photos. Cate surmised that one was a younger Era with her husband, a gentle looking man with a cookie-duster mustache. Another photo might have been of the same man, except for the stern expression and more prominent jaw. In an overexposed snapshot, a young girl she presumed to be Kiki stood awkwardly beside a saguaro cactus, squinting in the bright sun.

The women were talking excitedly when another knock on the door announced the arrival of Virgil. Hunched over his rolling walker, he wheeled in and lifted his imaginary hat. "At your service, ladies." They stepped aside so he could scuttle over to pat Era's shoulder. "You have had quite an adventure, young lady."

"I certainly have, Virgil. And I thank you for coming."

"You are most welcome. I would take exception to your handling things so well that you prevented me from performing my chivalrous duties," he said, looking into her eyes, "but from what I hear, you conducted yourself with great valor."

Era giggled.

Cate stood back in awe, not only of the network that dispersed information with the speed of light, but also of the welling spirit of community and support. They surrounded Era, praising her for her quick wits, and asking her a jumble of questions. In no time, they'd started to make plans in case the perpetrator should return.

Her cell vibrated in her pants pocket and she backed away to answer it. Robin had gotten a call from her mother and was wondering if she should come immediately.

Cate said, loud enough for the others, who had stopped talking, to hear, "I think the residents here are handling everything quite well without our help." She winked at Virgil, who winked back. "They're already setting up a schedule for checking on each other and have decided to travel in pairs for the next few days. Right now Frannie is sitting down the hall with Edie where they can see both the elevator and the stairway. Iris has her camera ready to take a picture of anyone she doesn't recognize. Rose, with the help of Mighty Carlton, the Wonder Dog, is patrolling the halls at this very moment."

Robin laughed at her description. She reluctantly agreed to stay away until tomorrow.

Not aware that it had been Era's intent nearly an hour earlier, Daisy suggested she might want a little nap after her ordeal. The others saw the wisdom of that.

"The rest of you can get back to what you were doing. I'll just sit here if I may, and work on my puzzles." Daisy pulled pencil and folded newspaper from her pocket.

"Do you think he'll come back?" asked Virgil.

"Ha!" said Era. "Not until he's recovered."

Virgil chuckled. "You hurt him pretty badly then?"

Era smugly replied, "I hope I hurt him badly enough, the little bastard won't be able to procreate."

When they were done laughing, they went on their way, assuring each other they could handle whatever came along, just as they always had.

14

Era's would-be kidnapper rocked himself and moaned. He'd managed to stumble down the stairs to his truck in the tuck-under garage. "I do not believe this shit!" he bellowed as he drove out of the parking lot. Turning left at the street, he drove four blocks up a small hill and, after almost clipping a mailbox with his extended side-view mirror, he decided to pull into the parking lot of a Burger King. He swung the vehicle around so he could see the entryway of the old people museum where the old woman lived. Even if the cops arrived at the parking entrance instead of the front entry, he should at least be able to hear the sirens.

Gingerly clutching himself through the denim, he uttered some of his favorite expressions containing the effenheimer, as his mother called it. With each curse, he could taste the Irish Spring soap in his mouth and picture the shriveling expression of disapproval his mother wore whenever her eyes fell on her only child. The way his mother saw the world, all babies born in Wayzata and other bastions of good breeding came out in perfect little packages with a preppie imprint, destined to marry others of pedigree to make a new generation of preppie babies. The message had been fed to him in his baby bottle along with whatever concoction she gave him that was engineered to replicate, and yet improve upon, mother's milk. The message that besides breeding with other elite, his fate was to be one of the political and entrepreneurial movers and shakers, and leaders of society.

That message had not changed even when his father's investment strategy, thanks to Winston Dudley, had rendered him bankrupt and practically suicidal, even when they'd had to move to the Little Cottage—his mother's term, as if they used the quaint two-bedroom, two-bath bungalow as a cozy break from their palatial estate.

Derek had continued to hear the drumbeat of entitlement even when he'd managed to bollix up any chance of a soccer scholarship after he and a friend named Shane had temporarily occupied the vacant lake home of a magazine editor, a divorcee who spent weeks at a time in New York. For seventy-nine fun-filled hours, the two had enjoyed cruising Lake Minnetonka in the woman's boat, picking up girls at Fletcher's and bringing them back to watch sunsets on the deck. The third night of their unsanctioned stay, Derek stepped out of the hot tub, leaving Shane and the girls to be buffeted by the powerful jets while he fetched champagne flutes and bubbly.

He was opening the small downstairs refrigerator, when it had happened without warning. A meaty hand gripped the top of his shoulder, squeezing a nerve so hard he almost blacked out. The guy spun him around and he found himself looking up into the blazing eyes of the owner's ex-husband, a boozed up Bill Murray type, who apparently was on friendly enough terms to have a key to the place. The other three scrambled to get dressed. He himself was bare-ass naked when the police arrived.

The owner and her ex were utterly humorless. Derek never understood what all the righteous indignation was about. After all, they hadn't broken or vandalized anything, and he'd offered to fill up the gas tank of her cabin cruiser and pay for the liquor they'd drunk. Besides, the owner obviously couldn't live in two houses simultaneously, so what was the BFD? As it turned out, the girls were never charged, since all agreed they had not been told that the high school boys were there without permission. And because Derek and Shane were both minors, the whole prank was pled down to a misdemeanor, which was all it should have been in the first place, with the record being expunged if they had no further offenses.

But nothing could reinstate his soccer scholarship, and with his father's fortune gone, so was his future.

He pulled up to the drive-through and ordered a Dr. Pepper before resuming his lookout. Leaning back, he closed his eyes only to find that the face of the old Dudley woman had been imprinted on the inside of his eyelids—her wrinkled, ancient face dwarfed by round, thick glasses which made her eyes look huge. She had looked utterly harmless until she suddenly went all ninja granny on him. He could not freaking believe it! First Kiki's grandfather, old Pruneface, who had played with Derek's family fortune like it was Boardwalk or Park Place, and now the old bag of bones whacking him right in his man tonsils with her cane! Jesus, what kind of an old lady does that?

His balls had ached in a whole different and pleasurable way that night he'd first seen Kiki at some party he'd crashed. He was chilling with a drink, loving the idea that everyone assumed he'd been invited by someone else, when this Kate Moss look-alike bent over to light a cigarette off a candle, her sweet little booty hovering only inches from his face. She sat on the loveseat across from him, took a long drag, and then puckering her lips, she blew the smoke out in a thin stream. Her skirt was short enough to see all the way to Caracas. She seemed unaware that he stared. She was uncultured, had regrettable use of the English language, was pierced and tattooed, but extremely cute in a trailer trash kind of way. Everything his parents hated.

All the stimulation had been visual, right up until he overheard her say something about her "Grampa Dudley." He'd locked onto the name. "What does your grandfather do?" he'd asked casually, inserting himself into the conversation. The second she told him, Derek's mind had begun whirling with the possibilities. When

Derek's father had been making money hand over fist, he'd referred to his financial guru as Dudley Do-Right, but the nickname quickly turned to Dudley Do-Wrong when his two largest investments turned to fool's gold.

Derek and Kiki hooked up that night. It had been easy enough. Kiki was new in town, a little misfit looking for a place to fit in. She dug him. He had a pretty good understanding of what girls saw in him. He was surfer-tan and ripped, and he came across as confident, even when he wasn't. The clincher, though, was something more elusive, the aura of Bad Boy, something most girls found irresistible.

After that first hookup, they started doing it right in Winston Dudley's own house. Kiki never connected the dots, never once suspected Derek knew anything about her grandfather. And she had even more reason than he did to keep their relationship a secret. He might have lost interest in her, except for two things. First, he loved to imagine bringing her home to the Little Cottage to meet mummy and daddy. Second, it was a dependable turn-on just knowing what he was doing to Winston's beloved little granddaughter was the same thing Winston had done to his family. It came as quite a surprise when he realized he'd begun to fall for her. He had even begun to let himself think that they might actually get married. If that ever happened, it would not be just for the money. She was a pretty sweet package all by herself, and smarter than she let on.

He peered down the street at the apartment building. Why hadn't the cops come yet? Maybe they were driving around the neighborhood right now looking for him, going on whatever description the old lady had given them. Maybe if he was lucky, her eyesight and memory wouldn't be as accurate as her aim.

* * *

SHE HATED COMING BACK HERE, but she had to get more of her stuff. Every time she thought about it, she remembered what she and

Derek had done there—in the living room, in her bedroom, and once he'd even wanted her to do it in her grampa's bed, but she couldn't go through with it.

Most of the clothes she had were for summer. Not like she had tons of winter stuff, coming from Arizona, but she did have the boots, the wool coat and the lined gloves her grampa gave her money to buy almost as soon as she got off the bus. A couple weeks later, he gave her three hundred-dollar bills and told her to get some sweaters and stuff, too. She was pretty excited about it, even when he said he wanted to see everything she bought. She'd been careful, knowing he was going to have judgments about some of the things she really liked. He wound up approving of everything she bought, and even said he was proud of her for stretching the money by buying most of it on sale.

She hadn't even pulled into the driveway when she saw something had torn up the front yard. At first she thought the marks were tire tracks, but when she got closer, it looked more like some giant bird had clawed it with its talons. Something else looked goofy, but she couldn't figure out what. She went over and stuck her key in the lock, almost expecting somebody waiting for her inside.

She had not been this scared in a long time. She squared her shoulders and walked in.

It was just as she'd left it, except a little stuffier. She got a big knife from the kitchen and held it up in front of her, ready to use it if she had to. She checked the rest of the rooms. Upstairs, she looked in closets and finally decided she was safe. When she snapped on the closet light, it got bright, fizzed and went out. She thought he kept light bulbs in the basement, but that basement always creeped her out, even when her grampa was home. Besides, she'd been brave enough for one day, just coming here.

As soon as she opened the blinds, she saw what she'd missed earlier. A big branch of the oak tree, the one that always looked like a big old finger pointing right at her window, was gone, broken. There was a splintery stub where it had been. The scratches in the lawn made sense now. They were right where the branch would have fallen. She sighed out loud and relaxed for the first time since she'd come.

She considered for all of a nanosecond that her grampa had come back and had hauled the branch away. She sighed heavily. It was probably just Conrad.

After making two trips to her car with most of her warm clothing, she locked the front door. At the end of the driveway, Kiki was backing into the street when she happened to look to the left and just about wet her pants. Their neighbor stood next to the hedge that separated the two yards. Just watching her, with his hands in his pockets. He looked unfazed, as if he'd known she'd been there.

No wonder she'd felt spooked!

By the time she pulled herself together, it struck her as odd that he still hadn't moved. She rolled down the window and said, "Did you take away the branch?"

"I did."

She tried to stay calm when he sauntered over and leaned his left arm on the door with his hand draping in through the open window.

"It came down two nights ago in the wind. I lost a few too."

Looking at his smile, or maybe it was more of a smirk, she felt uncomfortable. Her gaze shifted to his hand dangling in front of her. "Where did you get that watch?" The question fell right out. Immediately, she wished she'd kept her mouth shut. If he was a thief—She wondered if she should lean on the horn.

His smile got wider. "Do you recognize it?"

She made sure the door was locked. And then suddenly her fear turned to anger. "It's Grampa's! He thought I stole it! He blamed—"

"Whoa, whoa," he said, stepping back. "Take it easy. I didn't steal it either." He unbuckled it and slipped it off his wrist. "I was just making sure it belonged to him. It's an expensive watch." He handed it to her.

She quickly looked it over, certain it was his. "If you didn't steal it, how come you were wearing it?"

He started to chuckle as he stuck his hands back in his pockets.

Her hand went to the gearshift. If he did anything funny, she was out of here.

"I lost a big branch on my elm. It darn near fell on my roof. In the morning I went out to assess the damage and I scared off some crows."

She couldn't believe he'd just completely changed the subject. "Why are you talking about crows? I didn't ask about any crows."

"Hold on. I'm getting there." He pointed to the place on his lawn where he had similar gouges and scratches. "There's been a crow's nest way up in that tree and after the branch broke, those crows sat on top of the branch and set up such a ruckus, I figured their nest had fallen, and there it was, barely showing under the big tree limb. It was broken, of course, but it was still full of their stash, all the little treasures they'd collected. There were coins, a button, some foil candy wrappers, that kind of thing."

What a crock! "You're telling me a crow took my grampa's watch off him and he didn't even notice?"

His smile was back. "No, I doubt they took it off his wrist. It probably fell and the crow picked it up. They like shiny things."

Kiki actually saw a show about that. Some woman had lost her necklace and went back on the trail just in time to see a crow swoop down and fly off with it.

Remembering the show, she relaxed and then they both laughed. "Okay," she said, strapping it on her own wrist. It was too big even on the first hole. "Well, thanks."

"If you back up another foot or so, you can see how big the nest was. It's still lying on the ground.

"Wow, that is big," she said when she saw it. His garage door was open and there was a lawn mower inside that looked just like the one at her grampa's.

He turned to see what she was looking at. He tried to look casual. "Oh, yes, I meant to ask you if I could borrow Winston's mower. Mine broke and I don't want to replace it until they go on sale in the spring."

"Well, you didn't ask me, and it looks like you already borrowed it."

He looked like he was going to apologize, but instead he said, "You may not have noticed, but I've not only mowed the grass over there, but I also removed the branch and hauled off all the debris.

She instantly felt bad. "Yeah, I did notice. Sorry." She thanked him and told him he could use the mower as long as he needed to.

He might as well, she thought as she drove off. What am I going to do with all his stuff if he never comes back?

Era's pocketbook was not gone after all. One day after the incident, a visitor to Meadowpoint Manor found the worn black leather purse near the top of the stairway and Mary Gumm returned it to her. Era opened it to find the bills in her wallet—about what she'd expected, two tens and six ones—along with her Visa card. A new tube of eye drops, her hankie and a folded plastic rain cap were there too, unscathed. The little creep must have dropped it as he fled, because otherwise he would certainly have taken her money and credit card. Picturing the nasty creature in headlong flight from her—her of all people, a ninety-six-and-a-half-year old woman—she began to chuckle.

"You must be relieved to get it back," Mary Gumm said.

"Of course. Wouldn't you be?"

"How do you suppose it got there?" Mary played with her rubber wristbands as she glanced around Era's apartment. Era knew the pink band was for breast cancer and the light yellow for prostate cancer, but what was the purple one for, and the red? All those causes! Did people really think they accomplished anything by wearing bracelets? It was about as effective, she wanted to say to Mary, as the lucky charms the Bingo Bunch brought with them every Friday evening—not just a rabbit's foot, but cigarette lighters, troll dolls, jewelry, even a fishing lure. There was no end to the silliness.

"How do you think your purse wound up in the stairway?" Mary asked again.

There was something in her demeanor, Era thought, as if she were assessing her competency. She fervently hoped they would not start that nonsense again. She remembered the story Wanda and her daughter had cooked up to avoid exactly this dubious reaction. She drew herself up in indignation. "I take the stairs now and then."

"Really!" Mary's expression changed to one of concern.

"I do indeed. It must have fallen when I was coming back from our little gift shop. I'll bet my pocketbook slipped out of my hand when I shifted my . . . my purchases back to my right hand at the top of the stairs. I always hold onto the railing for safety. You just can't be too careful." She tugged at the sleeve of her sweater to make sure the growing bruise wasn't visible. "Thank you, Mary, for returning this to me. I'm just about to make my rounds again. I walked for thirty minutes already this morning. May I walk you back to your office?"

* * *

THERE WERE TWO THINGS Kiki liked about both of her jobs. The very best thing was the food smells—muffins and fresh coffee and quiche in her morning job, French fries, sizzling steak and wood-fired pizza at the restaurant. The second was watching people. In the coffee shop right now there were thirteen people inside and one guy sitting outside, even though it looked like it might rain. The two women sitting in the puffy upholstered chairs ate scones and let the crumbs get all over the chairs. She'd have to get the hand vac out as soon as they left.

Two guys, regulars, talked mostly to each other, almost completely ignoring the short-haired woman at their table. Fag hag, that's what Derek would have called her. Sometimes his comments like that really pissed her off.

Some people sat alone with their computers. And then there were the same four guys who came every week. Their voices got louder when they started in on Can You Top This, like they always did, whether they were talking about work or women or money. Three women at the other end of the room were playing the same game, but their competition involved smart children and all the things their husbands did that they hated.

The guy sitting alone at the outdoor table had tipped her a dollar for his soy latte. He was sort of a regular and he always wore gear like he'd just been hiking. He tried to read the newspaper but the wind made it hard to keep the pages from folding over. He seemed nice enough, but the dog sprawling next to his chair was a real sweetie. She was an Irish setter, the guy told her, and she wore a different bandana every time she came. Today it was lime green with pink polka-dots.

She really wanted a dog. And a fat gray cat. She'd always wanted pets.

The women in the puffy chairs got up. One brushed crumbs off her big chest, which stuck out like a shelf. Before they made it to the door, Kiki scooped up their mess and wiped the table. In the back pocket of her gray jeans skirt, her cell phone vibrated. No number or name showed up. Her stomach started to hurt when she guessed who it was. Pressing the button she heard Derek's voice, all smooth and sexy. "I can't get you off my mind," he said.

"Funny," she said, ducking around the corner to the hall that led to the restrooms, "because I don't have any trouble at all getting you off mine."

"Aw, babe." He said it soft and low and even though her brain said he was a giant loser, she got tingly that way she did when he breathed those words into her ear.

"What do you want?" She went into the ladies room and locked the door behind her. The air freshener had a sickening fake flower smell.

"Are you at the coffee shop?"

"Yeah."

"I miss you. Want to hang out tonight?"

In a flash of insight, she knew how her grandfather's watch had gone from his desk drawer to wherever the crows had found it.

"Why? So you could come over and steal something else?"

In the second or two it took for him to answer, Kiki thought he might have hung up. But then she heard him breathing and he said, "What are you talking about?"

She felt cold. Not shivery cold, but cold-hearted. "I know you took Grampa's watch."

His voice went up a couple of notes, which was not at all sexy. "Why would I do that? I don't even wear a watch, you know that. When did you ever see me wearing a watch?"

She hadn't actually ever seen him wear one. "Well, he got all in my face and blamed me, and I know I didn't take it."

"I swear I don't have it."

Well, of course he didn't. It was now in her locked glovebox until she figured out a safe place for it.

"Maybe he lost it. He's old."

She tried to remember if she'd ever seen him be forgetful or lose things. Nothing came to mind.

"You should've called me."

She leaned back against the toilet tank. It felt cool, even through her tee shirt. "I did call you. You laughed at me."

There was another weird pause before he said, "That was days ago. You still should have called."

Why did she ever think he was hot? "I did. You didn't want to see me."

"I didn't mean ever. I just had a lot going on, babe."

"You had a lot going on," she parroted. "That's why you called me a spoiled brat, because you had a lot going on? That's why you called me a —"

"Hey, I was a jerk, okay?"

She certainly could agree with him on that. Did he really expect her to forgive him and tell him it was okay?

"Are you still staying at Ashley's?"

"Yeah." Why did she even answer him?

"I miss you."

Her knees started to shake. "Good," she said right before she punched the END button.

She found a box of baking soda in the pantry, shook a little pile into her hand and tipped it into her mouth like a tequila shot. Derek, she decided, had everything to do with the way her stomach felt.

When the phone vibrated again, she did not answer it, but looked instead at the time display. Her shift ended in fifty-two minutes and then she'd have four hours until her other job at the restaurant. She suddenly knew who she wanted to see. She pictured the look on her great-gran's face. It wouldn't be a smile, exactly, at least not compared to Daisy's smile, but she knew there was love in the way Great-Gran would move her eyes over Kiki's face, like she was memorizing it so she could hang onto it even after Kiki went away.

She pictured that look the whole time she drove, and all the way to the apartment door. She just wanted to be with the one person left who thought she was special. All she needed was to disappear in Great-Gran's hug and cry and tell her she was so, so, so worried about her grampa and about her own stupid life.

It took her great-gran a while to come to the door and even from that first glimpse of her, Kiki thought she didn't seem very much like herself, a little smaller maybe, and without that special thing she usually had. Kiki didn't know what to call it, but it was the sparkle or buzz or fizz which kept her from being just some other little old lady. She knew Great-Gran wasn't going to live forever, but Oh, God! She wasn't ready to lose her too!

Instead of the big hug she'd pictured, Kiki hugged her like she might break. There was no way she could tell her about what was troubling her now. It could just push her over the edge. "Are you okay? You look so tired."

* * *

ERA WAS ABOUT TO SAY the same thing. Even thinner than usual, Kiki had dark smears under her eyes that did not look like makeup. The child's life had not been an easy one—that was putting it mildly. Even at her young age, she bore the weight of the world on her insubstantial shoulders. Era could not, in all good conscience, give her one more bogeyman to worry about. It took her a fraction of a second to decide not to tell her about her attempted kidnapping. Of course, Frannie was the only one referring to it as such. Others used words like *mayhem*, *fracas*, *brouhaha*. She herself thought of it as an altercation. Iris told her not to get into any more brawls, and Virgil had said, "You look astonishingly well after your kerfuffle."

"Well, come in, sweetie," she said to Kiki. "Have you eaten today?" Era sat in her favorite chair and beckoned her to sit.

"I had a blueberry muffin." Kiki crossed her legs and tugged at her hair.

The poor thing had been raised mostly on fast food. "That's how you fuel your body for work? Well, never mind. There's a fresh peach, cottage cheese and some deli ham. Help yourself." If she hadn't had Dudley blood in her, Era had thought many times, Kiki might not have survived, and it was that genetic strength she was counting on to get her great-granddaughter through. Looking at her, she noticed that the previous piercing on her eyebrow was healing and almost unnoticeable. And while her hair was still black as pitch, the neon streaks were gone.

"Are you sure you're okay, Great-Gran? You really do look tired. Am I keeping you from a nap?"

"Heavens no. It can't even be noon yet." Era pushed up the sleeve of her sweater to look at her watch.

Where'd you get that bruise?" Kiki jumped up to examine her wrist before she could cover the telltale marks.

"I bumped it."

Bending over her, Kiki examined her arm. "On both sides? Oh, my God, I've heard about nursing home abuse and if—"

Era sat up straighter. "This is not a nursing home and I am not being abused. This place," she pronounced with great dignity, "is the cat's meow."

That made Kiki giggle. "The cat's meow. That is too funny." She knelt and gently massaged the non-bruised portions of Era's arm. "But really, you have to be careful."

"I will," she said solemnly. "And you, my dear, have to make yourself some lunch."

"In a minute." She continued to massage the arm with just the right amount of pressure, avoiding the sore spots, her thumbs circling downwards to the palm of her hand, before concentrating on each enlarged knuckle and the spaces in between.

Touch was so important, Era thought, and yet by the time people got to be her age, hardly anyone touched anymore, except for the medical people, and you had to be sick for that to happen. This touch was special, though. Kiki had done this even as a child, this caressing of her hands, and it had continued to be a comfort to both of them in stressful times. "You've always had the gift of healing," she told her as she stroked the back of Kiki's head with her unoccupied hand.

"Really?" Tears filled the girl's eyes.

"Really. You could pursue a career in the health industry, you know. Have you ever thought of being a nurse?"

"Great-Gran, I just do this with you 'cause I love you so much." Kiki's tears spilled over. "Besides, I'd rather work with animals than with people. I could be like Betty White, taking care of animals even when I'm your age." She stood, pulled a used Kleenex out of her pocket and blew her nose. "But it's like eight years of school to be a vet, and that's after I finish—" She stopped herself. She'd never told her grampa or his mother that she'd dropped out of school.

"I'm fully aware that you have not finished high school." Era kept stroking her hair. "But you will. If you truly want to be a veterinarian, you'd better buckle down now. How have your grades been up to now?"

She brightened. "Actually, pretty good. Not so great in English, but A's and B's in everything else and straight A's in Biology." The corners of her mouth pulled down. "But there's no way I could afford college."

Era took her hand, sodden tissue and all. "My dear, I may not have much time left in me, but I do have money, and I can't think of a better use for it."

16

"Will I have to meet him?" Cate asked. She was fully aware of her petulant tone, but couldn't seem to help herself. Without answering, her mother pulled a pair of light wool gloves from her jacket pocket and slipped them on. They crossed the street and picked up the walking trail that led around a pond and marsh.

Cate stopped to button her sweater up to the neck. Facing into the wind, she unclipped her hair and gathered up stray strands to redo her ponytail in its leather clasp. "I mean, do I have to meet him this time?" Cate's attitude about her newfound brother—Ricky—shifted from day to day. Sure, she had some compassion for her mother's role in all this, but it was still a betrayal. For five decades she did not know of his existence. Those years could never be reclaimed.

Every time she felt the least bit excited at the prospect of meeting him, it quickly turned to apprehension. Would they have anything in common? Would she like him?

Perhaps more disturbing, would he like her? If she had to admit it, the small part of her that was still a child wondered if her mother actually, deep down, loved him more, this child she had not raised. She thought about some of the cruel things she'd said to her mother when she was a teenager, words she could never call back. Going through endless variations in her head of how the first meeting with her half-brother might play out, she found every one of them awkward as hell.

Wanda's scarf billowed in the wind and she retied it more tightly over her hair. She was wearing the new sensible shoes Cate had bought her. "You don't need to decide today about meeting them. Ricky and Bunny won't be here for a few days."

Cate stopped. One eyebrow shot up. "Bunny? His wife's name is Bunny? Oh, that's just perfect!"

Wanda did not meet her gaze. Slipping her arm through Cate's, she nudged her forward along the groomed trail. "My darling daughter, I want you to open your eyes and look at the beauty all around you." She swung her arm to encompass the fall scene.

Slowly and grudgingly, Cate set aside the prospect of an excruciatingly uncomfortable meeting and let her downcast eyes take in morning-damp grass, the single rusty oak leaf blowing along the path and a perfect trio of mushrooms. The wind grazed her cheeks and blew her hair across her face, bringing with it the pungent odors of the marsh. From its perch on a cattail, a red-winged blackbird shrilled, and children called to each other on the nearby playground. Despite the wind, it was a lovely fall day, whether she was in the mood for one or not. She knew she should savor the moment.

They passed three smallish girls huddled under the arching boughs of a pine tree, and when a boy approached them, they shrieked and giggled. "Mom's looking for you," he said, and one girl immediately crawled out, brushing pine needles off the seat of her jeans.

Cate felt a sudden weight on her chest. Why had it never occurred to her to ask? "Mom, does Ricky have kids?"

Her mother's grip on her arm tightened, but her answer had a lilt to it. "Yes, he has a grown son."

Of course he did. But that apparently wasn't enough of a blow.

"And he and his wife are expecting their first child."

Cate's breath came out through pursed lips. She thought she'd gotten over the sadness of not having children, but here was the old ache of unfulfilled desire, layered with the guilt of not being able to give her mother grandchildren. Although her mother hadn't burdened her with that expectation, she sometimes wondered if her life would have more meaning if she didn't know she was the end of the family line.

Without realizing it, her strides lengthened and her pace picked up. She walked several yards before realizing her mother had let go of her. Turning, she saw Wanda standing on the trail looking very small. Walking back to her she said, "You must be ecstatic. Son, grandson, great-grandson, all in one fell swoop." It was hard to keep the bitterness from her voice.

"I don't know what I feel. I've sealed away that part of me for so long." She pulled a ragged Kleenex from her pocket and dabbed at her eyes.

The sentiment was so like her own, it made Cate's eyes sting, but she wasn't done with her little punishment yet. "I guess you'll have no trouble getting used to being called Grandma." The pleasure she'd felt a moment ago as she looked at the scene around her was replaced with bleakness.

Wanda waited for Cate to make eye contact before she said, "My dear, I believe you are getting ahead of yourself again. Things will happen however they happen." Her voice did not waiver. "I can't force a relationship on anybody, but Ricky has reached out to me, and I have decided I will be open to whatever possibilities there are in this situation, both good and bad. If he has anger, I owe it to him to listen. If he decides, after meeting me, not to contact me again, I will have to live with that too. What I will not do is worry myself sick over the past or the future. It's just plain foolish to focus on the could-have-beens and the what-ifs at the expense of what is."

* * *

LOUISE WORE A BLACK VINTAGE blouse with ruffles which came up high on her neck, and a becoming half-hat made with green feathers—a live mannequin in her own antique shop. She leaned over the table to pour Robin's tea into a china cup, a translucent and iridescent beauty in the shape of a water lily. Moving about the table, she captured the feeling of an era long gone.

She gestured for Robin to sit, and even though Louise had said the dainty iron chair was more comfortable than it looked, Robin's hip ached as she tried to find a better position. She sniffed the tea. "Orange rind?"

Louise lowered herself into the matching chair, her movements fluid. "I don't think so. I'm thinking orange blossom. They won't give any details of their proprietary blend except to say it's a black tea."

She sipped. "It's delicious. Strong, but not bitter. This would be a good choice."

Louise and her partner Dean were considering opening up the back room of Past Tense Antiques as a tearoom, to be used only once or twice a month. For a set price, one would get tea, a small selection of nibbles and some kind of presentation on antiques. "I don't want it to get too fussy. In the first place, I want to keep the cost down, and for another, the kitchen here is cramped and, well, antiquated."

Robin laughed.

"Besides, I certainly don't want to be doing a lot of cooking and baking on the premises. The important part of these tea parties, besides the tea, of course, is to do some kind of themed presentation. For instance . . ." She rose from the low chair and picked a footed bowl from a glass case, placing it into Robin's hands.

As the only book club member from the South, Louise had a slight drawl. Today, Robin thought she was laying on a bit thick.

"This is a berry bowl. Louis XV. I thought for one of the teas I could have only things that are served in bowls—berries, of course, with crème fraiche, spiced pecans, stuffed buns, mini cream puffs—I haven't really worked it all out yet. But the idea is to introduce a grouping of things I carry, and give the history and a little lesson on why this bowl is worth what it is. I want to whet their appetites."

"I think you're onto something. But once you're done with serving pieces, what theme food goes with . . ." Robin's eyes settled on a grouping. "What goes with the old fashioned tennis racket, the croquet set and the bocce ball set?"

Louise considered for a minute. "Food in spheres. Maybe truffles, goat cheese balls, cherries, that kind of thing, all served on my green and white Limoges on grass green tablecloths. We can learn about how lawn sports evolved."

"How do you come up with these ideas?" Robin shifted toward the right so she could press the sore spot on her hip. She wished she had some way of determining whether such pain was just normal wear and tear or—

"Is that a bad chair for you?" Louise asked. "I can get you something with a little more padding."

"I thought I had enough padding of my own." She tried to smile, but it turned into a wince.

Louise looked concerned. "Robin, what's—"

"I'm okay, really. Probably just arthritis." She poked at the juncture of hip and thighbone. Maybe she'd fire up the heating pad when she got home.

"I know Cate complains of creaky knees, but I didn't know you had arthritis too."

"I don't actually know if it's arthritis. What I do know is my cancer treatment shut down my estrogen and that isn't a happy situation for my joints."

"Hmm." Louise poured more tea.

Robin was not comforted by the way Louise's brows pulled together. She wanted to bring the conversation back to something other than her pain. "I really love this tea thing. It's brilliant. Ladies meeting regularly to discuss something intellectual and eat wonderful food, all in beautiful surroundings—does it remind you of anything?"

Louise grinned. "You mean like our book club?"

"Naturally."

"So you think this could really catch on? I've actually been thinking about your little ladies over at the nursing home."

Robin sighed. "It's not a nursing home." What did she have to do to change that misperception? "It's senior living, and the people I've gotten to know over there live quite independently."

"Well, that's better yet, because I assume they're mobile and still have their faculties."

"They do. In fact, I can only hope I'll age as well. What do you have in mind for my 'little ladies'?"

Louise extracted the large pin from her feather hat, removed the curved headpiece and set it back on its stand in the alcove. "I thought for my very first tea—it would be kind of a dress rehearsal, actually, so I wouldn't charge them—but I thought we could make it kind of a party, since I'll be practicing on them, you know. I could introduce a segment of Americana with practical items that your ladies knew firsthand, something nostalgic from their childhoods. I have washboards, a marcel curling iron, hair combs, darning eggs, fountain pens, that kind of thing. That apothecary cabinet is from the early 1900s, and I have several tin ceiling panels from the bank they tore down two miles from here. If anyone has the stories to tell, it's your bunch over at the senior, uh, place."

They talked excitedly, brainstorming the food and how they would transport the tea party guests. Robin made a list of which women to invite. Era, of course, and the Flower Children, her mother and Cate's mother . . . What about Frannie? She could be so dour, but maybe she was shy and waiting to be included.

Maybe Frannie's experience wasn't that different from Robin's in grade school. She remembered returning to school after her long year away in her father's care. After the teacher had everyone in her fourth grade class clap to celebrate her safe return, the other kids backed off. She was no longer one of them. They looked at her and whispered. She sat by herself at lunch, waiting for someone to beckon her to their table, but they did not, and so she doodled pictures on her napkin and ignored her classmates. She added Frannie to her list.

When she stood to leave, she sucked in her breath and grasped the tabletop as a sharp pain drove through the top of her thigh.

Louise touched her shoulder. "Honey, you really need to get that checked out."

Brad had said those exact words just yesterday.

17

Winston came to her in a dream. He was as handsome as the day he'd headed off to the university. Although he never uttered a word, his very presence communicated such reassurance and love that she wanted to reach out and take his face in her hands. "You came!" Era breathed the words so as not to make him disappear this time.

He smiled.

"Did you come for me?" she asked.

Still smiling, he shook his head.

She reached out for him, but he wasn't there

* * *

AFTER POSITIONING ROBIN'S LEG at an unnatural angle, the x-ray tech bustled out of the room and the machine buzzed.

Until yesterday, the only concern Robin allowed herself had been the pain and discomfort. Arthritis had been cropping up more and more as a topic of conversation, and was certainly a common ailment among her friends. She'd almost convinced herself that calling her primary physician yesterday had been only to get Brad and Louise off her back, but then her doctor had wasted no time getting her in for x-rays—nineteen hours, to be exact.

Lying on the metal table, she ran her tongue inside her mouth, feeling its dryness.

The tech returned. Her blue scrubs fit her poorly, as if she'd recently lost weight. She fussed with the markers on the table and did not make eye contact. "I need another shot. Same position." Tilting Robin's leg inward again made the dull pain more acute.

Another buzz, another wait, another angle. She rolled onto the hip that hadn't hurt until it dug into the hard table.

More than two years ago when Robin's mammogram showed spots of microcalcification, she had been more surprised than anxious. There had been a flurry of tests: a second mammogram, ultrasound and then a needle biopsy. This was followed by a meeting with a doctor of Brad's choosing for a second opinion, and then a very long appointment with the general surgeon who ultimately performed the mastectomy. She'd also met with a plastic surgeon, and even though she initially resisted the idea of reconstruction, she was mostly pleased with the results.

The surgery had been easier than she'd anticipated, the chemo harder. Oddly, the greatest challenge to her bravery and composure was losing her hair. There was no logic, but she'd heard from several other cancer patients that they also had struggled emotionally with that temporary side effect of chemo. Then last year she decided to have her other, healthy breast removed, despite her husband's insistence that it was unnecessary. She'd finally convinced him that she'd worry less about the cancer's return if she had the second mastectomy. Once that was over, she told herself she'd done all she could.

And yet here she was, with worry gnawing at the edges of her thoughts.

"Don't move," said the tech, once more slipping out of the room.

So she lay as still as she could, trying one of the visualization techniques she'd learned. She had felt empowered during her treatments back then when she'd aimed her imaginary laser beam at the aggressive cancer cells that had infected three of her lymph nodes and watched them vaporize. She was aware some aberrant cells might have survived, mutating further during a brutal course of chemotherapy, and be lurking even now, waiting for the right time to strike. Bones, liver, lungs and brain. That's where she'd been told the cancer would likely metastasize if it had the chance. That chance, according to her oncologist, was about one in three. Every tumor had its own "fingerprint," as he put it, and was based on stage and grade of tumor, plus a number of other factors, including receptivity to hormones. It was sneaky that way.

"Okay, we're done," the tech said. "You can get dressed."

Later, exchanging her hospital gown for a simple cami, cotton shirt and jeans, she felt a little silly for allowing even a moment of worry about a fairly routine test. Hadn't Cate said, just the other day as she'd rubbed her knee, that she could feel winter coming? And Foxy had announced a couple of months ago she was no longer taking more than three massage clients a day because the deep tissue work they most valued was so hard on her thumbs.

Robin decided she'd been hanging around the people of Meadowpoint so much lately, she was picking up some of their aches and pains by osmosis.

Any other time, she would have turned to Cate, who would, with a mixture of humor and comfort, make her feel better. Cate had been preoccupied lately, and frankly a bit odd. On her way to the parking lot, the newly chilled wind whipped leaves and dust into a frenzy and made her eyes water.

* * *

ERA AND KIKI SAT SIDE by side on the velvet loveseat. Kiki picked at a hangnail and looked at how a beam of light from the window made a stripe across their knees, and made Era's clasped hands look colorless against her navy slacks. She reached out her hand and rubbed the wrinkly old knuckles more gently than usual. She didn't want to break her.

"Don't worry, they're not made of barley sugar." Era smiled.

"Barley sugar?"

Her great-gran's laugh sounded dusty. "It's from *Mary Poppins*, child. Didn't anyone ever read that book to you? It's a classic."

Kiki shook her head. "I saw the movie, though."

"Mary Poppins had a friend named Mrs. Corry, who had fingers made of barley sugar. She broke them off and gave them to the children to eat and then she grew new ones."

"Gross!" She made a face. "I don't remember that in the movie."

"Rather inventive though, don't you think?"

"'To let people eat her fingers? That's truly warped!"

She didn't bat an eye. "You might know of something in nature like that. Did you know starfish can regenerate whole new arms if one is broken off?"

Kiki tilted her head to see if Era was kidding her. "Really? That's cool."

"Yes, it is cool."

Thinking about those barley sugar fingers, whatever the heck barley sugar was, Kiki stopped rubbing and stared at the old hands. Somehow, she was pretty sure if she broke off anything on an old person, it wouldn't magically grow back.

"So what do you think happened to him?" Kiki asked. She didn't want to look at her great-gran. Crossing her legs, she let the top leg swing like the metronome her piano teacher used to use. She remembered the distinct sound of metal on hollow wood. It didn't say tick-tock like an old clock, but tick, tick, tick, like a time bomb.

Era didn't change the subject like she did last time. "I think my son is no longer living." Her tone wasn't all sad like it should have been. It was the same way she sounded when she'd said, "I'll have to get my winter boots out of storage pretty soon."

Kiki puffed out her cheeks and let the air come out in a long, skinny breath. She looked hard at her, but her great-gran didn't take her words back. No longer living. That was just another way of saying the word she was trying so hard not to think. She squinched her eyes shut and took some deep breaths, but she couldn't keep the tears from coming.

She covered her mouth and jumped up. Rushing to the bathroom, she bent over the sink and tried to throw up, but nothing came out, and after trying for a while, her throat burned and her neck muscles ached. She gave up, but stayed to splash water on her face and get her breathing calmed down. When she looked at herself in the mirror, she thought she looked like a little kid again. Except for her eyes. They looked like they belonged in an older person's face. Maybe if she lived to be ninety-six, she'd be able to think about death without crying.

She pulled herself together and went back to sit on the loveseat. Her voice only cracked a little when she said, "If you think he's not, y'know, living, what do you think happened to him? I mean, he has to be somewhere, doesn't he, whether he's alive or, or not."

"Oh, yes, he's somewhere."

Once she'd seen a show on TV where the magician made an elephant disappear. But the thing was, the elephant was really there the whole time and the magician had just tricked everyone into not seeing it. She balled her hands into fists and rubbed them along the tops of her thighs. "I have to find him." She started crying again and her words sounded like someone was choking her. "How am I gonna find him, Great-Gran?"

"I do not know." She emphasized every word.

Kiki blinked away her tears and thought her great-gran looked like one of those apple dolls Daisy had carved herself, an old man and woman, and dried them in the oven. "I just hope he wasn't afraid. Do you think my grampa knew he was gonna die?"

Era closed her hand over Kiki's and held on. Kiki could feel her eyes on her, and after a minute she looked back. Her great-gran's mouth was kind of lopsided, like she was too sad to smile with her whole mouth. She said, "Sweetie, it doesn't matter any more. He's okay now. Your grandfather loved you very, very much, and I can assure you he doesn't want you to spend any more time being sad about him. He's quite happy, actually."

Kiki watched how the wrinkles of her face quivered when she spoke. "How do you know?"

When she sucked air through her nose it made a whistling sound. "He has his way of letting me know."

Kiki felt her mouth fall open. "Did you have like a séance?"

Again, with the dusty laugh. "Not exactly. The first time my Winston came to me, I wasn't sure if I was dreaming or hallucinating from whatever they gave me in the hospital."

"You mean his ghost?"

"Hmm, I suppose that's one way of putting it, but I have seen him again since that first time in the hospital, and I have no doubt he comes to reassure me he is fine."

Fine? Was she fucking kidding? Kiki pulled on her hair until it hurt. "So fine's just another word for dead?"

"There are more things on heaven and earth, Horatio, than are dreamt of in your philosophy."

Was she having a stroke or something? "Great-Gran?"

"Shakespeare, dear. I don't suppose you were exposed to the classics in that school either."

Was that some kind of put-down?

"It's never too late to learn. Kiki, you have an excellent mind. I want you to remember that."

Kiki felt a big fat tear dribble down her face and fall on her arm. "How about if you just keep reminding me."

She did the lopsided smile again.

Her eyes stung and more hot tears rolled down her cheeks. "Great-Gran, how come he doesn't come to me?"

"Ah, that's an excellent question, and I happen to have an excellent answer." She pulled Kiki back to rest her head against her shoulder, like when she was little. "Two answers, actually. The first is that I carried Winston under my heart for nine months and that bond is not easily broken, even by death."

Kiki sniffled and made a hiccupping sound.

"The second answer is one that I do not expect you to understand for many decades to come. I'm old, Kiki, and when a person gets to this point, they know more people on that side than on this, and I won't be sorry to leave this old body when the time comes. The thing that may not make sense to you is this, I'm much, much closer to the next world than you are. The curtain between the worlds has become very thin for me, and I believe I can see through a particularly thin spot. Don't you think, at my great old age, I should be allowed a little glimpse into eternity?"

Since they were heading into the weekend, Robin did not expect to hear from her doctor until Monday. Nevertheless, she tucked her cell phone into the pocket of her apron as she moved around the kitchen. Making dinner was a pleasant distraction. Both she and Brad appreciated gourmet food, but what they really loved was a simple, down to earth meal like the one she was preparing. And unless one of his patients went into premature labor, or false labor, as had happened last night, they would be able to eat together at a civilized time.

For her, the comforting that came with comfort food began with the preparation. She inhaled the aroma of the stewing chicken with celery stalks, onions and garlic. Lifting the dishcloth off the bread rising in an oiled bowl, she sniffed the familiar smell that became even stronger when she punched down the puffy dough and shaped it into a loaf. It was all so homey and reassuring, and yet she found herself glancing too often at the clock.

Her unconscious thoughts migrated to the forefront. When she pressed the Talk button on the phone, the dial tone told her it was operational. It was the weekend, she told herself—she would hear nothing until Monday. In an effort to suppress memories of this morning's x-rays, she turned on the radio. The song on the jazz station was a bit frenetic, so she turned to MPR, where there was a discussion of how term limits could plague the Minnesota legislature with even more gridlock. Was that even possible?

Soon the rhythmic chopping of vegetables had a soothing effect, and her mind wandered until her only conscious thoughts were of her upcoming interview and photo shoot with Era. She pictured how it would go. She would shoot in black and white, with the mid-afternoon light deepening the character lines of her face. Era would not be reticent to talk, but Robin had a few questions to put her at ease and get her started, if needed, questions about childhood books, her favorite teacher or her first dance. She would have no trouble eliciting stories that would leave the readers with no doubt Era Dudley was remarkable at any age.

When the bread had doubled in size she turned on the oven. Yeast intrigued her. She read up on the process once. It was just a simple fungus that worked by consuming sugar to form carbon dioxide, which created air bubbles in the dough. Impressive, she thought, that it can double and redouble in one afternoon. Another image inserted itself into her mind—cells dividing rapidly and out of control. Closing her eyes the image remained.

Yeast. Cancer cells. Damn it all!

Shoving the loaf pan into the oven, her wrist contacted the upper metal rack. She jerked back and swore again as she grabbed an ice cube, gliding it over the fresh burn. When the phone in her pocket rang, she jumped as if she'd received a jolt of electricity from the ice cube.

It was her doctor, as she'd known it would be.

The first part of his sentence was drowned out by the buzzing of her brain. She caught his words midstream. ". . . a couple areas of luminosity," he said. "Since the femoral head is a common site for metastasis in breast cancer, we need to rule out the possibility."

The femoral head, she vaguely remembered, was that knobby top of the thighbone that fit into the pelvis. "Of course," she heard herself say. "Are there any other possibilities? Anything else that would show up as, how did you put it, 'areas of luminosity'?"

His answer was quick, though not particularly reassuring. "Let's not get ahead of ourselves."

Bones, liver, lungs and brain, her inner voice taunted.

"Someone from the imaging lab will call you later with an appointment time. Hopefully, they'll be able to get you in right away Monday morning."

"Such a rush," Robin almost whispered into the phone.

"Yes, I suppose so, but I'd like to get on top of it now rather than—"

Buzz, buzz, buzz.

She had always thought when this time came, she'd be afraid, breaking down into uncontrollable tears. Instead she was numb. The numbness lasted only a few minutes though, replaced not by the worry that had been nagging at her for days but by a strange calm, as if she were outside of herself, watching events unfold.

This self outside of herself looked around her kitchen, appreciating anew the attention she'd paid to detail when they'd remodeled—how the starkness of stainless steel appliances and granite countertops was offset by warm wood floors and hanging copper-clad pots. Again, she closed her eyes, inhaling the familiar smells of chicken soup and baking bread as if for the last time.

Life has been good, she thought. *And bad. But mostly good.*

She already knew she wasn't going to call her daughters at school, one on each coast, and worry them, maybe needlessly, about the CT scan until she got definitive results. But should she tell Brad? She had a strong understanding that, although she was surrounded by people who loved her, there were parts of this journey that could only be traveled alone.

Her eyes fixed on the set of photos on the far wall. She had taken them both at their property in Wisconsin the summer before she was diagnosed. It would always be one of those events that delineated her life: BC—Before Cancer. The top one was of their cabin, which existed now only in photographs. She and Brad had discussed rebuilding, and had had some blueprints drawn up, but would Brad even want another cabin now, if her cancer had returned? She had usually been the one to go there by herself or with friends, while Brad's job more often than not kept him from going with her. They'd had a good marriage, but were not Super Glued to each other like some couples. Maybe that was for the best, because if he was going to go on without her, he would not be adrift.

The lower picture was one of her favorites, a woodland path that began in bright sunlight and led into—She tried to focus on the shadows of the photograph. "Where does it lead?" she said out loud.

* * *

IT WAS SATURDAY MORNING, and as soon as Cate's husband Erik left for his game of racquetball with Brad, she heated water on the stove. Unwrapping the tea set she'd bought in Stillwater, she washed it, enjoying the pleasing shape of the teapot in her hands. Simple grace, she thought. She filled a tea ball and remembered the first time she'd served this particular blend to Robin and told her it was called Maui sunrise. Robin had asked, "Are you sure we shouldn't be smoking it?" And then after drinking two cups, she'd claimed it had given her "the munchies."

It had been a while since she and Robin had gotten together and laughed like they had that day. Lately they seemed to be on different tracks. Cate had been sensing it for a while now. At first she'd thought it was Robin who was creating the distance between them, but in the last couple of days, she'd come to realize part of it had to be her own preoccupation with her mother and the startling discovery she had a half-brother. There was no one, not even Robin, who could understand how utterly surreal the whole thing was for her.

And so she'd picked up the phone last night after dinner to do whatever she could to reconnect to her dearest friend. Robin had sounded floaty and far away, and the conversation was halting.

Cate grabbed the teakettle before it whistled, and filled the pot. Each tea bowl was slightly different, the mark of hand-thrown, non-production pottery. She chose the one with a blue flash of color shot through the ruby glaze. Holding it in her hands, it felt good, just the right size and shape for her hands, but as soon as she filled it with the aromatic tea and put it to her lips, she became anxious. Sometimes she had clear intuitions about things, but this anxiety was fuzzier, and since she had just been thinking about Robin, she suspected her uneasiness had something to do with her.

With other stressors in her life, mainly her mother and her brother—and now, as it turned out, a nephew—she wondered why it was Robin who was so heavily on her mind.

When they'd first met in college, there had been an instant bond, despite their different lives. Robin was an English literature major and Cate was in fine arts. Robin was northern European pale and Cate's coloring came from her Native ancestors, setting her apart from most of the other students. Yet for decades, the two of them had shared secrets and fears and joys. They had laughed until their sides ached. They had taken turns being in crisis and being the one to offer comfort through the crisis. When the burden had been too heavy for one, bearing it together had made it possible. But now Robin seemed out of reach, just when Cate needed her support.

She set her laptop computer in front of her. Checking her e-mail, she deleted over sixty new messages. It didn't matter what spam filter she used or how many messages she blocked, there was a bottomless cesspool of unwanted mail. She'd somehow gotten on a senior dating service, and each time she blocked the sender, the message came back the next day from a slightly different address. The same was true of refinancing offers, astrological advice and magical treatments for cellulite or belly flab. At one point, she'd blocked certain words that showed up in the Subject line, and that list of blocked words itself looked like the porn she was trying to avoid. As she stared at the screen, another e-mail popped up, this one offering multiple orgasms.

Disgusted, she pushed her computer away from her, knowing as soon as she did it that it had been a mistake. She heard the teapot hit the floor and the sound told her it had not survived the fall. Groaning, she bent to look under the table.

Tea splashed across the floor and baseboard. The spout had broken cleanly away, the lid was shattered and the rim of the pot was chipped. She unwound a wad of paper towels and dropped to her knees to pick up the pieces. Standing up quickly, she got a head rush and had to put a hand on the table to steady herself. The pieces she dumped into the garbage bag made her think of potsherds found at archeological digs.

Although she thought she'd memorized the phone number, it didn't come immediately to mind, so she looked it up in her planner. Dialing the shop in Stillwater where she'd bought the tea set, she waited only two rings before Jillian answered.

"Good news!" Jillian said without preamble. "We've already sold two bracelets, one with the little copper twist in the center and the other one with the dangly clasp, but they didn't buy the matching earrings."

Cate had to think. "There weren't matching earrings."

"I thought they went with the little triangle ones on the French hooks. I displayed them together."

"Ah," Cate said, trying to come back to her reason for the call. When Cate explained about the broken pot, Jillian said she'd call the potter, Jon Nord.

"I called him just yesterday to let him know his anagama pottery has been a big hit. One woman was absolutely gushing about the glaze combinations he uses."

So much for my jewelry, Cate thought. The hot new potter had relegated her to obscurity.

"I asked him to stop in sometime in the next few days with more pieces. I'll call him to see if he has other teapots that might work for you. Even if it's not exactly the same, his pieces are all so individual. You don't want matchy-matchy anyway, right?"

After they hung up, Cate noticed her finger was bleeding. She must have cut herself on one of the shards.

Era was in fine form for her interview. She wore a smart brown wool dress and pearls, and had just had her hair done in the downstairs beauty shop. Her table was set with pretty china, an African violet in bloom, and an assortment of pastries from the little bakery next to the beauty shop. She set two stemmed glasses of milk out for them.

Across the table from Robin, and positioned to face Era, was a picture of Era's husband in a crude wooden frame. It was not the studio photo Robin had seen earlier, but a snapshot of a man with dark hair and eyes and wearing a bulky sweater.

"Is this Winston's father?"

Era smiled. "It is indeed. That's my Gordon." She cut a croissant in half to reveal the soft chocolate filling. With a little flourish, she put half on each plate.

For the first time since her arrival, Robin noticed a third plate in front of the empty chair, and remembered how some of the women had talked about Era setting an extra place for her dead husband. This had been the basis for some people wondering if she had dementia. That, and the odd expression she had used when telling Vivian about the photo. "Oh, he doesn't talk," she'd said.

Well, he doesn't talk, Robin thought. She was right about that.

She took note of the fact that Era had not heaped pastries on his plate, a good sign she didn't believe he was actually eating anything. "He looks nice, kind of like a young Ernest Hemingway," Robin said.

Era chuckled. "Oh yes, we heard that more than once. Luckily, Gordon was blessed with a better disposition than that bastard." She dabbed her lips with a napkin.

Hearing a proper lady like Era using improper language made Robin chuckle.

Era concentrated on cutting a date muffin in half and putting half on each plate as well, urging Robin to eat while they were still warm. "Gordon was such a dear man," she said, looking at the picture.

"May I?" Robin picked up the photo to get a better look. "Yes, I can see kindness in his eyes."

Era's sigh sounded like the rustling of dry leaves. "He doesn't come around much anymore and when he does, he never says a word, which really isn't like him at all."

Robin set the photo back.

"He could tell a story, Gordon could. When he was in a room, he could make scintillating conversation about absolutely anything. In fact," she said, chuckling again, "sometimes, I would find myself wishing he would get laryngitis." She paused and stared off into space. "Oh, I don't mean I didn't enjoy him talking, but sometimes my ears needed a little vacation."

Robin laughed.

Touching the glass protecting the picture, Era said, "And now you see how it is. I would give anything to hear his voice again." Shaking her head, she raised the croissant to her mouth and took an unladylike bite.

As Robin had guessed, Era needed no prompting to tell stories of her youth. Some of her favorite memories, she said, were when her father would come home from work at the bank and tell her about all the people he was able to help with loans. It made her feel like a grownup to have him tell her about these people. She knew some of them. They might have come asking for money to purchase boat tickets for their parents to come over from the old country, or perhaps they needed another plough horse or a new windmill for the farm.

"One time he told me about a man who wanted to pay the freight for a new bride he'd never met, and my father asked him how his current wife would feel about that." Era snorted.

As Era talked in her animated fashion, the sunlight streamed in for optimal lighting. Robin took out both of her cameras. She had Era tell about the history of items in her glass curio cabinet while she took the first few shots, swapping back and forth between her Nikon and her little digital camera. Although the photography for this next book would be strictly black and white, she might make use of the color shots.

Maybe she'd put some on her website, whenever she got around to figuring out more than the basics, with slideshows accompanied by music or nature sounds. The learning curve for the program was steep, and what took the twenty-somethings minutes might take her hours or even months.

She asked Era about the photos grouped on the end table. Era named the people: her parents, a grandmother, her older brother who was killed in Dunkirk and a much older sister she barely knew before she married and moved to Nova Scotia.

They moved to the upholstered chairs by the window. At one point, Era's head tilted slightly to the right, eyes closed, and Robin was not certain if she was recollecting something or had dozed off. Then she smiled and looked at Robin. "Gordon was not my first beau. No, I was quite the glamour girl, with curly, strawberry blond hair and an eighteen-inch waist." She sat up straighter. "Why, the men were like moths to the flame."

Robin clicked the shutter. "Of course they were."

"Life was one big party for a while, but when Gordon began courting me, I knew things were about to take a turn. It was a turn for the better, of course, but I had to let my other beaus go. There was one of the young men—his name was Alfred and he was smitten with me, but he was not my cup of tea. He simply assumed we would marry, although I truly didn't give him much encouragement. When he heard about my engagement to Gordon, why, he rushed right over and insisted on talking to me alone, so I agreed to walk with him down by the river. When we got to where we could see the high bridge over the Mississippi River, he threatened to jump off it if I married anyone but him. Can you imagine such a thing?"

Robin shook her head.

"Well, I thought about it for all of three seconds, and decided if I let him coerce me into marriage, I'd be subjected to that kind of extortion the rest of my life, so I said, 'Well, Alf, old chum, I shall miss you.'" She cackled at the memory.

Robin caught that on film.

"I left him standing there with such an expression I shall never forget. But do you know he was a bald-faced liar! He did not jump off that bridge or any other, not then and not ever. In fact it was not even two months later he got married to a girl we called Mopey Molly. They had seven children and all of them had that same downturned mouth of their mother's."

Robin laughed with her.

"Oddly enough, not a single one resembled Alf."

Robin looked up to see Era bugging her eyes out in mock innocence.

She smiled back, then snapped a few more pictures . . . "So you married Gordon," she prompted.

"I did. He was the real McCoy. If he said he would do something, he did it." She looked away and said in a small voice, "He said he would never leave me."

The words settled on Robin and she felt the weight of them. Picking up his photo once again, she looked at it more closely. "Oh,

I thought he was standing in front of a white stucco wall, but this is a snowbank, isn't it?"

Era sucked in her breath to say something, and started choking. Robin sat helplessly as the poor woman wheezed and hacked until tears trickled down through the maze of wrinkles on her cheeks. Robin jumped up to get her a glass of water, but Era flapped her hands and said, "No, no, stay where you are. I'm fine." When she'd finally recovered, she redirected Robin, saying, "You were asking about the picture. Yes, that was snow, all right, several feet of it."

Nothing wrong with her memory today, Robin thought. "It looks like the snow was higher than his head."

"Oh yes, it certainly was. That was the Armistice Day Blizzard, November 11, 1940." She got a faraway look.

Robin decided not to interrupt her train of thought, even though the silence went on for a while.

Finally Era continued as if there'd been no break. "That was a blizzard like we'd never seen before. It started out as rain and then it turned to snow. For two days it kept on coming down, and all the time the temperature dropped and dropped and the wind blew harder and harder. By the time it was all done, there were snow drifts as high as—Well you can see how high this one was. Some people had drifts all the way up to their second story windows."

Robin had heard people refer to the Armistice Day Blizzard, but she'd never heard a firsthand account. "How did you get out of the house?"

Era laughed. "We couldn't use the front door, of course. That's where it drifted the highest, over ten feet in places. The back door wasn't much better. But from the upstairs windows we could see that the snow cover wasn't uniform, and so I got the idea to open the window downstairs in the dining room where the snow thinned a few feet from the house. Well, you can imagine, when we opened the window, all that snow just fell right into the room, and so we scooped it up with pots and pans and put it in the kitchen sink and the laundry tub and even the bathtub until it melted, and then we scooped some more."

Robin decided to look up whatever she could about the storm when she got home. Surely there would be photos online.

"We worked and worked to clear a passageway so Gordon could get outside. I don't know why it was so important to get out. It's not like we had anything we had to do out there, but I suppose it made us feel less trapped to know we could. He crawled through the little tunnel to the side yard, took one look around and crawled back inside. He said, 'Well, Mother'—He called me that even before Winston was born—'Well, Mother, I think we should break out the Christmas brandy and sit by the fire.' And that's just what we did."

Robin was charmed not only by the narrative, but also by the mental picture of Era as a young woman.

"It had never occurred to us that we might want to have a snow shovel inside the house." She shook her head. "But we did from that day on."

"Thank goodness you were home when it hit," Robin said, trying to picture it.

"That blizzard claimed a lot of lives, a hundred and fifty or so. You see, we didn't get weather reports like New York and Chicago did, so people were caught quite by surprise. They were out doing whatever people do, and without a clue of what was coming, they were dressed inadequately for the storm. About a third of the ones who died were out hunting, duck hunting on the little islands in the Mississippi River as I recall. By the time they realized the storm wasn't going to let up, some tried to swim to shore and didn't make it. Some stayed where they were and died of exposure. But the ones who lived to tell the tale said that the storm blew in enough ducks to feed them for a year."

Robin knew how Minnesotans loved to talk about weather. Stories like this were the reason for the preoccupation.

Era sat back. Sunlight shone through her white hair, making a halo of light. She blinked with heavy lids.

"I hope I haven't worn you out. Maybe we should call it a day."

"Don't worry about me. Talking about those days, I feel like a spring chicken. A mouth in motion tends to remain in motion. It's one of Newton's laws."

Robin would have to put that in the book. "Are you sure? We don't have to do it all in one day."

Era leaned forward, twirling her arthritic hands in front of her. "All right, Mrs. DeMille, I'm ready for my close-up."

She snapped the shutter. After a couple more shots and several more stories, all of them entertaining, Robin noticed the lines of fatigue once again settling on Era's features. Tuning off the recorder, she jotted down some notes. Noticing Era's eyes were closed, she took one last picture.

Era's eyes sprang open. "Do be careful, dear, there are places you should not go," she said in a surprisingly strong voice.

Where did that come from? "I'll be careful," Robin answered, like a child to an overcautious parent.

"Not alone." Her voice was weaker now. "Tell your friend . . ." Her voice trailed off.

She wondered if Era might be having a TIA, but then she was again lucid.

As she saw Robin to the door, Era thanked her profusely, saying she'd made her feel like "the belle of the ball."

Walking down the hall, Robin mused about the warning. Tell my friends what? Don't take any wooden nickels? Don't drink your bath water?

* * *

AT HOME, ROBIN COULD HARDLY wait to tell Brad all about the interview.

He looked up from his project, gluing and clamping the frame of a wobbly kitchen chair, and said, "You're absolutely jubilant! She must be quite a character."

"Oh, she's that, for sure."

Sitting on the high kitchen stool while he worked, she transcribed her few notes onto her laptop, stopping to tell her husband snippets of the conversation with Era. Going back to get her camera, she felt the small weight of the cell phone in her pocket. Only then did she think about turning the volume back on, and saw that there were missed calls and voice mails. Her involvement with Era had served so well to distract her earlier, but once again she experienced the dark, hollow sensation as she listened to the messages, one from the imaging center and one from her doctor. Her CT scan was scheduled for 10:15 a.m. on Monday.

She looked at Brad, happily working away, unaware of how his world might soon and without warning be turned upside down. The intense love she felt for him at that moment was infused with sadness.

Once more she had the sensation of being outside of herself as she took the camera downstairs to her darkroom to immerse herself in the routine that, although familiar, demanded her concentration. She loaded the 35 mm film into the developing wheel and put that into the stainless steel tank. She poured in the developing solution, agitating the small tank to coat the film and setting her timer for six minutes before pouring it out. The stop bath was next, followed by the fixative, which took ten more minutes.

The fifteen-watt red light gave off its usual eerie glow. After hanging the treated film up to dry, she trudged upstairs, wondering if she would be able to sleep tonight, knowing what was coming Monday morning.

But oddly, when she went to bed that night, what popped up in her mind were the peculiar words of caution Era gave her as she was leaving, something about places she shouldn't go. Had it been a throwback to the way she had cautioned her son as a small boy, the way parents did? Don't talk to strangers, don't dawdle on the way, don't cut through the woods . . . And then there was that bit at the end, which had been hard to hear, but she thought Era had told her to tell her friends. But tell them what, she wondered? Was she supposed to tell her friends about Era's interview or encourage them to buy the book when it came out? Or maybe—

She stopped herself from a lifetime pattern of perseverating on such things that had led to serious insomnia for years. As a therapist had once suggested, she dumped her obsessive thoughts onto paper. She could return to them if, and when, the time was appropriate. On the notepad at her bedside, she wrote, "places I shouldn't go," and below that, "tell your friends." She drifted off to sleep with the thought that maybe the word was not *friends* but rather *friend*.

Most of the shops in Stillwater were open on Sunday and, although there weren't nearly as many shoppers as on any weekend during the summer, Cate still had to park a block away from the store. Inside, Jillian stood at the cash register, ringing up a purchase. Cate was pleased to see she wore one of her bracelets.

When she saw Cate, she said to her customer, "Here's the designer of that lovely silver and gold cuff you were looking at." She introduced the two women.

The customer, a silver-haired woman dressed in all black, asked to see the cuff again and then pointed out to Cate that if it had curved just so over her wrist bones, she would have bought it. Cate handed her a card and invited her to call to see the rest of her collection. Such an invitation rarely resulted in a sale. Sometimes people feigned interest as a way to save face, a way to avoid telling the artist to her face they weren't buying.

When the customer left, bearing her purchase of hand-made paper Christmas ornaments, Cate thanked Jillian for calling her.

"I'm really sorry." Jillian wrinkled her freckled nose. "Jon was supposed to be here at noon, and here it is after one o'clock, and I haven't heard a word. He was going to bring several pieces from his latest firing, too."

Cate pulled her mouth to one side, and sauntered over to the area where Jon Nord's pottery was displayed. She held up a large bowl. "He did say he has more pieces with this glaze, right?"

"He thought he did. As I told you, he said he'd bring two different teapots with that beautiful red glaze."

Maybe if he had a teapot like that, she would invest in some other pieces as well. If he showed up. To Jillian she said, "I guess I could mosey down the street and get a late lunch. If he hasn't come in by the time I'm back . . . well, let's just hope he does."

The glorified coffee shop had opened just over a year ago, and Cate wasn't sure it would be around for long, judging by all the empty tables. The décor was a bit fussy for her tastes, but the place was clean, and the food tasty, although overpriced. She dawdled over the tomato bisque and turkey ciabatta, and then ordered a latte, stalling so she wouldn't have to drive back another day for a teapot which was beginning to feel like way too much trouble. The round trip was just over fifty miles, so it wasn't a huge deal, but it irked her to have to wait. Some artists she'd known had little concept of time, and she had more tolerance for that attitude than most. But honestly, she thought, if you're going to be in business, at least be businesslike!

A ruckus at another table drew Cate's attention. A mother in an expensive-looking sweater and long acrylic nails talked on her cell phone while her three small children finger-painted the plate glass window with their smeary hands. The youngest, a toddler, blew spit bubbles, much to the amusement of the other two. Remains of their lunch—hot dogs and macaroni and cheese—dotted the tabletop like an expressionist painting. From behind the counter, the owner watched the tableau, her jaw set.

The middle child, about three-years old by Cate's estimate, squirted more ketchup onto the tabletop, getting a dollop on the sleeve of his polo shirt that bore the Ralph Lauren logo. Edging his sister aside, he climbed onto the extra-wide windowsill and promptly fell off, whacking his head against the table leg. His mouth formed a perfect rectangle when he howled. More annoyed than concerned, the mother shut her phone and tended to him, careful not to let him touch her clothing with his grubby hands or his condiment-stained shirt.

Cate stood up to pay her bill. She felt compelled to leave an overgenerous tip, knowing full well it was a futile attempt to compensate for someone else's bad behavior. So often in the past, Cate had watched other people's children behaving badly, and had thought how she would have done a better job. Today, though, she wasn't so sure.

Taking languid strides, she headed back to the gift shop. When she walked in, Jillian was on the phone. Gesturing to Cate, she said to the person on the other end, "Hold on. She just walked in. Do you want to talk to her yourself?" She covered the mouthpiece and spoke to Cate. "He can't make it in today—some complication—but he really wants to make other arrangements with you."

Cate took the phone and talked to Jon Nord. Her eyes rested on the shelf of his pottery. None of the glazed pieces appealed to her as much as the broken teapot had, but she did like the bowl. It would make a nice housewarming gift for her mother.

The potter apologized for inconveniencing her. "I had another artist lined up to help with the firing a couple weeks ago, but he bailed on me, so I was left to do it on my own. It's not a one-person job. I stayed up three days stoking the kiln by myself."

"I can't imagine." She rolled her eyes at Jillian.

"So, I pretty much crashed for a couple days."

Cate couldn't see how his problems two weeks ago would have affected the commitment he had made just yesterday to bring in a load of pottery.

"And if that wasn't bad enough, when I unloaded the kiln, I discovered the big pot I was firing as a favor to this other supposed friend had exploded and wrecked several of my pieces. It never would've happened if he'd wedged the clay properly. Amateur mistake."

For someone who portrayed himself as beyond amateur status, he did not impress her as professional. He was young, according to Jillian. There was more than a hint of arrogance in his tone. Having done her share of art shows, Cate knew some of the artsy types affected a certain persona when they were promoting their craft. The fact that so many did made her think it must appeal to some of the moneyed patrons.

He was still talking about his kiln. "But bottom line is, I did manage to salvage a teapot that would match your set. Problem is, I won't be driving into Stillwater until next week."

"Okay, thanks." She was about to hand the phone back to Jillian when he said, "Hey, if you want to drive out to my place, you could see what else I have, and I'd be happy to show you around."

Annoyed as she was, the offer intrigued her. "I would love to see the kiln—actually your whole setup. I took a little class in pottery years ago, and always thought I'd like to give it a real try someday."

"You're the one who does the metal jewelry, right?"

"That's me." She looked out the window and saw the mother from the coffee shop coming toward Jillian's store, and was grateful her jewelry was relatively safe in a glass case. All three children were walking ahead of their mother, with the little girl pushing an empty stroller, which she abandoned to bang on the window. She waved at Cate like she was a favorite aunt.

"But listen, if you don't need the teapot for a while and want to wait until I do the next firing, you can be part of the crew," Jon was saying to her. "I always need extra people around to take turns stoking the fire. What do you think?"

She rarely turned down a chance to see how things were created. There was so much more to art than the finished product. But staying up for three nights? She hadn't even been good at that in her younger days. "No, I'd rather come out soon."

He told her where his shop was. It was north and west from her mother's new place. But as soon as she indicated that she'd like to take him up on his offer and tried to pin him down on his next firing, he seemed to backpedal. "Yeah, well, it's hard to say. I have a lot of pots to throw before that happens. I mean a lot. I'll need to do at least two more firings to have enough inventory for the juried art shows I have coming up."

She knew what that was like, at least the time and inventory part. Luckily, since she'd taken up jewelry making, Erik's income had meant she didn't have to be a starving artist. "Congratulations. Which shows?"

He kept talking as if he hadn't heard her question. "Getting into the juried shows is the only way to do it. I don't know if you do regular craft shows with your jewelry, but if you do, you know how demeaning it is. People look at craft shows differently. They have no idea what's involved in your work, and they always think your stuff is overpriced."

She laughed. "True." She'd spent many a sale with a forced smile, cheerful in the face of people who came expecting, even demanding, to buy one-of-a-kind, handcrafted pieces of art at prices lower than what they were accustomed to paying for items mass-produced in China.

"But call it 'art' and ask five times the price at a juried show, and they treat you with more respect," the potter said.

Cate agreed.

Having found a sympathetic ear, Nord went on about the lack of respect the world showed him, like the Rodney Dangerfield of the art world.

She rolled her eyes at Jillian again. "I need to free up the phone here," she said. "How about if I call you when I'm going to be in the western suburbs."

* * *

ROBIN FELT BLOOD PULSE in her temples as she bent over the photographic paper. She hadn't been aware of how long she'd been hunching over the bench, working until her head began to throb. The muscles in her neck and shoulders told her it was time to quit, but she was almost done. The images had been enlarged and most of the black and white stills were pinned to a corkboard that took up the wall space between her enlarger and cutter that she kept on the side of the room designated as the dry side.

Even though so many photographers had switched to digital photography, there was something about the traditional darkroom she loved. She looked at her shelf of chemicals. Right after she was diagnosed with cancer, she blamed herself for putting herself in a toxic environment, but after talking to her oncologist and doing plenty of research, she figured it was not the probable cause. Early on she'd switched to a line of products with the least toxicity, and she always used tongs when using the developer, stop bath and fixer. Besides, her darkroom was well ventilated. Even now, with the chemicals sealed in airtight containers, the powerful exhaust fan was going.

Despite any real or imagined risks, Robin loved the magic of making images appear on blank paper. It had taken several years to feel proficient at controlling the timing of the chemical baths and fine-tuning subtle differences the average person did not notice, but that's what made the difference between an amateur and a professional.

With the main, fluorescent light on, she pinned a new print to the corkboard, and noticed an odd area of light on the print she'd put up earlier. It was a candid shot of Era, as most of them had been, and taken toward the end of the session. She looked again. No, it had been the very last picture she'd taken. Era sat in her chair about thirty inches from the camera, her jaw dropped slightly and her eyes were closed. Looking at the photo now, Robin did not think Era had been asleep at that moment. Robin had once taken a series of photos of school children listening to music, and they'd had the same expression of wonder and pleasure.

The natural light from the window played on Era's face, accentuating some of the wrinkles, but in a pleasing way. The focus had been just right, and yet . . . had she smudged the print somehow? She looked at the area of dappled white over Era's shoulder. It seemed to be lit from another source, even though she hadn't used a flash. It was faint, a blur of light which, if she moved in closer and used her imagination, looked a little like a face turned at a three-quarter angle toward Era.

When she stood back, it was just a wisp of light again, and try as she might, she couldn't see the face again. Cate would probably say it was an aura or a ghost.

Her photography teacher would have called it a simulacrum, something that appears to be something else—the mind trying to make sense of random patterns. It was not uncommon for someone to show such incontrovertible photographic proof of the spirit world, only to find out they were seeing what they wanted to see. It was like finding objects in the clouds—dragons or the face of Jesus or a pair of overalls. People saw things differently, although one of the most universal things the mind comprehended was the human face. She had read a whole blog about the phenomenon, complete with photographs of faces in the wood grain of a kitchen cupboard, in the shadows on a school playground and in a Petri dish loaded with bacteria.

Robin knew there was also the strong chance the light from the window reflected off some surface, maybe a white book jacket or the glass in a picture frame. Or it could be due to improper fixing on her part, or her own thumbprint on the lens.

Still, there was that peculiar expression on Era's face, which was turned, oh so slightly, in the direction of the dappled white shape.

On Monday morning they were both up long before the alarm went off. Neither was interested in breakfast or even coffee, since Robin's stomach was rebelling and Brad seemed anxious to leave.

She hadn't even planned to tell him about her x-ray until she'd gotten results from this next scan, but then last night after she finally emerged from the darkroom, Brad had surprised her by telling her he was taking the day off, and suggested a leisurely day trip to Northfield, a small college town south of the Cities where they liked to go for lunch and a stroll along the river.

She'd had no choice but to tell him about her appointment. She had braced herself for his angry outburst and his response had been predictable. After all, she had intentionally shut him out, and he hadn't had time to prepare. Besides, she'd lived with the man long enough to know that his worry always came across as anger, at least initially.

What she hadn't prepared herself for was her own reaction. It wasn't that she was indifferent exactly, but she felt walled off from what he was going through. As long as she could remember, she'd been the caretaker of all things emotional in her family, beginning with her parents. She'd tried, even as a young child to moderate their arguments, and after failing miserably at keeping them together, she'd borne the burden of guilt for their divorce and all that ensued.

After years of therapy, she knew it hadn't been her fault, that her mother's depression and her father's inability to get her mother the proper help had played the major role in their divorce. And it was not, her therapist kept telling her, her fault that her father had chosen to override the custody agreement, taking Robin away from her mother. It had been a decision born of frustration and fear, and, she'd come to believe, his need to control. But despite the academic understanding of the situation, her inclination had always been to make sure everyone else was okay, to smooth her daughters' ruffled feathers when Cass or Maya got their feelings hurt, to give Brad space when he needed it and attend to his wounded ego if necessary.

But something had shifted in these past days. For now, she knew she could hold only enough space for her own feelings. Her husband and everyone else would have to deal with their own feelings.

Brad slammed back his cup of coffee, grimacing as the hot liquid made its way down. Overnight his anger had subsided, and he had become overly solicitous, pulling her chair out for her, and taking her elbow as if she were some kind of invalid. Frankly, she preferred the anger.

On the drive to the imaging center, he rambled on about an article he'd read about unnecessary episiotomies being done, and a new study of nerve damage resulting from childbirth. This was a familiar pattern, with Brad finding comfort by retreating in his own vast base of knowledge whenever he was unable to control events around him. She knew it calmed him to focus on science rather than emotion, just as he'd done when his father had been dying. He'd cornered nurses to discuss care options, offered his expertise to his father's cardiologist, and regaled family and friends with little-known medical facts.

As they neared the imaging center, Brad reached for her hand. After he parked in the physicians' lot, he rushed to open her car door, something he rarely did. All the way to the front desk, he kept up a one-sided conversation, but the only words that echoed in Robin's head were "bones, liver, lungs and brain."

* * *

CARLTON TUGGED ON HIS LEASH, eager to get on the elevator, but when Cate gave him the signal to sit, he obeyed without protest. In his training as a therapy dog, the black lab had been the star pupil, as if he fully comprehended the honor and the responsibility of his job. Evidently, Carlton now thought every time he came to Meadowpoint, it was Animal Day, and he was the chief attraction.

When they stepped off on the third floor, Frannie sat knitting on the bench near the elevator. She set her needles down next to her and held her hands out for the dog, who went to her with his head down, ready to be scratched behind the ears.

Cate was concerned Carlton might wag his powerful tail and knock someone over, or leave bruises on the legs of the elderly residents, so she had worked with him not to wag his tail too vigorously when he was in therapy mode. Frannie stroked his back and crooned to him. He whined almost imperceptibly and his tailed quivered with pleasure.

Virgil passed them, touching his forehead in greeting. Frannie nodded back, but said nothing as he veered over to pat the dog's flank before moving on to the sunroom.

Cate was about to take her leave when someone called to the dog by name.

Iris rolled toward her, grinning broadly. Carlton waited for the wheelchair to come to a stop before resting his head in her lap.

When she could stay no longer, Cate said, "I need to check in with my mom for a bit." She left them, pleased that Iris and Frannie were chatting amiably. Until today, she'd thought Frannie was antisocial.

Partway down the hall, Cate picked up the scent of gingerbread. She was pretty sure it didn't come from her mother's apartment, since, although her mother was a passable cook, the only bakery goods she had were store bought. Cate used to wonder what it would be like to have June Cleaver for a mother. Heck, at one time in high school she would have traded in her parents for Gomez and Morticia Addams. For a few seconds, she let her mind conjure up the family photo, with her newfound brother as Lurch and her as-yet-unknown nephew, Pugsley. She grinned at the thought.

Her mother came to the door looking like she hadn't slept in days, which is exactly what she said when Cate told her she looked tired.

"What's going on?" Cate asked.

Wanda just shook her head and led Cate into the living room. She moved a book and a box of Kleenex off the loveseat for Cate to sit. Plunking herself down in the small barrel chair, Wanda sat uneasily and said, "I'm too nervous to sleep."

Cate waited for her to continue.

She fretted with the beaded zipper pull of her jogging suit. "I'm finally going to meet your brother for the first time since he was a newborn. Can you blame me?"

Cate hated how casually her mother slipped the word *brother* into the conversation. A person grew up with brothers, had pillow fights with them and played together with the neighborhood kids. Big brothers bugged their little sisters and looked out for them in turn. They didn't just pop up half a century later. She raised one eyebrow in a way her mother found annoying. "Really!"

"Yes, really. Oh, I couldn't be more excited, but it's going to be hard. We've talked, of course, your brother and I. So it's not like we know nothing about each other, and he sounds really nice on the phone."

"But . . . ?" Cate prompted.

"But even though he says he isn't angry at me for my decision, I think, well, he has to feel rejected, wouldn't you think?" Her lips quivered.

How was it possible to feel so much love and so much anger towards someone at the same time?

"I gave him away, Cate. I just handed him off to the nurse." The corners of her mouth pulled down as she shook her head. "How can he not have some judgments about me?"

Cate allowed that he might indeed harbor some bad feelings. "But Mom," she added, "that's not unique to your situation. I mean, kids who grow up with their own birth parents have judgments too." She knew it was a mistake the minute she said it.

Wanda's red-rimmed eyes turned on her. "Yes, I suppose you do." She straightened her shoulders. "And you'd be right to judge me. I have certainly made my share of mistakes." Tears welled up, and Cate could see her jaw muscles working in an attempt to keep from crying.

Carlton shoved his muzzle against Wanda's knee and she automatically riffled her fingers through his soft fur.

Cate sucked in her breath as conflicting emotions warred within her. "Please don't take it that way, Mom. I didn't mean I'm judging you, I just meant . . ." What had she meant? Maybe her mother's observation was more astute than she gave her credit for.

Wanda stood up and went into the kitchen.

Cate heard water running. "Mom?"

"Never mind."

Cate waited until the sound of clattering dishes subsided. "So, when is he coming?"

"He's not sure when they can get away, but they're aiming for the end of the week. Maybe not until next week. He said they'll call when they're certain."

They. So Ricky and Bunny were both going to be here.

Her mother's voice was clogged. "When Ricky said they wanted to meet you too, I didn't know what to tell him." She walked in carrying a big plastic tumbler of water, sloshing a little onto the carpet before setting it on the end table next to her chair.

Cate wanted her answer to be as noncommittal as possible. "It depends. Where are they going to stay, anyway?" *Surely not here*, she thought, looking around the small room.

Wanda shrugged and took a swallow of water.

Carlton's big brown eyes rolled over to give Cate a look, and she felt instantly defensive. She couldn't be expected to put them up, could she? She and Ricky might be related, but they were perfect strangers! Besides, her guest room was a chaos of items she was storing for the animal shelter benefit. Things like dog bandanas and catnip-filled mice. Somehow or another it had fallen on her to store all of these donated items, and Erik had been agitating for some time now to have her find someone else to take over the responsibility.

In response to the news of her having a sibling, Erik had beamed at her and said it was wonderful to have siblings, a comment she thought odd coming from an only child. "And isn't it intriguing," he'd felt the need to point out, "that both you and your brother are so deeply involved with animals?"

"Genetics are fascinating," she'd said with an edge of sarcasm.

Sitting between the two women, Carlton kept his eyes on Cate, who finally said, "I guess I could talk to Erik about it."

Her mother seemed to be waiting for her to say more, but that was as much as she could muster, and so they sat in an uncomfortable silence. Wanda took another swig of water, which made her cough and slosh more water onto her slacks. "Crud," she said, brushing the water off. "Now I'll have to change my clothes."

Cate checked the wall clock and waited. By the time her mother came out of the bedroom, she said she had to go.

"You have no idea how much the other people are looking forward to your next visit," said Wanda. "You know, with the pets."

Other people? Cate blinked back tears at the inference that it was only other people who looked forward to her visit. She and her mother hadn't had much conflict over the years, at least not since she became an adult. A fairly relaxed parent, Wanda had not saddled Cate with a lot of expectations, as some parents had. She'd encouraged Cate to be her own unique self from a young age. But ever since she had moved up from Florida, the two of them seemed unable to be in each other's presence without this prickliness. Cate longed to talk to Robin about it, but Robin had not returned her call last night, which was unlike her.

Wanda stood and sighed heavily.

Feeling her shoulders slump, Cate got up. Carlton stood too, touching his nose first to Cate's hand and then Wanda's as he rolled his big eyes from one to the other. He could not have been more eloquent if he'd stood on two feet and said in perfect English, "Why don't you two just get along."

It appeared word had gotten out that Carlton was in the house, because as Cate neared the elevators, she saw several people had gathered in the sunroom. "There he is," Virgil said loudly, and they turned. Seeing their eager faces, Cate knew her mother had been right.

* * *

BRAD TOOK ROBIN OUT TO LUNCH on their way back from the CT scan. One of their favorite new restaurants was a place with lots of earth tones and a grand, stone fireplace, a mix of Southwest and Italian country. After they put in their order, Brad took her hand in his and held on, rubbing his thumb against her palm.

She smiled at him, still feeling oddly detached. At the hospital clinic, his behavior had been almost comical, letting everyone know he was a doctor and therefore would be making sure his wife got the very best treatment. Embarrassing as that was, she believed if it weren't for Brad's pressure to speed up this process, it might have dragged on for weeks.

Just as they'd been leaving the clinic today, the receptionist had turned to them and covered the phone. Addressing Brad, she said, "I'm talking to Dr. Singh right now. He said to tell you he'll take a look at the scans as soon as he gets them." To Robin, she explained, "It's all electronic now, so it won't take too long. In fact, he hopes to talk over the results with you after six this evening." By the time they'd left the imaging center, they already had a provisional appointment for a full-body bone scan the following afternoon, just in case, as the receptionist put it, "they still need to rule something else out."

Robin had learned, often the hard way, what it meant to be a doctor's wife, and it wasn't all perks like this. It was helping him financially and emotionally throughout medical school, only to have him act as if he were ashamed of needing her help. People who envied her life should have witnessed those years of his residency when he was always sleep-deprived. Try as he might to be an attentive husband in those years, she didn't kid herself about his priorities. They were the same as hers: to make sure he succeeded in this highly competitive field.

Even when his practice finally took off and he was home more, his schedule was erratic. Unlike several of his classmates who went into gynecological surgery, Brad stayed with obstetrics, with its unpredictable hours and greater chance of malpractice suits. Brad also refused to be drawn into the fashionable practice of inducing patients, timing a baby's birth to the doctor's schedule. Although it meant a life of disruptions, Robin loved him for sticking to his principles.

When their daughters came along, Robin had much of the companionship she'd been missing, and she took Brad's sudden departures more in stride.

There was that one time, though, when she and the girls all had the flu. Although Robin was dizzy, she'd bundled both of her daughters up and took them to the clinic. On the short drive, Maya strafed them with a spectacular case of projectile vomiting, causing a chain reaction in her sister. When Robin and her two little human geysers got back from the clinic, Brad, who'd just gotten home himself, made the mistake of asking her how he could help. He wound up cleaning her car.

But this time, he was right here, holding her hand in a lovely restaurant, at a table near the fireplace. This time he was not only giving her all his attention, but making sure all her medical people did too. Even as he smiled at her, she saw his concern just under the surface.

When their food arrived, Robin inhaled the wonderful aroma of her seafood pasta. "I'm starved," she said. In that moment she knew that whatever the doctor had to tell her today or any other day, she would be able to deal with it. As soon as her mood brightened, Brad's spirits were lifted as well and they both enjoyed their meal. Before they left, Robin wrapped two jumbo shrimp in a paper napkin to take home to the cats.

When they walked in the door of their house, Samson and Delilah were waiting for them. They stopped their yowling as soon as Robin placed the peace offering in their twin dishes.

Then, after thanking Brad for all his ministrations, she gathered up her cameras and digital recorder for her afternoon photo session and interview at Meadowpoint.

22

As far as Carlton was concerned, every visit to Meadowpoint Manor was a chance to spread the love around. Virgil got choked up as he stroked Carlton's velvety ears, and pretty soon he started telling stories about his old hunting dog that could retrieve any bird he shot, even when the dog's eyesight was failing and he had to rely mostly on his sense of smell.

Era appeared to be the most senior citizen there, but when she petted the black lab, Cate suddenly saw in the old woman's face the child she once might have been, with bright, snapping eyes and a sense of wonder.

Of course Carlton got something out of it too, basking in all the attention lavished on him. Cate had to restrain one of the women from slipping him a cookie, but Carlton had not missed the gesture, and his eyes followed the cookie as it was transferred from the woman's hands to her sweatshirt pocket. When she went down the hall, taking the treat with her, he stared after her, whining.

Frannie lingered after the others had gone. "Wouldn't it be a wonderful thing," she said, speaking directly to Cate for the first time, "if we could adopt pets here, not just to keep in our rooms, but what if Meadowpoint Manor had pets that we could all share? That way, when one of us dies, the animals won't have to adjust to a new owner. They grieve too, you know."

Cate was deeply touched. The words echoed her own thoughts. In the past couple of years, she and other volunteers at the animal shelter had discussed expanding their adoption process to include companion animals becoming permanent nursing home pets. It was all about matching pet to owner, or owners in this case.

When she finally tore Carlton away from his fans, Cate headed for the elevator, mentally running through the possibilities. One of their newest dogs, a Basenji, was a perfect pet for someone, unfortunately not for Meadowpoint. His breed was referred to as "barkless," but the sound he made was akin to a child's scream. Their oldest shelter cat was just too much a part of the facility and shouldn't have to adapt to a new home. Cate thought through several other options, knowing if Robin got wind of her idea, she'd give her a hard time, calling her a "pet pusher." Well, there are worse things to be, she thought, already working on her defense.

She brought Carlton to a heel and pressed the down arrow. His tongue lolled to the side.

And then Cate remembered another of the shelter's residents, the little Boston terrier with a brindle coat who'd been left behind when his owners were evicted. He was still young, and had a delightful disposition to go with his clownish smile. He would be a huge hit here.

The elevator doors opened, and before it even registered with Cate who was inside, Carlton bolted into the elevator car, wagging his tail so that it slapped against the metal walls like a snare drum. He licked Robin's hands and pranced in delight.

Surprised to see her old friend, it took Cate a moment to order Carlton back to her side. He and Robin exited together, with the dog pressing against her thigh.

"I called you last night," Cate said to Robin, dismayed to hear the scolding tone in her own voice.

Robin opened her mouth and shut it, and her eyes darted away briefly before resting on Cate's. She said, "I heard your message. Sorry I didn't call back." She winced and shifted her camera bag on her shoulder. "What's up?"

"I just haven't talked to you in a while. Why haven't you called?" Hearing her own voice, Cate had a vivid memory of saying the same words, and in the same wheedling tone, to a guy she'd dated briefly. He'd told her to stop pestering him. The memory still stung.

Robin's shoulder rose in a shrug. "I . . ."

Cate couldn't stand it. "I mean, here we are, both at the same place where both our mothers live, but you're coming and I'm going. Literally. It's weird." She gave a tug on the dog's leash, trying to make him sit again.

Robin looked anxious to get away. "I guess I've been wrapped up in this thing, this new project, and . . ." She frowned and set her things on the floor. "The people here have had interesting lives, really interesting. I'm just having such a good time talking to them and hearing their stories." Her smile was strained.

"You used to think spending time with me was a good time," Cate wanted to say, but Robin's words so strongly echoed what Cate's mother had said about other people looking forward to her visits. She'd felt unlovable before, but until now, it had never been Robin who'd made her feel that way.

In that moment, she made up her mind to plow ahead as if these feelings were not based on reality. "I understand," she said, although she didn't. "Want to stop by the house later?" Seeing the frown lines between Robin's brows, she revised the invitation. "We could grab a glass of wine closer to your house if you want."

Robin looked away again, just for a split second, but it left Cate with the conviction that she was hiding something. "I can't. It's . . . We have something . . ."

What the hell was going on? Cate frowned. All she'd done was ask if they could get together later. It was a question they'd asked each other dozens, if not hundreds, of times over their long friendship, but she couldn't remember ever getting a response like this. Having pushed the point this far, though, she figured she might as well keep pushing. "How about tomorrow? Do you have anything going tomorrow? I know! Maybe you could come with me in the afternoon. I was thinking about making a little trip out to—" She stopped when she saw Robin shaking her head. "What?"

"Cate. I can't. I'm sorry." Again, she winced and shifted her weight and, although she looked directly into Cate's eyes, it was as if she'd made herself intentionally blank.

Tears of humiliation springing to her eyes, Cate turned and punched the elevator button. "Well, okay then, I won't keep you." Carlton gave a backward glance as she tugged him along.

* * *

DAMN IT ALL! Robin took a detour into the empty laundry room to collect herself. The last thing she wanted to do was hurt anyone's feelings. But now she had to question just who she was trying to protect with her silence, Cate or herself. She knew if she told Cate about her medical tests, Cate would be gearing up like a warrior, taking charge of Robin's care much the way Brad had tried to do. In fact, it was exactly how Cate had behaved when Robin was first diagnosed, and although her fierce protectiveness had been welcome at first, over time it made Robin feel more powerless. She couldn't articulate why. Back then, she'd had a fighting chance of beating this rotten disease, but now if the cancer had metastasized—She threw up a mental barricade, knowing this path led to destructive worry and sleepless nights.

Still, there was the issue of Cate's feelings. Even though it wasn't Robin's nature to be selfish, she had a pervasive sense that she had to conserve every spark of energy she had for herself and whatever was coming next. She could not afford to use it dealing with other people's reactions or consoling the people closest to her. That time might come soon enough, but not now. She tried not to think about her daughters hearing the bad news for the first time. The thought was unbearable.

She knew what the possibilities were, but it was premature to ramp up the worry machine Catherine and Brad and her mother represented to her. The thing she was coming to realize was that she needed time to come to terms with her own mortality, in her own time and by herself.

Once at lunch today she'd been able to glimpse a concept out of the corner of her mind, a glimmer of something profound. She'd sat in wonder at what was beginning to form in her mind. It had seemed so perfect at that instant, a concept of life and death being the very same reality, but seen from different vantage points.

But then Brad had started talking, offering her butter for her bread and asking her if she had any questions about the bone scan scheduled for tomorrow. By the time she tried to recapture the moment, the idea had lost something essential and slipped away.

She heard the almost imperceptible sound of a wheelchair as Iris came around the corner, a canvas bag of laundry on her lap. "What's on your mind, Kiddo?" Iris asked after greeting Robin. "It looks like you've got the weight of the world on your shoulders."

"Sorry, I'm just going through a list of what I need to do."

The look Iris gave her was dubious. "I know you're going to see Daisy today, but if you have time to stop by my place afterwards, I'd like to show you something. I just unearthed a box of pictures. They've been in my storage closet so long, I forgot I even had them."

"I don't think I have time today, but I'd love to take a look when I come next time."

"That's fine. It was just a silly thought." She navigated the wheels with practiced ease. She wore a short-sleeved cotton shirt today, and Robin could see that her arms were more toned than most people thirty years younger.

Robin backed up to make room, effectively blocking her own way out. She saw Iris reaching to open the lid of the washing machine and stepped forward to help her.

"I've got it," Iris said and wedged her chair into the small space, held the lid open and tossed a load in. "I must have looked at those pictures for three hours last night. It's funny, I used to think the man I married looked like a movie star, with his chiseled features, as we used to say." She leaned forward to pour detergent powder into the machine. Then she sat back with her hands in her lap, her wheelchair blocking the small space between washers and dryers.

Robin didn't mind staying for a bit longer. She was already caught up in the story of an abusive husband, and this woman who was undaunted by her useless legs.

Iris touched manicured fingers to the pink foam rollers at her temples and the nape of her neck. "Oh, he dressed the part in his imported suits. And the way he strutted around like a peacock! For a time he took to wearing a mustache like Clark Gable's. Oh, the women liked him, and he liked them. Since I was such a Plain Jane, I wondered how long it would last before he tired of me. And those women at his office thought nothing of flinging themselves at him. At least that's what he told me."

Robin felt a stab, comprehending the power he'd held over her.

"I don't know why I believed what I did, but everyone thought he was such a catch. Once I talked to my aunt about him, and all she could say was that I should count myself a lucky woman to be married to him. Of course I found out quickly that life with him was no picnic, but still I believed I ought to be grateful."

Even now, Robin could see that she must have been quite attractive. She was about to say so when Iris wheeled backwards and into the hall.

Following her, Robin was compelled to know where this story was headed.

Iris didn't pause in her narrative. "But I want to tell you, when I opened that box of pictures yesterday, I found photographs taken at a charity ball. It was before I was like this." She gestured to her legs. "I remember that event to this day, although for the life of me I can't remember who it benefited . . . a hospital or an art museum or something. It was so long ago."

Robin walked alongside her, leaning down and straining to hear her. "But I remember the socialites were there, as they always were, bragging about the money they'd inherited or married into. Their questions ferreted out people like me, with no pedigree. That One knew how I hated to go to those things, and I took great care to make him proud of me. I was wearing an emerald dress my mother had made for me, with a rhinestone brooch just over my right bosom. I'd had my hair done up, with a jeweled clip. Just before we left the house, That One made some remark about me looking matronly, and I spent the whole evening feeling like one of the Ugly Stepsisters at the ball."

Robin began to commiserate, but Iris cut her off. "Oh, I put on a brave face. I even danced with most of the men there. I could cut a rug in those days."

They stopped in front of her apartment. Iris put a restraining hand on Robin's arm, and, with a hint of wistfulness, said, "I'll just finish my story before you have to go."

Robin had hoped she would.

"When I looked at that picture after all these years, I expected to see the man I remembered, a man with a cold heart but movie star looks, with his arm around his dowdy young wife." She laughed. "But That One looked like any stuffed-shirt lawyer, and I was the one who looked like a movie star. I couldn't believe it. I had to look twice." She turned her key in the lock. "Why, at first I thought I was looking at Myrna Loy." She fluttered her eyelashes. "Are you sure you won't come in?"

Tempted as she was, Robin had to decline. She'd already glimpsed Daisy in the sunroom, all decked out for her interview, wearing a garnet red pantsuit and gold-trimmed shoes. Robin got a lump in her throat, seeing the eagerness with which the residents of Meadowpoint Manor looked forward to a chance to talk about their younger days. It was as if she was offering them a sip from the Fountain of Youth.

23

She was picking up the bin of dirty dishes when she saw him coming toward her. The minute he sauntered through the coffee shop door, Derek's oily smile told Kiki everything she needed to know. Whatever his reason for dumping her in the first place, he now expected her to throw herself at his feet and beg for him to take her back. Holding out open arms to her, he said, "Miss me?" He used his soft bedroom voice.

Like I miss the swine flu, Kiki thought. "What are you doing here?" She carried the bin to the sink and plopped the coffee mugs and plates into warm, soapy water.

"I had to see you." His voice was close behind.

She turned to glare at him. "You're in my way."

She backed up, positioning herself behind the counter that held the espresso machine. He came around to the other side like he was going to order something, which he didn't. She checked the air pots and started brewing more decaf Sumatra, keeping busy so she didn't have to look at his face. It felt good to have all that stainless steel between them.

"Ki Ki." He said it like two words. "I can't stop thinking about you." The way he let his head drop and raised his eyes to meet hers made her think of a naughty little kid that wanted to get out of his punishment. "Don't you ever think about me?"

Yeah, along with all the other things I have to worry about. You're somewhere between bedbugs and STDs. That's what she wanted to say. Instead, she stared at him until he blinked and said, "Derek, we're over. Didn't you get the memo?" She had a wet rag in her hand, and she pictured herself smearing it across his face.

Just for a second his eyes looked like they were made of metal and then he smiled and they went back to normal. He hadn't shaved in a couple of days. She used to think the stubbly beard thing was so hot. He bent toward her, leaning his hands on the counter space between them and she wondered for a minute if he was going to try to kiss her. Even with the fresh aroma of brewing coffee, she smelled him. It was the smell that used to make her all melty inside.

There were two customers in the shop, sitting at separate tables and clicking away on separate laptops. They paid no attention to the drama going on.

"Hey, I've been doing a lot of thinking about us."

"Isn't it a little late for that?"

His eyes got shiny. "I really hope not."

His voice sure sounded sincere. That was not fair! He couldn't cry and make her feel sorry for him. He was nothing but a player. She had to keep telling herself that.

"Kiki."

The way he said it, she remembered the soft way he said her name in bed. She took a deep breath, looked him straight in the eyes and said, "Are you going to order anything, or what?"

He jerked his neck back and did an exaggerated blink. "Yeah, sure, a large coffee."

Pulling out a mug, she filled it, putting in a caramel shot the way he liked it. She always used to give him the coffee free, but before she decided whether to charge him or not, he put a ten-dollar bill on the counter. She snatched it up and plunked his change down. He took the coffee, but left the change there.

The guy by the window snapped his laptop closed and left. There was just one other customer left now, a girl with an eyebrow ring, a bracelet tattoo and spiky hair. She reminded her of herself, not very long ago. Kiki tugged at a strand of hair over her right ear. It was now a deep shade of brunette.

She watched Derek walk right past the girl's table without even noticing her. His swagger was gone. She had expected him to do a double take at the girl. He slunk off to a table where he slouched back in the chair, his legs stretched out before him. His boots were scuffed and covered in dust. He sat, sipping on his coffee and looking out the window. As much as she wanted to hate him, she couldn't. He just looked so sad, sitting there all by himself.

She took some of the breakfast things out of the display case and put them in the cooler, and then restocked the cookies and bars in the case. Sighing, she put a frosted brownie on a plate. When she headed in his direction, Derek was staring at his hands that were spread out on the black tabletop in front of him. His knuckles were red and roughened and he had white stuff under his fingernails, so she knew he was still putting up drywall. Or maybe he was painting. Either way, she figured he was alone a lot.

He jerked his head up when she got close and gave her that hopeful look like her friend's dog used to do whenever anyone got near the refrigerator, but when he saw the brownie, he shook his head. "Thanks, but I'll have to pass. I'm tapped out." He reached in his back pocket and flipped open his wallet to show her that it was empty.

"Just take it." She whacked the plate down in front of him and sat on the empty chair facing him.

He broke off a piece and chewed like he wanted to make it last.

That's when she noticed the dark hollows under his eyes, like he hadn't been sleeping again. "Are you really that broke?"

He swallowed hard. "No. Well, yes, but not permanently. I've got a few things going and I have to get to the bank. You don't need to worry about me." He brushed a crumb off the table.

She wrinkled her nose. "I don't. Jeez, I've got enough to worry about."

He reached out to cover her hand with his.

She flinched, but she didn't pull her hand back.

"Kiki. You don't understand. I have big plans, and the only thing I want is for you to be a part of it all."

She clenched her jaws and gave him a look to say she wasn't buying it.

"I'm not going to be poor forever. I'm going to be discovered. Just give me a little time. I promise you that one year from now, when you say my name, people will know who I am."

What an ego trip! Does this guy even hear how he sounds? "Why are you telling me this?"

"I'm a little cash poor right now, but that's all going to change."

"And you think I'm going to inherit a boatload?"

He stopped talking and got a look on his face like it had never occurred to him, and then it turned into that hurt look which made her feel like a creep for saying it. She fought the guilt by telling herself he was just acting.

A puff of chilled air came through the open door as the last customer left.

"Whether you have money or not, I want you in my life. Don't you know that, babe?" Leaning across the small table, he put his fingertips on her lips, running them around the edges. His hands were rough. "I want to sleep with you in my arms every night and wake up in the same bed with you every morning. Don't you want that too?" The words were warm and syrupy in her ear.

His fingers slid down to the little hollow of her throat. The spot he touched almost vibrated with pleasure.

"Ki Ki. What do I need to do to get you back?"

She pulled back. "When you had me, you treated me like a big pain, like I was just some annoying little kid." For a second she thought she was going to break down and cry, but she ground her teeth together and the tears dried up.

"I was wrong." He looked away and pressed his lips together like maybe he was about to cry too.

"Wow. I never thought those words would come out of your mouth." She meant it to sound sarcastic, but he took it a different way, and she realized that maybe she'd actually meant it that way.

"I was wrong," he said again. "Thinking you might be in my life again is what makes me want to live." He took a shuddering breath and sat back. "Otherwise . . ." He let the word hang there in front of her like it was her problem to solve.

She knew emotional blackmail when she heard it. God, she'd seen that game played all her life. Her loser mother was still manipulating people with that line.

And yet, his eyes were so full of pain, and even though she knew it wasn't her fault, well, still, she didn't want to be the one to hurt him.

She started to cry then, big goofy sobs like when she was a kid. She jumped up and ran to the back room. She was blowing her nose on a rough paper towel when she felt him behind her, pulling her head against his chest and holding her tight.

When she was five years old, she'd had a babysitter named Leah who had long hair that she used to wrap around her like a yellow scarf. One day Leah was reading her a book she'd brought with her and they'd stopped on the page with the picture of Peter Pan teaching Wendy and John to fly. Kiki had said, "People can't fly." Leah, looked at her with a twinkly smile and said, "It's a story. You just have to let yourself believe with all your heart, and then you just let yourself fall into the story. And anyway, how do you know you can't fly? You never know until you try." The next morning, Kiki had climbed up onto her mom's dresser. For just the tiniest minute she believed that just maybe she could fly. She closed her eyes and jumped. And then she hit the floor so hard her teeth cracked together, and at the same time she felt excruciating pain in her leg. She had fallen, all right, but not into the story. The whole time she wore the cast, she blamed herself for the broken leg. After all, she had not truly believed she could fly, not with all her heart.

Was it possible that Derek really loved her? Could she believe it with all her heart? You never know until you try. Kiki closed her eyes and let herself fall.

* * *

IN HER DARKROOM AGAIN, Robin prepared the chemical baths for her new batch of photos. Her time with Daisy had been delightful, as she'd known it would be. Like Iris, Daisy wanted to show her photo albums, grinning broadly as she pointed to a picture of herself lifting the hem of her dress to show off a pair of shapely legs, which she referred to as gams. "My husband called them my Betty Grables." When Robin had given her a blank look, Daisy said, "He thought I should insure my legs for a million dollars, as Betty Grable had."

It amused Robin to think of Meadowpoint Manor as the retirement home for movie stars and fictional characters—Iris as Myrna Loy, Frannie as Madame Defarge, Virgil as Don Ameche, Era as Helen Hayes, and Daisy's legs standing in for Betty Grable's.

She was having so much fun with her little flight of fancy that she forgot, for almost an hour, to think about the words of Dr. Singh when he'd called after dinner. He'd used the word *ambiguous* to describe the results of the CT scan, and said she needed to keep her appointment tomorrow for the full bone scan.

Brad had been calm, at least outwardly. A couple of years ago, when she was first diagnosed, he'd withdrawn from her, pouring himself into his work. He'd concentrated on doing what he did best, removing fibroid tumors and prescribing birth control, and delivering bad news as easily as he delivered healthy babies, knowing that his skilled hands and soothing bedside manner were just what his patients needed. But when he couldn't cure his own wife's disease, he had avoided her and become emotionally absent.

Now, she was the one withdrawing—literally, into her darkroom.

She held up the treated film for inspection, and had the sudden conviction that at this very moment, someone was looking at her scans, finding something they had not seen before. She closed her eyes and whispered the words of Julian of Norwich to herself. "All will be well, and all will be well, and all manner of things will be well."

Today Kiki was working a split shift. She'd opened at six in the morning, which was fine because she hadn't slept all night. Not after what Derek had told her. It was just so weird, after all the jerky things he'd done, to see him like this. *Contrite.* That's the word her grampa had used when he talked about his daughter, Kiki's mom. He told her more than once that he couldn't have Diana, his own daughter, in his life until she acted contrite. Being contrite was what had to happen for a relationship to work, she knew that now.

As soon as she saw that Derek understood how rotten he'd been to her, everything had changed. He told her he wasn't going to let her go now that he realized how much he loved her. She thought he'd stay with her at Ashley's apartment, but instead he'd gone home last night to make room for her to move in with him. Not just live together, but actually get married. Like, really soon, he said, because he'd already wasted enough time being stupid.

In a little while, he was coming over to pick her up between shifts and they were going to look at rings. She'd put on nail polish this morning to go ring shopping, not the electric blue she'd been wearing, but pearly pink.

She'd never even been to Derek's place. It was weird when she thought about it. One time her mom was totally in love with this guy who never took her to his house and it turned out he was already married. He had kids too. Kiki had followed the guy on her bike and found out where he lived, which was only a couple miles away. It was so easy for her to figure it out, and she wondered how her mom could be so stupid. God, she hoped she wasn't making the same mistake! Well, she'd find out soon enough, when he drove her out to his place.

When they first started hanging out, Derek said he thought it was "hot" to make love at her grampa's house when he wasn't home. It was kind of fun, she had to admit, sneaking around like that. But then her grampa disappeared without a word. She never ever imagined he would do that to her.

She'd thought about it from every side. Maybe he really was dead. But maybe he'd figured out about her and Derek and what they were doing, and he got so disgusted with her, he couldn't look at her anymore. He'd cut off his own daughter, hadn't he? Or maybe he was on the Riviera, wherever that was, and was just teaching her a lesson by not telling her he was okay. The more she thought, the more her stomach twisted. She hung onto the stainless steel counter, and sucked in her breath.

But the thoughts didn't stop, even for a minute. After she'd moved out of her grampa's house, she and Derek never went back. It was too freaky. She tried to remember how it had happened that they'd fallen into a pattern of Derek sleeping over with her at her friend's apartment. It was just easier somehow. Besides, it was closer to both of her jobs, and his work was in a lot of different places, so it didn't matter.

Derek said the house wasn't huge, but it was on eleven acres, which was a whole lot bigger than what her grampa had, and his house was filled with a lot of beautiful things he'd collected or made. She could live with that. Now that they were going to get married, maybe he'd tell her about his big plans. The way he talked about it, he was going to be famous, but whenever she wanted to know more, he acted like it was some big secret. She stood up and wiped sweat from her upper lip with a rag.

With her freshly painted fingernail, she scraped a gummy drip of flavor shot off the clock. Derek would be coming for her in forty minutes.

Last night they'd talked for over an hour in the closed restaurant. They split a blueberry muffin and a pumpkin bar, and he told her not to give up hope on her grampa, but she said that at some point she and Great-Gran would have to. They'd sat at the corner table where she could see the streetlights come on, and were still talking when the light at the liquor store went out.

He'd been really sweet the way he told her over and over that he would never leave her, not like her mom did, and not like her grampa did, without even saying good-bye. It was like he really understood. She'd always had fantasies about somebody who would love her like this. He was wearing the shirt she liked with the blue stripes, and he kept trying to smooth down the little cowlick on the back of his head.

It was all so weird. First she was in love with him and thought he loved her back, but then the way he jerked her around, she couldn't stand being around him.

But then last night, he held her and said he wanted to hug her until she wasn't sad or scared anymore. He promised her he would never call her names or lock her out if they had a fight. He'd said, "How could I ever do anything to hurt you again?" It was something she'd wanted for so long.

Once they were married, she would finally have a place to live. She wouldn't have to worry about that ever again.

Now, in the light of day, she hoped last night was real. The door opened and two women came in with a baby in one of those carriers, and the way they acted, she figured they were a couple. The baby was asleep, with its little mouth all puckered up. They both ordered chai lattes and sat in the comfortable brown chairs in the corner.

She wondered if Derek wanted kids. They'd never talked about it, but she was pretty sure he'd want some. They'd have dark hair, since both of them did, and maybe they'd be smart like her grampa. Thinking about him made her sad. She'd always thought Grampa would be alive to see her grow up and have kids. She wished he could meet Derek and see he was going to make something of himself. Then maybe he'd know she wasn't like her mother.

Her stomach did another flip, and as soon as she brought the chai lattes to the table, she slipped back through the bathroom door. Why did this keep happening?

Pay attention to your body. That's what her great-gran told her. Sometimes it tells you you're making a decision that isn't good for you.

Well, that couldn't always be true. Sometimes it was just the flu or food poisoning. She put her head between her knees until the spasm passed.

The afternoon person came. Darcy was older, in her forties, and had been hired about the same time Kiki had been. She had maroon hair and a contagious laugh. After tying on her apron, she gave Kiki a squeeze. "You don't look so hot," she said.

Kiki blew air out of her cheeks so it made her bangs flap. "Just my stomach. Again."

"Well, you told me last week you're not pregnant. So maybe it's something else. You ought to get it checked out. My sister had the same thing and it took a while to figure it out, but they finally diagnosed her with celiac's. She doesn't eat gluten anymore and she's fine." Darcy opened the refrigerator and checked the milk jugs. When she stood up, she said, "Uh oh. Trouble."

Kiki looked up to see Derek standing there. She suddenly felt embarrassed at the thought of explaining to Darcy that Derek was back into her life. "Things are different now," she said, tugging on her hair.

Darcy grunted.

"Ready?" he said, and gave her a lopsided grin.

It was a good thing she didn't tell Darcy they were going shopping for an engagement ring, because almost as soon as she got into his truck, Derek told her the bad news. "I just can't catch a break," he said, tilting his head against the headrest. "I went to get paid this morning for that big remodel I was telling you about. And that smug bastard said he had to get to the bank first. He said he'd have it in a couple of days." He put the truck in gear and squealed the tires pulling away from the curb. He pounded the dash. "Fucking corporate fatass! His car is worth more than some people's houses and he can't come up with enough to pay me without going to the bank? When I'm rich, I swear I will never do that to someone who's working his ass off for me! People like that don't deserve to have money."

Kiki just let him go on, and pretty soon he started to calm down. At a light, he grabbed her hand and pulled it up to his mouth and kissed it. He said they could still pick out the ring she wanted, and as soon as he got paid, he would come back and get it.

She didn't want him to see how disappointed she was. She could see he already felt bad enough, and anyway, it wasn't his fault. When they walked into the fancy jewelry store, she understood how hard it was for him.

The woman with long black hair led them right to the case with the most expensive rings. Kiki could see it made him uncomfortable, and she thought of all the times she'd been embarrassed by the way people looked at her or her mom because they didn't live like other people.

Derek ducked his head down and mumbled something to the woman and they went to another glass case with smaller diamonds. His jaw tightened and loosened over and over.

They found a ring she loved, though. It was super sweet, with a band that kind of swirled around the diamond. The woman said she'd keep it for them for a few days.

They both felt better on the way back to the coffee shop for her second shift. Kiki was so excited she could hardly keep from bouncing up and down in her seat, "I really want you to meet my great-gran," she said. "Wanna go there tomorrow? You will love her."

"Yeah? Do you think she'll love me?"

She saw the way his hands got tighter on the steering wheel. People always said someone was "white-knuckled," but his just got redder. His hands were usually rough and red, though, from the manual labor he did.

* * *

THE NEXT DAY KIKI wasn't scheduled to work. Derek woke up horny, and she decided to tease him by going into the kitchen to make coffee wearing just her little red panties. He followed her in, as she knew he would. He had her up against the refrigerator with his body pressed into hers when the door flew open, and her roommate stomped in, slamming a plastic bag on the table. A small carton fell out of the CVS bag and onto the floor. Kiki recognized the pink and white box. It was a pregnancy test.

"Shit," Ashley said when she saw the two of them looking at her, and tears welled up in her eyes.

Kiki ran over to her, and without thinking she was practically naked, she threw her arms around her. "Oh, Ash, don't cry. It's probably negative."

Ashley shook her head. "It was positive yesterday. This is my second one."

"Oh!" Kiki let her arms drop. "Does Josh know?"

"No. I'm scared to tell him." She took off her gray hoodie and flung it across the room. "We were so careful."

Kiki thought it was probably true. Ashley and Josh were the kind of people who paid bills on time and never left dirty dishes lying around. "He's a really nice guy. He'll be happy."

Derek snorted and they both turned to look at him.

"What?" Ashley said. "You don't think so?"

Derek made a face like he thought the whole thing was gross. "I don't know the dude all that well, but I know I wouldn't be jumping for joy if I found out—" He stopped.

Kiki felt the blood drain out of her face. "Found out what? That I was pregnant?" Her heart was beating so loud she thought he must hear it. She threw on jeans and a sweatshirt.

Derek turned her around, holding her arms so she couldn't even wipe her runny nose. "You're not, are you?"

"No."

As soon as he got dressed, he said, "I need to get out of here." When she asked where he was going, he shrugged. Detouring around the table, he headed for the door.

He stopped with his hand on the doorknob. "Are you coming?"

He drove fast out of the parking lot.

Kiki had no idea where he was taking her. She wiped away a tear and hoped he hadn't seen it.

There was so much she wanted to ask him, but she kept her mouth shut. He could be such a moody asshole sometimes! Maybe if she didn't say anything to set him off again, he'd get over it and they could have a real conversation about babies after they were officially engaged.

And right now, there was no way was she going to bring up her idea again of going to meet her great-gran. Maybe it was better, anyway, if the first time they met, she was wearing her ring, so Great-Gran would see he was serious. Having Era's approval was too important to her, and the way he was acting right now, he wouldn't exactly make a good impression.

She had less than three hours before she needed to be at Meadowpoint Manor by herself—so wherever he was driving, he'd better get her back in time. She'd promised to take her great-gran to some kind of tea thing that Robin's friend had arranged, and she was supposed to dress up. "Wear something pretty and feminine," Era had said. Kiki supposed her lacy red panties didn't count.

When she'd told Derek about it yesterday, he'd said, "What do you do at a tea party? Drink tea?"

"I guess." She'd giggled. "I've never been to one. Maybe I'll run into Alice and the Mad Hatter."

Pretty soon he doubled back to Ashley's apartment. By the time they got there, Ashley was gone. Kiki hoped she was in Josh's arms, and he was telling her how happy he was about the baby.

Derek took off his nice jacket and put on his ratty tee shirt and a sweatshirt with paint on it. "I think I can finish that tile job in Orono today." He kicked one of her tennis shoes out of his way. "The kitchen in that McMansion is practically as big as this whole apartment. Bastard'll probably stiff me too."

She could tell he was still upset, but asked anyway. "Are you coming over tonight?"

"Naw, the job's closer to my place. And I have a few things to do tomorrow, like going back to that other guy's place again. This time I'm going to stay there until he pays me. I want to put that ring on your finger, and I'm tired of waiting for my, uh, our life to begin."

Now that he was starting to calm down, she could see all he wanted was to be with her, just like he said. When he caught her looking at him, he smiled, showing his one crooked tooth, and the icy place in her heart warmed right up. He gave her a long kiss that stayed on her lips for a while after he left. Maybe tomorrow night, after he got paid and had time to think about the whole thing with Ashley, she could ask him about having kids.

25

When she got off the elevator, she didn't see her great-gran right away, but then someone called her name, and there she was, sitting on a bench next to Daisy. Kiki figured her great-gran had just had her hair done because it was more lavender than usual, or maybe it just looked that way because of the purple sweater jacket she was wearing. She looked pretty, her eyes bright with excitement. Kiki bent down and gave her a kiss on the cheek. "You look good," she said.

Era stroked Kiki's cheek. "I'm as good as I'm going to get."

She laughed. "Oh, I don't know. I think you just keep getting better and better."

Era looked mischievous when she smiled. "I do, don't I!"

Kiki didn't want to leave Daisy out, so she complimented her, too.

"I was just thinking how becoming that outfit is on you," Daisy said to Kiki. "Very flattering."

She didn't say she'd borrowed it from Ashley. The only skirts she owned were super short and tight, nothing like this copper colored skirt with three layers of ruffles that came a couple of inches above her knees. There was a little black jacket with it that had a copper chain belt. It reminded her of something Barbie might wear.

Robin's mother came down the hall with another woman. Kiki thought the woman was maybe forty or fifty, tops, but as they got closer, she was surprised at how old she really was, because she dressed like someone a lot younger. Not a hootchie mama—God knew she'd seen plenty of those—but a whole different breed from these other ladies. Her skirt was no longer than the one Kiki was wearing, and she wore skinny knee boots with high heels. Her feather earrings almost touched her shoulders and she wore a bunch of wrist bangles that clinkled when she walked. Clinkle was the word she made up for the noise her mother's drinks made.

Her great-gran introduced her as Wanda. "I thought you weren't going to join us today," Era said.

Wanda's feather earrings swung when she shook her head. "No, no, I signed up for the tea next month. My daughter's picking me up to go shopping. She says I need boots and a winter coat."

"That you do," said Era. "I thought you used to live in Minnesota."

Wanda's eyes got sad, just for a second. "I got rid of my winter clothes when I moved to Florida. I did not expect to be living here again. This is not my climate."

Yeah, Kiki knew what that was like. But Arizona with her mother, and whoever she was shacked up with, was a nastier climate than anything Minnesota dished up.

Wanda took the elevator down.

Daisy's daughter Ann came. She didn't look a lot like her mother, except for her smile. She talked to Kiki like she was a real adult and not just some kid that was tagging along. Robin was like that too. "Where's Robin," Kiki asked Vivian.

"She had an appointment that ran a little late. She's on her way. We're still missing two people, right?"

A voice came from the little sitting area. "Just one. I'm here."

She looked over and saw a plain, lumpy woman with a pile of knitting in her lap. She'd been right there in plain sight, but Kiki hadn't even seen her.

The woman stood up and lumbered toward them. "So we're just waiting for Mabel."

"Who's Mabel?" Two people asked at once.

"Me." A woman came out of the library. Her hair was a weird orange color and she had deep wrinkles all around her mouth. The woman stood next to Kiki, who recognized the look that went with the smell of stale cigarettes. One of her jobs had been to empty her mother's ashtrays.

"It's Mabel, but you can call me Sparky. Everyone else does." She nudged Kiki with her elbow and grinned.

Oh, that one. Great-Gran had told her about the woman who lights her hair on fire when she smokes. She looked more closely and saw the uneven bangs. Weird, but funny.

* * *

LOUISE STEPPED BACK to get all of them in the picture. Only the sweet woman with mauve hair, Era, had worn her own hat, a brown cloche with a pale pink ribbon and fabric flower. The rest of them had spent several minutes trying on hats from her own collection in front of the cheval standing mirror.

Once she'd cleared out the extraneous clutter from the back room of the shop, Louise had immediately seen its potential, but today it was more beautiful than she'd imagined, with flowers scattered about the room and three tables set with three different sets of china and pastel tablecloths. The table with buttery yellow linens was set with the Limoges rose-patterned china. The blue table had vintage Haviland china, and on the pink lace tablecloth, she'd put her Japanese cherry blossom pattern. The centerpieces were stand-up paper dolls.

Louise tried to memorize their names, using the skills she'd learned in a memory course she and Dean took at the senior center.

Rose, Iris, Daisy and her daughter Ann sat at the yellow rose table, making it easy for her to remember Rose's name. Three flowers and an Ann—make that Queen Anne's lace and we have four flowers, she said to herself. Sitting at the table with Robin and her mother Vivian was a woman nicknamed Sparky. Louise had no trouble with that one, since the woman's hair was a washed out flame color.

Then there was Frannie, the name of her old piano teacher. Then Era, the oldest, whose name meant a long period of time, and her great-granddaughter, Kiki, who without knowing it, had provided Louise with the perfect memory device by leaving her keys on the table next to her water glass.

Robin snapped several pictures as the women grinned and held up their empty teacups, then posed with one at each table pouring tea. Louise was thrilled they'd gotten right into the spirit of her little party. After all the work putting this together, seeing the joy on their faces was all the reward she needed.

She ducked into the mini-kitchen that was partitioned off by a pair of dressing screens and cued up the music Dean had selected. "Sentimental Journey" began playing in the background. She returned with a silver platter of crustless sandwiches, placing three on each plate.

Kiki, she noticed, sat back and watched the others, mimicking their actions, as if afraid she might make a gaffe. Era winked at the girl and she relaxed.

For her Dolls of Our Childhood theme, Louise had put together some tableaux. The most elaborate was a doll tea party, with four jointed dolls and a Raggedy Ann doll, all dressed in finery and sitting at their own miniature table, which was set with Blue Willow doll dishes. Two porcelain babies in white lace were propped in a small wicker doll buggy, pushed by a large doll dressed as a flapper.

Louise was excited to tell them the history of the cloth dolls made in Milwaukee as a WPA project, and given to children in hospitals and nurseries. As soon as she poured a second round of tea, she began her spiel.

* * *

ERA LOOKED AT HER FRIENDS, who were just as fascinated as she was. This Louise had really gone all out, she thought. She finished her tea and nibbled on the iced gingerbread girl cookie, starting on the left leg as she always had, ever since childhood.

Her eyes rested on the little Tudor-style dollhouse sitting on a tea cart. Era had no trouble remembering the one her father had built her for her sixth birthday. It had had six wallpapered rooms plus an attic. Her father had hand-painted the blocky furniture and her mother had dressed the dolls—mother, father and daughter—in the latest fashion. Her eyes teared up just thinking about the kindness she had grown up with, which had not been the case for all of her classmates. When the Great Depression struck, her family had been shaken, but remained solid, while her very best friend had to move away to live with relatives after her father went off to find work.

She pulled her hanky from her sleeve and dabbed at her eyes.

Frank Sinatra was crooning, "I'd rather have a paper doll, to call my own." That's when men sang like men, she thought, and you could understand every word.

Louise was talking about the Dionne Quintuplet paper dolls when Era stood up, her pocketbook in hand.

"Are you looking for the powder room?" Louise asked.

Kiki and Robin both offered to go with her, but Era declined. Did they think she was incapable of going to the bathroom by herself? Thank the good Lord, she could still manage that much!

Louise instructed her to go out through the curtain and then turn right. At least that's what Era thought she'd said, but when she turned right and opened the door, it wasn't a bathroom at all, but what looked like the old pantry in her childhood home. Her mother had always kept that pantry well stocked. Never once during the Depression had her family ever gone hungry. She wondered if the stairs to the cellar were around the corner, as they'd been in her old house. She didn't want to stumble upon a flight of stairs in the dim light. At the far end of the pantry, she pulled aside a heavy velvet curtain and peered out into the sunlit room.

It took her a moment to realize she'd taken a circuitous route and blundered into the main part of the store. "You old fool, getting lost on your way to the bathroom," she chided herself.

Against the bright light, two men stood in conversation. She squinted at them, but couldn't make out much, since they were little more than silhouettes in front on the window. She hoped they didn't notice her. She didn't want to explain that she'd gotten turned around. Oh, Lord, I don't mind losing my way. Just don't let me lose my marbles!" she said under her breath.

She stood utterly still for a few heartbeats until she got her bearings, and then turned and retraced her steps, putting one sturdy orthopedic shoe in front of the other. Ahead of her, in the hallway, she saw the door which had to be the powder room.

26

Derek pulled the small bundle out of his jacket pocket and folded back the tissue paper to reveal the Japanese carving. He watched the guy's eyes carefully for a clue as to whether or not he really wanted the netsuke. At the last shop, the woman had had no idea what she was looking at. She called herself a dealer, but wasn't even familiar with this revered art form. What a moron!

This place seemed less pretentious, more legitimate and not crammed to the rafters with tchotchkes.

He couldn't bring himself to sell his favorite, the shishi lion-dog biting its tail, even though it would have brought top dollar. But it was also the one which made him the happiest to hold. Its theme of rebirth reminded him he was not stuck forever in this dismal life of a day laborer, living from one late payment to the next.

And now, it looked like he might get to have the life he wanted, after all. Kiki's great-grandmother couldn't live forever, and from what he understood, Kiki was the only living relative the old lady had anything to do with. So he'd hidden his promise of rebirth with his other treasures and had gone back to Winston Dudley's house.

This time he'd chosen the pair of carved monkeys that looked like they were playing patty-cake. He didn't think of it as stealing, so much as a small compensation for the ruin Winston Dudley had brought on his family. The monkeys were nicely done, even though the detail and artistry just couldn't compare with the shishi.

The antique dealer raised his eyebrows. That was a good sign. He was burly and had veins of silver in his thick head of hair. His face was full of wrinkles. The deep ones around his eyes deepened as he examined the tiny ivory carving. He screwed his mouth to the side and made a noise like he was savoring something delicious.

Derek scanned the room for security cameras. Nothing. He shifted his weight from one foot to the other.

The guy put on a pair of glasses and rolled the netsuke in his hands to see it from all angles. "I want to do a little research on this. Could you leave it with me for a day or two?"

Derek shook his head. "I can't do that." He didn't want to tip his hand and say he needed the money today. "How about if I call you in a couple days? See what you're thinking."

He seemed reluctant to give it back.

A ripple of female laughter came from somewhere behind the counter. Derek jerked his head up, startled. He hadn't known anyone else was here.

The guy chuckled. "That's Lou's new venture. She's always coming up with something. Now, she's turned the back room into a tea room and she's got a whole gaggle of women back there."

Tea room? Derek stopped breathing. Was it possible that he'd managed to walk into the same place Kiki had taken her great-grandmother? Who would ever think someone would have a tea party at an antique store?

Just then the heavy curtain at the corner of the shop was pushed aside by a hand, and a tiny figure stepped into the light.

He thought he must be hallucinating. She looked like Mrs. Dudley all right, the woman he'd tried to recruit to help him out with his little cash flow problem. Her purse, probably the same one he'd dropped at the apartment, was clutched in her hand. His balls ached at the memory.

She turned and looked directly at him.

He let out his breath like he'd been gut-punched. It was her, no doubt about it.

"If you want the leave your number, I'll get back to you as soon as I've done a little checking around." The guy put the netsuke in Derek's outstretched hand.

Derek tried to process the situation. "Uh, that's okay." He gestured with his thumb. "Say, what's behind that curtain?"

"That's the hallway to the bathroom. I keep meaning to put up a sign."

With his fingers curled around the carving, Derek quickly rewrapped it in tissue paper and stuffed it back into his pocket. Ignoring the guy's expression, he said, "I'll use your bathroom before I go, if you don't mind."

When the curtain closed behind him, there was very little light, but he could see, down at the end of the hall, a door was just closing on what he assumed was the bathroom. Just ahead of him, on the right, was a side exit. He quickly slipped the bolt and twisted the lock, poked his head outside, and then walked back through the showroom. "I'll call," he said as he passed the guy at the counter.

Sprinting out the door and past his truck, he ran up the steps and reentered through the side door. He held his breath. Could she have gone back to the tea party already?

But then he heard the sound of a toilet flushing, and with quick strides, he got to the door just as it was opening. Moving aside, he was able to partially conceal himself behind the door.

She stepped out. No cane this time—maybe his luck was changing. His hand shot out to clamp over her mouth. He felt her body sag and with his other arm he grabbed her at the waist, tucking her up close to his body so her feet were off the floor.

Hanging onto her, he backed up to the door, where he realized he'd have to let go of her with one hand so he could turn the handle. He still remembered the way she'd screamed the last time.

He took the chance of holding her tight against him with his left hand on her mouth while turning the lock with his right. Wedging himself in the doorway, he dragged her onto the steps outside, awkwardly making his way down the three steep steps without losing his hold on her. This time she didn't put up a fight at all.

All he had to do was get her to his Tundra, which was in the front corner of the small parking lot, close to the street. And somehow, he had to do it without being seen. He looked toward the back of the store. What he'd thought was an alley was actually a small space for a couple of cars, and now he could plainly see that Kiki's car was in it. Why hadn't he even bothered to look around before he'd parked here? If he'd seen her car, he never would have gone inside!

Listening for traffic, he waited for a car to pass and then hauled her to the passenger side, ripping her purse from her grip before stuffing her into the truck. He locked the door before slamming it shut, then hustled to the other side and vaulted in. She was already fumbling with the door handle. Grabbing her arm, he jerked her toward him.

"Leave the door alone. You're not getting away from me this time." Before turning on the engine, he reached under the console vault and lifted the towel covering his revolver. He didn't want to think he'd ever have to use it on her. He might move a few things from the Dudley side of the ledger to his own, but he didn't want to hurt her. He didn't have the stomach for violence.

Still, it didn't hurt anyone if he just showed her the gun to make a point. Especially after the way it went the last time. Flashing Winston Dudley's own Smith & Wesson at her to squeeze some money from his own mother—now, that was downright poetic. Call it the Dudley Surprise.

She was staring at him. Her expression was not one of fear, but of contempt.

"I have a gun," he told her.

"It's you!" she said as if she hadn't recognized him in the store.

Was that possible? If she honestly hadn't recognized him a few minutes ago, it would mean he'd grabbed her for nothing. And now, she was sitting right next to him and studying his face so she could identify him. It was the kind of shit he always did. His father said he had knee-jerk reactions. The counselor his parents made him see told him he had to work on impulse control. Well, that was money well spent!

So he'd done another moronic thing on impulse. Now what? If anything happened to the old lady, the store owner would be able to describe him. At least he hadn't given the guy his phone number. Slamming his hands against the wheel, he yelled the word his mother had tried so hard to wash from his vocabulary. "Fuck!"

"You are a horrid human being." She folded her hands in her lap and looked straight ahead. "Why do you keep accosting me?" Her voice sounded like a scratchy old record.

In answer, he unzipped her purse and grubbed around for her wallet. He pulled it out, a purple snakeskin thing, and opened it. A few small bills, her Medicare ID, an AARP card, a Visa card and a yellow bank card. He flipped open the check register. She had over nineteen-thousand dollars in her account. Her checking account!

"If it's money you want—"

"I want you to help me. If you do what I say, I won't hurt you."

"And why would I help you?" She buttoned her sweater and sniffed.

"I have a gun. I already told you." He turned on the engine and pulled out onto the street. At the stop sign, he took a right onto a wider road lined with retail shops. He wasn't familiar with this part of town.

"And I already showed you that I can hurt you. I might not have my cane with me today, but old ladies can be crafty." She looked more indignant than afraid.

He almost groaned, remembering the pain this blue-haired biddy had inflicted on him. When he stopped at the light, he flipped her checkbook onto her lap. "Write a check. Make it out to cash. Fifteen thousand dollars."

"I don't have a pen."

He reached across her, opened the glove box and snatched out a pen.

She took it from his hand like he was too filthy to touch. Sighing, she flattened her checkbook with the side of her hand and scribbled something. "It's out of ink," she said, showing him that the pen hadn't made a mark.

A car horn sounded and he saw he was veering into the other lane. He jerked his wheel back. In the next block he slowed to let traffic pass. He applied the pen tip to the back of his hand and drew a line. "Try again, old lady."

She took the pen and when he saw that she'd written "Cash," he sped up again.

"Oops." She threw her hands up. "It slipped out of my old fingers."

Frustration filled his chest. He grabbed her arm and shook it hard, pronouncing each word emphatically. "Then. Pick. It. Up."

She bent in half and leaned forward so far he thought she might fall off the seat. Her spindly arms surely couldn't reach the floor. "I've almost got it." Her voice was muffled.

He turned at the next corner.

"Oops. I think it rolled in your direction."

"So get it."

"I don't think I can reach it."

"You're on my last nerve." Who did that sound like? It was one of his mother's favorite expressions.

She leaned, reaching.

His gun! He grabbed her by the hair and jerked her head back. "Any more stunts and I'm done with you. You're more trouble than you're worth." The growly tone was his, but the words were his mother's. He shoved her. "Move over. All the way over!"

She scooted her boney butt until she was against the door. "Red light!"

He hit the brakes and felt his chest heaving. This geriatric nut job was going to freaking kill him!

"Oh, never mind. There it is." She was holding the pen in her hand.

He groaned. "Fifteen thousand, cash," he instructed her again.

Once more she opened her checkbook. After writing the check, she tore it out and laid it on the space between them.

He picked it up, struggling to read her shaky writing.

"Green light," she said at the same moment a car horn sounded. She pointed over the dash with a shaky finger.

He lurched forward. Traffic was heavier now. If he didn't want to attract attention, he would have to keep his eyes on the road. He slipped the check into his pocket. He'd look at it more closely when they got to the bank.

As he slowed for the next light, she seemed anxious, swiveling her head around. "Oh dear, I think you just passed it. Is this fifth?"

He craned his neck to read the street sign, but it was at the wrong angle.

"You did. You missed my bank. It's back there on your left. I can see it way back there."

Leaning forward and twisting at a painful angle, he still couldn't see around or over the panel truck in the left lane, so he opened the window and stuck his head out to get a better view.

He heard a click and jerked his head back inside. By the time he made a grab for her, the old lady had slid off the seat through the open door and onto the pavement.

Lunging for his gun, he pulled it out by the barrel, but immediately held it down between his knees while he considered his options. Not a lot of good the gun did him now. There would be witnesses. A thrumming started in his ears

Horns honked and traffic began to creep forward. Before pressing the gas pedal, he leaned across and pulled the passenger door shut.

Just as he reached the intersection, he spotted the purple-haired figure on the sidewalk to his right. Era Dudley was talking to some Asian dude with a backpack. Her arms were waving around and the guy looked to see where she was pointing. Fortunately, where she pointed was back a few car lengths, to the place where she'd once again outfoxed him by slipping out of the car.

He got the hell out of there.

The shopping trip with Wanda was not going well. Cate tried steering her mother toward more conservative clothes—a simple black wool coat, a pair of flat boots with treads for a good old-fashioned Minnesota winter, and a brimless wool cap. Wanda met each suggestion with the same general insult—they were boring, dull, uninspired, tedious or dreary, in turn.

"You're a walking thesaurus," Cate said. She spotted a puffy, quilted coat in metallic grey. "Here, this will keep you warm." Sliding it off the hanger, she handed it to Wanda, who took it, but the down-turned corners of her mouth told Cate she was not going to like anything today, no matter how warm or stylish it was. "Just try it on."

"Ridiculous!" Wanda said, modeling it in the mirror. "I look like a giant hand grenade, for Pete's sake!"

Cate suggested they give up for the day. On the way out to the parking ramp, her exasperation caused her to blurt out something she'd been thinking for the last hour. She suggested her mother might make a better impression on Ricky and Bunny if she dressed more like a mother and less like a fortune teller. Even as the words left her lips, she regretted saying them.

Wanda stopped in her tracks, taking the blow as if it had been physical. After taking a deep breath she said, "That's an odd thing coming from someone who claims to have psychic abilities."

Cate's eyes stung with tears. Overlooking the veiled sarcasm, she put her arm over her mother's shoulder, and apologized. It wasn't enough, she could see that. Ricky and his family would be arriving on Saturday and she'd just dished up an extra serving of insecurity onto Wanda's plate.

The drive back to the Manor was quiet. Wanda invited her to come up, and although Cate had only a short while, she saw it as a peace offering. She shut off the engine.

"Unless you're too busy."

Cate decided not to bite. "It's okay, Mom. Maybe we can just sit and relax for a bit so we can leave it on a better note."

But almost as soon as they walked into her mother's apartment, she saw something that rankled her. The pottery bowl she'd given her mother as a housewarming gift, one of Jon Nord's larger pieces, sat on the kitchen table, filled with a bunch of papers and even a candy bar wrapper.

"Was there a problem with having the bowl on the shelf?" Cate sat at the table with her jacket on.

"I needed something for all that junk until I can sort through it. Honestly," she said, picking up a flyer for the grand opening of a fitness club, "Why do I need a health club? We have all that equipment in our exercise room." She tossed it back in the bowl.

Realizing she'd just spent well over a hundred dollars for a trash receptacle, Cate snagged an unopened envelope with a yellow postal sticker from the pile. "Mom, you need to open your bills right away and check the due date. It takes extra time when it gets rerouted through Florida."

"I'll get around to it. I have my system."

Cate shouldn't have pushed it, especially after the aggravation of their shopping trip, but she found herself saying, "I'm going to be seeing the potter who made this. I'm sure I can exchange this bowl for something you want." Her hands slid around the outside of the piece, tracking the subtle imprints made by the potter's fingers as he threw the pot. It really was a lovely piece. And as before, although not as strongly, touching his pottery gave her the sense that it retained some of the kiln's fire.

Her mother shook her head. "No, please don't. I really do like it, and I'll put it back on the shelf when I've sorted through everything."

Cate took her cell phone out of the pocket of her jeans and set it on the table so she could keep track of the time. It was almost two thirty. They hadn't set an exact time, but Jon Nord said she could come any time after two.

After Cate had checked the time once too often, Wanda stood. "I know you need to get home and make Erik dinner."

Cate stood too. "Erik is playing racquetball with Robin's husband, and they'll grab something to eat. But I need to go anyway." She didn't want to be driving after dark, especially to a strange place. In the detailed directions Jon had given her, she'd noted that the last two turns were unmarked.

* * *

NO ONE KNEW EXACTLY how long Era had been gone before they'd realized it had been too long. Iris was the first to notice. Louise went back to check on her, but she wasn't in the bathroom or the pantry. Hurrying through the pantry and into the showroom, she asked Dean if she'd wandered up front. But he hadn't seen her either.

Together, they made their way toward the back room, and at the same moment they noticed the side door was unlocked. Dean couldn't swear to her he'd locked it after he'd taken delivery of the chifferobe from an estate sale this morning. A glance into the parking lot told them she wasn't there.

The women were wide-eyed when Louise reported Era was nowhere to be found. She told them about the delivery door being open. Kiki looked shell-shocked when it appeared her great-grandmother had gone outside.

They figured that perhaps twenty minutes had passed by now, and made a hasty plan. It wouldn't do for all of them to be running in different directions, and so the younger ones, Robin and Kiki, Anne and Louise—Louise had to count herself in that number, considering the pool of candidates—exchanged cell phone numbers and set out on foot to find Era, each heading in a different direction.

After she'd inquired at the third business to her right, a yarn shop, Louise looked up to see a woman waving excitedly to her from the passenger seat of a bright blue Mini Cooper.

The driver stopped and backed up. She rolled down her window. "Do you know this lady?" she called out.

Louise bent to see Era in the passenger seat, wiggling her fingers in a wave. "Yes! We've been looking for her." When she saw Era was about to get out, she instructed her to sit tight for a minute. She ran around to the driver's side.

The woman removed her mirrored sunglasses as she spoke. "I was just getting into my car, and some guy came up and asked me if I could take her here." Her expression was worried. "He said she was wandering around, confused."

"Follow me. See the antique store just back there?" She pointed.

The driver made a tight turn in the street. They went the half-block, Louise on foot and Era still in the car. "Where was she when you found her?" Louise asked when the car stopped in front of her antique store.

She scratched her cheek with long red fingernails. "Not too far. Maybe four miles away, up by—"

"Four miles!"

She lowered her voice. "The man who asked me to take her said he thought she had Alzheimer's. I guess she was saying that someone took her."

"What do you mean, 'took her'?"

Era spoke, her voice so quiet that Louise asked her to repeat it.

The woman rolled her eyes. "She wants you to take her back to the tea party. See what I mean?"

Louise rushed to help Era out of the car. Era's legs seemed unsteady and she winced as she began to walk.

Dean rushed out, and when they each had hold of one of Era's arms, the driver took off. Inside, the others surrounded them. Iris and Sparky still wore their tea party hats.

Dean insisted Era sit on the fainting couch near the door while Louise called the rest of the search party to let them know Era was safe and sound.

Well, safe anyway. Louise figured if she were of sound mind, she probably wouldn't have mistaken the back door for a bathroom in the first place. Even if she'd been loopy enough to think the store had an outhouse, wouldn't she realize her mistake as soon as she opened the door and saw the stairs led to a parking lot? But the burning question was how, in God's name, had she gotten four miles away?

Kiki blew through the front door, followed almost immediately by the other two. Kiki knelt in front of Era, saying, "Oh, my God, Great-Gran where did you go? I was so scared."

Era mumbled something. Her hands trembled near her chest.

"What?" Kiki grabbed her hands and held them. "Are you okay? Is it your heart?"

"No dear. No. I'll tell you, just let me lie down for a minute." As soon as Kiki helped her lift her legs to rest on the fainting couch, Era's head fell back against the rolled arm. "I just need to catch my breath."

"Shouldn't we get her to the doctor?" Robin asked.

Though Era looked like she was asleep, with her hand over her heart, her answer was firm. "No doctor."

"Give her a few minutes," Daisy said.

Louise was surprised to look at the women and see several heads bob in agreement. Dean, standing a respectful distance back, cell phone in hand, raised his eyebrows questioningly at Louise. She shook her head and he closed the phone.

28

It wasn't that he didn't have a sense of right and wrong. Sometimes, it was true, he acted on impulse, but when he did stop to think things through, he didn't simply act on blind obedience, the way most people did. Intelligent people knew that ethics depended on the situation. For instance, was it immoral to steal a loaf of bread to feed a starving child? Of course not!

Any more than it had been a sin to take a few things from Winston Dudley's house over the past weeks—a silver letter opener, a couple of bills, a class ring from the University of Pennsylvania, nothing vital to Dudley's existence, or even his comfort. The silver eagle coin collection he'd found shoved in the back of a locked cabinet had been more useful to Derek. He urgently needed to pay his rent and was quite sure Winston hadn't even noticed the coins were missing.

The watch, though, that was a fiasco. He hadn't had it long enough to check on the model, but there were Patek Philippe watches selling on eBay for tens of thousands. How he'd managed to lose it between Winston's bedroom and his own truck, he didn't know. Either the band had broken or he hadn't fastened it properly, but somehow it had slipped off his wrist. He hadn't realized it until he was driving away, when he'd surreptitiously slid his hand under his sleeve. He'd almost driven off the road in his frantic attempt to find it in the truck. He didn't dare go back until the next morning when he knew Winston and Kiki were both gone. By then, it was nowhere to be found.

It was only a few days later that Kiki called him to tell him about the fight with her grandfather. She was practically hysterical, saying he'd flipped out about her hanging out with the wrong kind of people. Of course the old man would think Derek wasn't good enough for his precious granddaughter. And based on what? They'd never even met!

The more Derek thought about it, the more pissed he got, so the next day he'd left a little sack of flaming dog poop on his doorstep. Sure, it was stupid and childish, but also quite entertaining. Yeah, Dudley probably had to throw away the welcome mat, maybe even his shoes, but it was just a harmless prank. He had never planned for anything to happen to Winston Dudley.

Two days later, Derek went back. He'd wanted to be alone when he pocketed the carving. Winston Dudley's routine was precise, and Derek had timed it so the Cadillac passed by his parked truck exactly when he'd expected it to. Winston's driveway curved and sloped to give him privacy from the road, and he'd even taken the extra precaution of parking on the concrete apron to the right of the garage, where trees and shadow kept him virtually hidden from view.

He had allowed himself time to look around. Ever since he'd taken that first fifty dollars from the desk drawer, he'd realized something about himself. It wasn't strictly his need to come up with ready cash that kept him coming back, because even when he'd taken nothing at all, it was exhilarating to have free reign of the house. When he'd had the key made, he knew he would be back.

Memories of that day came to him in an endless-loop tape:

He'd felt the adrenaline boost as he crossed the threshold. This time he'd acted quickly, resisting the temptation to look around for other items. Opening the door just minutes later, he'd stepped into the sunlight and considered creating a little mayhem before he left, but resisted that urge too. The netsuke and cash were enough for now.

He'd stood on the doorstep, looking down at the spot where the welcome mat had been. Remembering Winston stomping on the flaming bag, he'd felt a twinge of remorse for pulling that juvenile stunt, and just for a second, he'd imagined what his old therapist would have to say. The flaming poop was exactly the kind of impulse he wasn't so good about controlling.

He was only paces away from freedom when, simultaneously, he heard and saw the approaching car, and saw the garage door begin to rise. He'd vaulted into the greenery, scratching his arm on the juniper bush and almost knocking over a planter. From this vantage point, he saw the black Cadillac slow and then stop. Winston, tall and gaunt, got out next to Derek's white Toyota Tundra and bent to peer through the windows. Then he straightened himself, removing his sunglasses to scan the yard and front step.

Derek held his breath, knowing at any moment he would have to raise his arms in defeat, but by some miracle he managed to elude detection. Winston's attention was back on the truck. He pulled on the door handle. It opened. He strode around to the passenger side. While his back was turned, Derek ducked out of his hiding place and darted behind both vehicles, ready to jump into his truck the second Winston pulled his Caddy into the garage.

What happened next didn't make sense, even to him. This was where the tape rewound, played again, rewound . . . He was not a violent person. And yet, his hand slipped under the tarp covering his truck bed, his fingers recognizing the shape of his wooden mallet, and curling around the handle.

Dudley's hands were in the glove box. Then they were unfolding the insurance papers. Hearing or sensing Derek behind him, he stood up suddenly, cracking his head audibly on the doorframe.

There was no thought that went into it, just the sudden urge to keep Winston from seeing his face. When he played it back in his mind, Derek wondered if it had been gravity alone that brought the mallet down on Dudley's left temple. The old man groaned and slumped forward, his forehead thwacking against the open glove box.

Before Derek had a chance to think, he'd stuffed Winston's limp body into a sitting position in the passenger seat of his truck and strapped him in, looking him over to make sure he was still breathing. There was no blood. When Derek jostled his shoulder, his head lolled to one side.

Snatching some paper towels from the side pocket, he jogged over to the Cadillac, which was still running, and pulled it into the garage, making sure he left no prints on the door handle or steering wheel.

It took him a few precious seconds to figure out that the automatic garage door button was built-in, just above the rear view mirror. He bolted out of the car and tried to scramble out before the garage door came down on him, but the motion detector caused it to rise. It took two more tries before he got the timing right.

Back in the truck, Winston snored. It was an obscene, gurgling mess of a sound. Just in case, Derek kept the mallet in his lap. As he drove away, he briefly considered whether Winston Dudley could have seen his face, but it had all happened too fast. Besides, there was a good chance the blow to his head had knocked out any memory of the incident. The man was out cold and even as Derek backed out of the driveway, he was formulating a plan to dump him in some out-of-the-way place before he ever regained consciousness.

He'd gone a few miles when the groaning began again. Derek acted fast. Pulling onto the shoulder of the road, he snagged two sweat-stained bandanas from under the seat, one to bind his wrists and the other as a blindfold. He did not want to think what he'd have to do if Winston could ID him.

He ducked his head when a car sped past, and then another. Christ, that's all he needed, to have someone report a trussed up old man in a white truck. He released the front seat and brought it forward as much as Winston's long legs allowed and reclined the seat-back to its maximum position. When he was fairly sure no one passing him would notice his slack-jawed passenger, he got back on the road.

Almost immediately, Winston began to cough.

"Aw, Jeez, not in my truck!" yelled Derek when the coughing turned into sounds of gagging, accompanied by the unmistakable odor of vomit. He clenched the wheel and berated the unconscious man, who, between weakening coughs, gasped for breath.

Stuck in the truck, having to listen to the disgusting gurgling and wheezing, Derek gasped for breath himself. "Choke on it, old man!" When the stench got worse, he pulled over a second time, throwing open his door just in time to spew all over his shoes. He pounded his fist against the door. "Look what you made me do, Asshole!"

More vehicles passed. Thank God nobody stopped to help. By the time Derek had emptied his belly and wiped off his shoes, the old man was silent.

He remembered a wooded area just a mile or so up the road, and decided that's where he would deposit Winston—minus the bandanas, of course—to sleep it off until he could walk to the road for help. With any luck, Old Mr. Dudley would never know how he'd gotten there or why he had such a ghastly headache.

When he got to the place, he parked about thirty yards into the widened turnaround, where the dense brush would conceal him from passing traffic. Rolling down the windows, he stumbled out, wading through tall grass to open the passenger door.

His passenger did not look so good, and it began to dawn on him why the stench had gotten so bad and why Winston had gotten so quiet. He put his fingers to the man's neck and felt for a pulse that was not there.

It hadn't been his fault. He hadn't intended any of it. Maybe the guy was sick anyway, and would have stroked out in his own living room if things hadn't gone the way they did. There must have been some reason Winston had succumbed from a little tap on the head while his decrepit old mother, who wasn't much bigger than a Munchkin, was still alive.

You aren't yourself lately," Erik had said to her last night. Cate had been about to prove his point by saying, "Well, who the hell am I then?" But she'd answered her own, unspoken question. She'd been behaving like her mother, at least the way Wanda had been behaving since she'd moved up to Minnesota—quick to take offense and sharp-tongued.

As she drove out to Jon Nord's place in the country, Cate rolled over in her mind the complicated nature of her relationship with her mother. It did not reach the level of her high school years, when things could escalate to full-blown war in minutes. No, this was a new, smoldering version, and she needed to do something before it became all-out conflict.

Wiping tears from her cheek, she wished she could talk it over with Robin. Nothing would be more healing than to grumble with Robin about her shopping trip with Wanda. They would laugh about her mother's hand grenade comment and she would begin, somewhere in the retelling, to see her mother in a more sympathetic light.

She'd never known why those sessions were so therapeutic, but usually when Cate put her feelings into words, Robin had the ability to elicit what was behind her reactions. And together, they could always wring the humorous tidbit out of even the most dire situations.

Traffic had picked up. When had rush hour started so early? It was only a little after three o'clock and, although traffic on Highway 55 was still moving at a good pace, drivers were suddenly edgier, cutting more sharply in front of each other and tightening the gaps between cars. Cate took a deep breath and turned on the radio, setting it to the jazz station.

She and Robin had had a few bumpy patches over the years, and it had always worked out. Sooner or later they'd sort it out and Cate would find out what she'd done to offend her. Not that it was always her fault. Sometimes Robin was just a little too tightly wrapped.

Like the time Robin's first born, Cass, fell at horse camp and had a concussion. Robin had fretted over it, blaming herself for letting her daughter go in the first place, and projecting that the girl might have long range consequences from her brain injury. Cate had told her to quit "awful-izing," and Robin had snapped back that Cate might understand if she'd been a mother herself.

She'd said nothing at the time, but for days afterwards, Cate had been aloof. Then one afternoon, Robin had shown up on her doorstep with a bag of potato chips and a bottle of Boone's Farm apple wine, a throwback to their college days. When she explained to Robin why she'd been so hurt, Robin said she couldn't even remember making the comment, but said, "What a horrible thing to say. I'm so sorry." And they'd gotten past it.

The radio crackled and she hit the button, changing it to MPR's "All Things Considered," but her thoughts were louder than the political punditry. She lowered her visor to block the direct glare of the afternoon sun. Just this morning Erik had been looking at the weather page of the Star Tribune and commented that the daytime hours and nighttime were almost equal. But today the sun was shining, and if you were dressed for it, the breeze wasn't chilly at all.

She passed through Plymouth and turned off at County Road 110.

Mitsy and Carlton would have loved to come along for a drive in the country. Going without her dogs to the remote shop of a man she'd never met, she felt suddenly vulnerable. And after all the flack she gave Robin about getting a dog for protection.

The rift she and Robin had their junior year at the U popped unbidden into her mind. It was all over Hugh, the guy Cate had been dating. After one drama too many, Robin said, "I'm done giving you advice just so you can ignore it, and then come back to me for comfort when it all goes to hell. Which it always does."

Not long afterwards, Hugh had hit her, and Cate had to admit Robin had been right. "What in the hell was I thinking?" she'd asked over and over. They started referring to him as Hugh What-In-The-Hell-Was-I-Thinking, and then, Hugh WITHWIT. Although she went on to date Doug Withwit, followed by a brief fling with Tom Withwit, her days of colossal mistakes were coming to an end. Over the following summer, Robin and Brad had set her up with his friend Erik, a fellow pre-med student, who treated her so well that at first she wondered what was wrong with him.

Remembering, Cate knew she and Robin would work through whatever the problem was. Maybe this time Robin had been the one to put distance between them, but it hadn't helped that Cate purposely scheduled the shopping trip with her mother to avoid the tea party.

Hoping she hadn't missed her turn, she wished she'd taken note of her odometer. The roads out here all seemed to have two names, a county number and a street name. In a few minutes she saw her turn.

Passing the sign for apples and then turning onto a dirt road just past the farm house, per his directions, she drove a few miles before seeing the pile of rocks that marked her destination. With a sigh of relief, she saw that she'd be on her way home well before dark.

The driveway went back a hundred yards or so. On the left was the double-wide mobile home and on the right, a log A-frame, just as he'd described. He'd told her the house belonged to his business partner, another artist. Parking near the trailer, she wondered why there were no other vehicles in sight. After double checking his directions, she swung her legs out of the car, slipping off her flats to exchange them for a pair of low boots. No one came out of either building when she slammed the car door.

Stepping over hummocks of dry mud and grass, she made her way to the door of the mobile home and knocked. And knocked again. The shade on one of the side windows was open just enough for her to see wood paneling and a television screen, but there was no sign anyone was home. "What a flake," she said as she turned away.

She breathed in deeply, listening to the subtle sounds of nature not drowned out by the city. A flock of ducks flew over, headed south. Something scurried ahead of her as she made her way over to the A-frame, scattering leaves as it went. The prairie grasses whispered as they caught the breeze.

The log structure had been recently built. Two rounds of concrete blocks marked what she assumed was the foundation for a garage. Ringing the doorbell, she expected no answer, and so she turned away after only one try.

Trudging down a well-worn path toward the back of the trailer she followed along a windbreak of pines. A maroon pole barn came into view, and beyond that, some kind of metal roof on stilts, under which was a strange, organic structure that could only be the kiln. It made her think of a whale or a giant slug, ungainly and yet beautiful.

Checking the pole barn first, she found it locked. She left the most interesting structure for last. As she got closer to the kiln, she could see it had two little windows, making it look less like a creature and more like a spaceship that had tunneled into the earth at a shallow angle.

On one end of the kiln, vaulting into the air and unprotected by the roof, was what appeared to be a smokestack. Nearby were three chairs, their canvas worn and stained, and an impressive woodpile. Her boots kicked up dust as she approached the entrance, where the smell of wood ash was strong.

Now that she could see into the mouth of the kiln, it didn't look nearly as large as she'd thought. The shelves at the back were similar to those she'd seen in gas or electric kilns. In the anterior slope, a single tier of flat rectangles atop columns had been constructed. Stonehenge in miniature. She wondered how Nord managed to load the shelves in a space where only a child would be able to stand upright.

Seized by the sudden sensation she was being watched, Cate froze. The shuffle of feet behind her made her spin around. She put her hand on the kiln to keep from losing her balance.

The man wore an odd grin, not exactly menacing, but not amused either. The way he stood, with his weight on the balls of his feet and his muscles coiled to spring, instantly put Cate on alert.

"Hi," she said, as casually as she could—not easy, considering that his sneaking up on her unannounced had nearly given her a heart attack.

"Hello." It was not a friendly greeting. The way his eyes moved over her, she knew he was reading her. She'd seen the same look in her bar-hopping days, men calculating how far they could take things. "You mind telling me what you're doing?"

"I was invited." This was surreal. "Are you Jon Nord?"

"Could be. Who are you?"

"Catherine Running Wolf." Normally, she would stick out her hand in greeting, but she wasn't keen on the idea of touching him. "Did I get the time wrong?"

He looked off to the side, as if trying to put it together in his mind, and then something shifted between them, a release of mistrust, and his shoulders relaxed. "Yeah, I'm Jon, but I guess you already figured that out." He laughed to himself and shook his head. "I completely forgot about you coming. Jeez, I'm sorry." He smoothed his hair.

Cate could see that she must have shaken him up a bit too. But now that neither of them felt threatened and her heart had regained a normal rhythm, she could see he was young, maybe in his twenties, and quite good looking. She had expected someone with the last name of Nord to look, well, Nordic.

He disarmed her with a grin. "Sorry, I have a lot on my mind. You wanted to replace a broken teapot, right?"

She nodded, and described the set she'd bought.

"I'll have to charge you."

"Of course. I didn't bring the broken one, but I have a pretty good color memory. I bought it at Jillian's shop in Stillwater."

"I know the one. Yeah, I think I have a couple that would work for you." He bobbed his head mechanically. "Yeah, okay, why don't you come with me." He gestured for her to follow him to the pole barn.

When he unlocked the door and flipped on the fluorescent lights, she was immediately impressed with the scale of his pottery business. The only potter she'd known had been able to fit into her basement everything she needed—her wheel, an electric kiln, a shelf for clay and glazes, tools and molds, and more shelves for the pots. In that small space, the potter had managed to create enough to keep her busy year-round.

From what she could see of Nord's operation, he was set up for more than a sideline business. She wondered if he could find a market for it all. After all, it took hard work, connections, and more than a little luck to break through in the art world. A lot of care had been taken here, and it had cost him no small amount of money to build and furnish this studio. His kiln was more elaborate than many she'd seen online last night. Even the simplest version of an anagama kiln cost several thousand dollars in materials alone.

Most of the shelves held materials, tools, and pottery in various stages, but there was plenty of space for more inventory.

He saw Cate looking at the only full section of shelves that held identical goblets, slender and graceful. When she commented on their pleasing shape, he said, "Those are for a little vineyard south of here." He picked up a goblet to show her the logo stamped in the clay. "I hate doing production work. There's nothing that stifles creativity more than throwing the same pot over and over. I might as well be flipping burgers."

She understood. She'd said something similar when Erik suggested it would be more efficient if she made duplicates of her jewelry. She tried to explain to him that creating a new design was the part she most loved.

Nord's walk became a swagger as he showed her around the studio, and he began to sound more like the man who had crafted that pompous artist statement. The more he talked about his work, the more off-putting she found him. Still, she had to admire his drive to have created this elaborate studio at a young age. It had taken her years to break into some of the juried shows for her little jewelry business.

Her eyes lit on the shelf that held several tea sets. "Take a look," he said, rocking back on his heels with his hands in his jacket pockets.

One teapot, in particular, would work as a replacement, she told him. He placed it in her hands. It was not exactly like the first one. The proportions were squattier, but she loved the splashes of color, which were similar to the first one. She ran her hands around it and checked the lid to make sure it wouldn't slip. It felt good in her hands.

"I'll give you a deal if you want to pay in cash," he said, naming his price. She handed him the bills and he stuck them in his wallet.

While he wrapped it up, she pointed to a vessel about four feet tall and almost three feet wide at the base. It obviously had not been fired yet. "How do you throw something that huge, much less fire it?"

"That one is going to take special care. That's a piece I will get top dollar for. Anyone who knows pottery knows it takes great upper body strength to throw a pot that size," he said.

He was slim, not at all the body builder type, she noted.

"Most potters don't even try anything that big, and the last thing I want is for it to blow up in the kiln." He explained that, although he usually let other people fire their pots in his kiln along with his own, he would not share his kiln when he fired this piece. "For that firing, I want only my own pots in there. See, not everyone is as careful as I am to make sure there are no air bubbles that will cause a pot to explode." He reached onto a high shelf behind him and handed her a mess of fired clay consisting of a wide-mouthed vase that was attached to a mug, and stuck to the mug was a cracked bowl and a brightly colored shard. "This is what happens when potters don't wedge the clay properly."

"Wow. Impressive." After examining the chimera pot from different angles, she handed it back. Pointing to the partition running the length of the building and ending well below the peaked roof, she asked what he had on the other side.

At first, she wondered if she'd offended him, but then he grinned and told her the other half was his business partner's studio. "He's not doing much lately, so I'm thinking if my business keeps growing and he doesn't need all of that space, maybe he'll let me use it as a showroom."

"Your partner lives in the log house?"

"When he's around, yeah."

She wanted to ask where his partner lived when he wasn't around. "Is he a potter too?'

He shook his head. "No, he does acrylic and oil, mixed media. He says he has a passion for other art forms, but as an artist, he's strictly two-dimensional. For a while, I tried to teach him to throw a pot, but he never really got the hang of it. You have to be centered yourself to throw properly. And you have to get spatial concepts." Jon snorted. "I mean, what kind of an artist builds a house with walls you can't hang a painting on?" He tented his hands together, like the angled walls of the A-frame house.

Picturing framed art hanging vertically from slanted walls, Cate burst out laughing.

"Right?" he said, bobbing his head. "He's got a few paintings on the back wall, but really, how dumb is that?"

"I've got to admit, it sounds pretty dumb."

He put her teapot in a double bag and set it on the work bench.

"I don't think I've ever been inside an A-frame."

He tilted his head, cracking his neck, and massaged his left shoulder. "I could let you take a look. He just called to say something came up and he won't be home today."

She was tempted.

"He doesn't care. We're pretty easy that way," Jon assured her. "I let him use my truck for hauling things, and he doesn't care if I borrow stuff. He comes and goes a lot, so I take care of things for him." He handed her the bag with her teapot. "Support the bottom with your hand. It's heavy."

She held it to her chest.

Sauntering toward the door, he commented on his partner, saying, "He's a good guy, but kind of a flake."

It takes a flake to recognize a flake, she thought, remembering she'd had the same impression of Jon Nord.

He's a Withwit!

The words popped into her head, as if Robin were saying them out loud. *Yeah, the world is full of Withwits*, she thought.

"Want to check it out?" He dangled a key from his fingertips.

"No, I'd better not. I just came to pick out one of your pots. Well, I'd hoped to get a little tour of your operation, too, so thank you for that. But I've definitely stayed longer than—" She stuck her hand in the pocket of her jeans to check the time on her cell phone. Frantically checking her other pockets, she said, "I must have dropped my cell phone." She cast her eyes around, and realized she'd have to retrace her steps.

Walking back to the anagama, she scanned the ground for the phone, wishing now that she'd kept the bright purple phone cover with rhinestones her mother had given her. It would make it easier to spot if she'd dropped that gaudy thing in the grass.

Vivian held the elevator door on the third floor, while her daughter and Kiki helped Era. It bothered her to see Era had lost the spring in her step. Wobbling a couple of steps on her own, Era paused in front of Frannie, who had gotten back to Meadowpoint well ahead of them, and was sitting on her usual bench.

"How are you feeling? Frannie asked.

"Just need to get my sea legs," Era said to Frannie before moving on.

Slowly they made their way to her apartment. When Vivian again broached the subject of calling the police, Era waved her hand in disgust. "Don't bother. They'll never believe me."

Could there be another reason she didn't want to involve the police, Vivian wondered? For the first time, she began to question Era's story—stories, actually. What was the likelihood that an able-bodied young man would get into their building without being noticed, try to kidnap some elderly woman, picking her at random, and then allow himself to be physically overpowered by her? Taken all by itself, it sounded absurd. Add to that the story of him stalking her to a public place, where again, unseen, he grabbed this same woman, this time at gunpoint, only to have her, once more, slip out of his clutches.

She glanced at Robin, and saw the same doubt playing across her features.

In her apartment, Era walked gingerly to her favorite chair and sank into it. Kiki propped a footstool under her feet and covered her with an afghan. "Your hands are like ice," Kiki said.

Vivian rushed to the kitchen. When she came back with a steaming cup of tea, Era's eyes were shut. Someone had taken her shoes off and replaced them with slippers. Crouching at her side, Kiki held her wrist in the way a nurse would check for a pulse.

Patting Era's other hand, Robin said, "Vivian brought you some tea. Do you think you could drink it? It will help warm you up."

Era slowly opened her eyes. "Tea? That's what got me in trouble in the first place." She eased her wrist out of Kiki's grasp so she could hold the cup with both hands. "You can stop checking me for a heartbeat," she said. "I'm not dead yet."

Vivian and Robin exchanged another look, and there was no doubt they were making the same calculations about the state of Era's health, both mental and physical. Even if everything she told them turned out to be true, it didn't explain why someone would target her, of all people, for such a bizarre crime.

Hearing voices, Vivian stepped into the hallway to find Iris, Daisy and Mabel—she could not bring herself to call the woman Sparky, even if she did smell of cigarettes and was missing an eyebrow. She told them what she knew, and said, "She needs her rest."

They went away, talking in hushed tones.

When she popped back inside, she saw Era had closed her eyes again, and decided to leave her in Robin's and Kiki's care. Instead of going to her own apartment, Vivian went to see if Wanda and Cate were back from their shopping trip.

When Wanda opened the door, Vivian could hear a recorded phone message playing in the background, a male voice saying he was excited to see Wanda this weekend. She could see how flustered Wanda was at having this private message overheard, and although

Vivian was dying to ask about this mystery man, she pretended she hadn't heard.

The message ended and Wanda invited her in. She had one foot over the threshold when Vivian heard what sounded like a parrot. She looked around for a cage. "Talk to me," the parrot said over and over.

Wanda looked startled. "Oh!" she said, spinning around. Her eyes settled on the table. "Cate must have left her phone here."

"Wanda, that isn't a phone ringing. It sounds like a parrot."

"That's her ringtone." Wanda snatched up the phone and answered it. The parrot went silent.

Vivian shook her head at the absurdity of a squawking phone. Pointing to the door, she indicated she was leaving. She went down to the second floor and was checking her mailbox when Wanda came up behind her. "Frannie told me you were here," she said.

Vivian laughed. "She's like Big Brother."

Inserting her key in the lock, Wanda pulled out her mail. "That was my son-in-law who called," she said. "He and Brad were supposed to play racquetball tonight, but Brad cancelled at the last minute. Something about wanting to be home when Robin got back."

Vivian frowned. "Why would Erik call you just to tell you that?"

"No, that's not why," Wanda said. When she shook her head, her chandelier earrings swayed. "He called Catherine's phone, and was expecting her to answer, so he just started talking. I cut him off to let him know he wasn't talking to Cate."

"Oh."

Vivian didn't know Erik well enough to understand his behavior, but she did know Brad, and the stated reason he'd changed his plans with Erik made no sense. She had observed how Brad and Robin were with each other. Somehow, she could not picture her son-in-law canceling his weekly game to rush home so he could be by his wife's side.

With a pang, Vivian realized her son-in-law wouldn't behave this way unless something serious was going on that she didn't know about. Her worries immediately zeroed in on Cass and Maya, at colleges on opposite coasts. So much could happen in those four years, when kids made mockery of all the good sense they'd been taught, and took stupid risks.

In the elevator, Wanda commented on how difficult it had been to hear Erik on the phone, with the dogs barking in the background.

"Maybe it was a ringtone."

"Ha ha! He said the dogs had been carrying on like that for a few minutes, walking on their toenails and barking. He said Carlton even howled. You've seen Carlton! He never howls. In fact, it was the dog's behavior that made Erik think to call and make sure Cate was okay. She's connected to those animals, you know." She shook her head and her earrings swayed again. "I can only imagine what Cate would make of that! She thinks she can understand what animals are saying. Robin calls her the Dog Whisperer."

The elevator door opened, and there sat Frannie, pretending not to notice when the phone in Wanda's jacket squawked. "Talk to me, talk to me, talk to me."

"Hello?" Wanda answered in a shaky voice. "Hi, Erik." She sat on the bench, forcing Frannie to move over.

Vivian gathered from the one-sided conversation that he wanted to know when his wife might be home and Wanda didn't know where Cate had gone or for how long.

"No, she just said something about going to some shop to look at pottery." After another pause, she said, "I have no idea where. I'm guessing she left a half an hour ago."

Wanda closed the phone and shoved it back in her pocket.

"Half an hour? We must have just missed her, "Vivian said.

Frannie, her lap full of her latest afghan, said, "You did. She left a few minutes after we all got back. That was about forty-five minutes ago."

"Do you know where she went?" they asked simultaneously.

"Not exactly. She was going to look at pottery. The place was west of here, about twenty or thirty minutes away." Her needles clicked away.

Wanda's mouth fell open. "How do you know this?" She put her hand on Frannie's arm, forcing her to look up.

"She told you." Before Wanda could protest, Frannie said, "No offense, but I find I can hear better if I'm not talking." She ducked her head and began to count her stitches out loud.

Wanda turned on her heel. Vivian followed.

They were almost to her door when Wanda and Vivian bumped into each other, startled by the grey blur that flew past them. "Is that Daisy's cat?" Wanda asked, her hand over her heart.

"Yep. Who would think that portly thing could move so fast?" Vivian was transfixed by the cat's behavior. Stopping directly in front of Era's apartment, the cat scratched the carpet frantically, and then stood on its hind legs to paw the door.

"Jane!" Daisy came around the corner, calling for her. No longer in her clothes from the tea party, she wore slacks and a sweatshirt. She thumped past them, using her cane. "I don't know what got into her!" she said as she passed. "She took off like a crazy thing and wouldn't come back when I called."

Vivian and Wanda followed close behind, forming a parade leading to Era's door. Wanda chuckled. "What makes you think she'd come when you call her? She's a cat!"

As soon as Kiki opened the door, Jane scuttled in and immediately leapt onto Era's lap, flattening her ears and narrowing her yellow eyes until Daisy, who was about to make a grab for her, backed away. Era, now awake and more like her old self, said, "Let her be. She's not bothering me." She stroked the cat's fur with her fingertips.

* * *

SITTING ON ERA'S STRAIGHT-BACKED chair, Robin watched all this with a sense of foreboding. If Cate were here, she would have a definite opinion about Jane's behavior. Robin had heard about a cat that made the rounds in some nursing home out east, taking up residence in the rooms of terminally ill patients and staying until they had passed on. No one knew how the cat sensed impending death, but it had been observed sniffing the patients before choosing the one he would curl up with. Rather than fearing the arrival of the cat, patients reported being comforted by its presence.

Her mother motioned to Robin to join her in Era's kitchen, and, speaking as quietly as she could, she began to tell her about Cate leaving her cell phone in Wanda's apartment, and how, not being able to reach Cate, Erik had talked to Wanda instead. Hearing about the dogs' barking only reinforced Robin's concerns about Era. She knew Cate had spent a lot of time with her dogs to train them not to bark unless there was danger. Between that and Daisy's cat, something was wrong.

She could feel her mother's discomfort and asked what was on her mind.

After some hesitation, Vivian said, "I'm concerned about something Erik said. Brad canceled his racquetball game with Erik because he wanted to be home for you. Does that mean something to you?"

Robin sensed her mother watching her for a reaction. She could feel her heart beating in her chest, and echoing in her ears. She had a pretty good idea what it meant. Brad being Brad, he had probably found some way to get her test results before she did. How, she wasn't sure, but he'd either had access to the clinic's electronic charts or had called in some favor to get around the HIPAA restrictions. His insistence on staying home to be with her could mean only one thing. She kept her voice calm. "I see. Did he say why?"

Vivian shook her head. "No, but I'm sure you could call him."

"I will in a bit." Uncomfortable under her mother's gaze, Robin turned and joined the others in the living room.

At Daisy's prompting, Era began to fill them in on a few of the missing details. Describing her supposed abduction, she said the man had taken her through the side door of the antique store. She explained he'd held his hand over her mouth while pinning her body to his chest to drag her down the stairs outside.

When asked for a physical description, she said he was "quite tall with light brown hair—just a kid, really." But when Daisy asked how she knew it was the same man who'd tried to take her from Meadowpoint Manor, Era said she recognized him by his dark hair. Era's story was getting more absurd by the minute, as she went into some detail about how this stranger drove her around and made her write a check. "He had a gun. I almost got it away from him earlier, but he pulled my hair when he saw me reaching for it."

Daisy was clearly bothered, whether by the stranger's brutality, or her suspicion that this whole thing might be fantasy. Tears ran down Kiki's face. Still on Era's lap, Jane rolled onto her side, draping herself over the woman's skinny legs.

Addressing the girl, Era said, "Don't cry, sweetie. I'm getting to the good part. My great escape!" She waved her hand with a flourish. Sitting a little taller in the chair, she said, "I was hoping that when we got to the bank, he would pull up to the window, and I would have to come up with something to get the teller's attention. So I wrote the check out to 'Cash,' as he demanded." She stopped, lowering her head while she thought. "Oh yes, I inverted the numbers so the numerical wasn't the same as the written amount."

"Did they notice?" Kiki asked.

"Oh, no, we didn't make it that far." She took a deep, shuddering breath. "I was hoping he wouldn't make me go inside. You see, if we had gotten that far, if he'd gotten me inside the bank and someone started questioning him, he had a gun, you see, and I didn't want him shooting up the place."

"But didn't you report your checkbook stolen when you lost your purse?" Robin asked.

"I did not lose it. My pocketbook was stolen. And the only items I reported were my credit cards. They sent my replacement cards right away."

"But how did you get away?" Kiki asked.

Smiling weakly, Era said, "I used a ruse. By then I'd figured out what he was trying to do the first time he kidnapped me. He was going to make me drain my checking and savings accounts and then he'd kill me. He would have no choice, since I'd seen his face. I knew the only way I would get out of there alive was to escape." She told them how she'd tricked him into looking the other way, which gave her a chance to open the door and simply walk away.

It was far-fetched, but the story began to coalesce in Robin's mind.

Daisy, too, seemed to be reconsidering her veracity. "Do you think you could identify the car?"

"It wasn't a car. It was a pickup truck." She said he'd kept the gun under the console, covered with a towel. Unable to identify the truck by model or license plate, she said it was either grey or dingy white, adding, "The temperature knob was broken and the clock was hours off." Folding her hands in her lap, she sat back smugly.

Suddenly Kiki bolted from the room. Even with the bathroom door closed behind her, they could hear her sobbing.

31

By the time they'd walked back to the kiln, she'd given up on finding her phone. Before turning back, she asked how he could load pottery in the low-ceilinged enclosure. "I don't see how you get in and out, much less how you'd do it, hauling a bunch of pots."

"You just crouch down. If you're working with a team, one person goes in and the others hand him pots. Go ahead. Check it out."

"Really?" Ignoring the sounds her knees made when she squatted down, Cate duck-walked into the kiln and immediately lost her balance. Planting her hands in the ashy rubble, she pushed herself up to a sitting position.

Jon talked to her from where he crouched near the entrance. "Are you okay?"

"I'm fine." She picked off the gravel that had gotten imbedded in the palm of her hand. One piece caught her attention. She held it up to get a closer look.

"Do you want a hand?"

"No, I'm just looking at this piece of bone. Oh, now it looks more like a tooth." She wished she had her glasses, but they were in her purse, right where she'd left it just outside the kiln. "How would a tooth wind up in here?"

"Hmm. It must have been in the soil. Probably from some wild animal." He gave a little chuckle.

Suddenly remembering the *Cat Who* book she'd been trying to recall in Jillian's shop, she said, "I read in a novel once that having organic matter in the kiln during a firing can give the pottery glaze all sorts of interesting effects."

"Yeah? I don't think that would happen. Fiction writers make up all kinds of shit."

When he came in, crouching at her side to get a better look, a beam of late afternoon light streamed in over her shoulder.

"Whoa," she said, dropping the tooth. "There's a filling in it!"

In the enclosed space, she could hear his breathing intensify.

"Give it to me. I'll ask my buddies if anyone lost a tooth." He held out his hand.

The sound in her head grew louder, until it became the roar of a fire. Images began to play like a slide show in her mind, accelerating at a dizzying rate. Nord's pottery, on the shelf in Stillwater, the lovely tea bowls and the single shard broken from her teapot, the gorgeous bowl her mother had turned into a waste basket. All with a slash of blood red.

He leaned closer. "What's wrong?"

"Somebody died in here." She didn't realize at first that she'd spoken the words out loud. In her mind, she leapt up and ran, but her body was paralyzed by the knowledge that she was about to die.

He began to back away, until his retreating shadow indicated he was standing just outside of the kiln, watching her. Neither of them moved. Breathing the ashes he'd stirred up, she coughed. Ashes, she suspected, that had once been a living, breathing human being.

"Who knows you're here?" His voice sounded tinny and far away, but his shadow did not waver.

"My husband and my friend. I told them where I was going and they're expecting me any time now."

The shadow's arm bent, and when it straightened once more, there was an object clutched in the shadow hand. "I don't think so."

She heaved herself to a crouching position, spun and flung herself at the entrance, aiming for his knees. He kicked her shoulder and she went down again on all fours. "Crawl back there," he said. "All the way to the back."

* * *

DAISY WAITED A FEW MINUTES before tapping on the bathroom door. Kiki, mascara smeared across one cheek, slowly opened it. She let Daisy lead her to the bedroom, where they sat on the edge of Era's bed.

"Your great-grandmother is safe," Daisy said. "It was a horrible thing for her to go through, but I think she's rather proud of herself, don't you?"

"I know she is, but . . ." She played with the ruffles on her skirt.

"But what?"

Kiki's voice was so soft, Daisy asked her to repeat herself. "Derek has a white truck." she said, louder this time.

"A lot of people drive white trucks," Daisy assured her.

She started swinging her legs so that her body bobbed forward and backward. "The clock doesn't work."

"Okay." Daisy stalled, thinking.

"And the knob is broken."

Daisy's skin prickled as the girl's words sunk in.

When Daisy tried to put her arm around the girl's shoulder, Kiki shook her off. "I knew something was wrong. Great-Gran says if you try to deny something, your guts will tell you it's wrong. Every time my stomach is a mess, it's because of him."

Daisy pulled away to face her. "That's good advice. She's a smart lady."

"I can't lose her! Great-Gran is all I've got." Her thin shoulders shook.

"I don't think you'll lose her—not yet." Daisy hoped that was true.

Kiki jumped up, went into the bathroom and came back with a roll of toilet paper. She unwound a hunk, wadded it up and blew her nose. "He's always going on and on about people who have money, and how they don't deserve it and he does."

Daisy definitely had a bad feeling now.

"I sometimes wonder if he just wants to marry me 'cause he thinks Grampa's probably dead and Great-Gran's gonna die, and then I'll be rich." She blew her nose again.

"He asked you to marry him?"

Kiki bit her lip. "We're kind of engaged."

Daisy was speechless. What had made her change her mind? And why would Derek jeopardize everything by abducting her great-grandmother, if he thought Kiki was going to inherit a fortune? There was no rhyme or reason to it.

Kiki shook her head as if to clear it. "I can't believe I ever trusted him. He always needs money and he gets really pissed when people don't pay him on time for the work he does. I heard him freaking out on the phone at some guy who owed him a lot of money." She stopped and blotted tears that had run down her chin. "I think it was, like, the next day that Grampa asked if I took his watch. Oh, I forgot to tell you." And then Kiki launched into a very strange story about a broken branch and a crow's nest.

Daisy interrupted. "Are you talking about Conrad, the man I met at your house?

"Yeah."

"What kind of vehicle does he drive?"

* * *

ROBIN'S PHONE RANG. Cate's husband was already talking when Robin held the phone to her ear.

". . . worried about Cate," he said. "I know it sounds stupid, but Mitsy tried dragging me to the door by my pants cuff."

She had never known any of their dogs to behave that way. "That is worrisome" she agreed.

"I know Cate went to see some man about pottery. I found a card for a potter named Jon Nord, but there's no address, and when I called the phone number listed, it rolls over to voicemail. I'm worried she might have had car trouble, and without a phone—"

"Give me the number." Grabbing a pen from her purse, and a magazine insert from the counter, she wrote what he told her.

He was still fretting. "If she got in trouble on some two-lane country road—"

Robin interrupted once more. "Give me a couple minutes. I'll see what I can find out." As soon as she hung up, she dug in her purse for her own cell phone and scrolled through her contacts.

When Jillian answered, she asked for Nord's address.

"I'll see where I send his checks."

She listened to fingernails clicking on the computer keyboard.

"Not sure what to do, here. I can give him a quick call and ask if it's okay to give out his address."

"He's not answering his phone. It's an emergency. My friend Cate—Catherine Running Wolf—went to see him and she's gone missing." Robin knew she was being overly dramatic, but Erik's worry had been contagious. She did not want to waste any more time. "I need to give it to the police."

That little subterfuge got Jillian's attention, as well as the attention of everyone in the room.

"Oh, my! Of course." As Jillian supplied the information, Robin wrote it down.

She hung up. After giving the *Cliff's Notes* version, she told those assembled in Era's apartment that she was going to find Cate.

It wasn't a great plan, but it was the best they could come up with in the moment. Leaving Cate's cell phone with Wanda, in case Nord should call to say Cate had never arrived, Robin and Kiki took off. The others would stay with Era, who agreed to call the police right away to report her abduction.

Almost as soon as they were on the road, Robin regretted allowing Kiki to come. It had been thoughtless and irresponsible to drag her—she was still a child, really—into whatever mess she was heading into.

She wasn't concerned for her own safety. As soon as she'd heard Brad was waiting at home for her, she'd assumed her cancer had returned. Oncologists treated advanced breast cancer as a chronic disease, with many patients living for years with it. But what would those years be like? More chemo and more pain? With this reference point, she understood why the residents of Meadowpoint Manor talked about sudden death as a better fate than a slow decline. On some level, Robin knew she would fight to live, but still, the quality of that life mattered to her.

Kiki, on the other hand, had nothing but possibilities ahead of her, and from the little Robin knew, whatever might be in the girl's future, it had to be an improvement on her past.

In the passenger seat, Kiki mapped out their route on her cell phone. With that phone in her lap so she could navigate, she punched in the numbers on Robin's cell phone and put it on speaker. Robin hadn't even known it had that feature.

The first words out of Erik's mouth were, "I know you think I'm overreacting." A sharp bark nearly drowned out his words.

"I trust your instincts." Robin told him she'd gotten the address and was heading there right now.

"By yourself?"

"No, Kiki's with me."

There was a pause. "What kind of name is that?"

"She's a friend." Robin rolled her eyes at Kiki. "And we're on speaker phone."

"Oh." Erik asked for the address, and Kiki read it to him.

"Erik, you don't need to come. I'm already feeling silly about this."

"Just call my cell phone when you know something."

Next, Kiki speed dialed Robin's mother, again putting her on speaker mode.

Vivian reported that they'd called the police, and someone would come shortly to talk to Era and make a report. Worry tinged her voice. "Honey, if you're concerned about Cate, why don't you call the police and have them check it out?"

"What would I say, Mom? There's nothing to tell. Cate's only been gone a couple of hours. The reason she can't call anyone is because she left her phone at Wanda's. There's no cause for alarm here."

Vivian cleared her throat. "Then why are you tearing off to find her?"

She couldn't explain it, even to herself.

For the next few miles, Kiki was silent. Robin imagined the girl might be suffering greatly if she believed she had brought such trouble into her great-grandmother's life. From what Robin understood about their relationship, Kiki knew very little about Derek. Was it possible she hadn't had any indication of his character until now? Or was it just because she couldn't bear to see the clues that had been there all along?

Cate had dated some unsavory characters in her day, too. Whatever psychic abilities she might possess, they never seemed to warn her and keep her from doing something stupid like she'd done today, going off on her own, without telling anyone where. Without her phone or her dogs. And after all the times she'd pressured Robin to adopt a dog for her own safety! What in the hell were you thinking, Cate?

But then it hit Robin that Cate may have tried to tell her when they'd run into each other yesterday at Meadowpoint. Cate had been about to invite Robin to go on a little trip with her. Was this the trip she'd meant? And she'd cut Cate off. Remembering the hurt in her friend's eyes when she'd gotten into the elevator, Robin got a lump in her throat.

Era's words came back to her, then. "Do be careful, dear," Era had cautioned her the day of her photo shoot. "There are places you should not go. Tell your friend." It had been *friend*, not *friends*. She knew that now. And she'd told her friend nothing.

"Turn here," Kiki said, pointing to the sign.

32

He paced outside the kiln. He couldn't freaking believe what was happening to him! Again! But this time it wasn't the Dudley curse. This time it was just some woman who liked his pottery, a nice person who happened to show up at the wrong place at the wrong time. He could hear her in there, trying to bargain with him, telling him she would never tell a soul if he let her go.

He knew that was a lie. It wasn't human nature to pass up a chance to hurt someone who'd hurt you. Some people just hurt others as a matter of course. Winston Dudley, for instance, didn't give a moment's thought to the little people he scammed. Derek knew Winston Dudley must have done something scammy, despite what his father had told him. Why else would the investment advisor not have put one single penny into the very mutual fund that he'd recommended to companies like his father's?

His father's company was inherited, just as Winston's money had been. Derek's family had lived in nice homes in similarly prestigious neighborhoods. They'd belonged to the same country club, where his father and Winston Dudley sometimes played golf together and threw back a few whiskey sours. This was the life Derek was supposed to inherit.

But that was all before Dudley Do-Wrong got greedy. Derek didn't believe he had actually been malicious. No, Winston Dudley hadn't thought about anyone but himself when he played with other people's savings like it was Monopoly money, playing it safe while advising others to overextend themselves to put hotels on Boardwalk and Park Place. In the end, the bank had scooped up all the money and all the playing pieces.

He heard sounds of movement coming from the kiln. His kiln, his fire-breathing dragon. His passion. When he looked inside, she was sitting at the back, doing nothing.

"Lie down on your stomach!" he ordered, and she complied. Sitting on his haunches, he watched her until he got a charley horse in his leg. He stood, keeping the kiln's opening in view, rocking back on his heels and forward on his toes, back and forth until the pain left him.

Pacing, he came to the conclusion there were no good solutions for the woman in the kiln, but he still racked his brains for one. "I'm creative," he said to himself. "I just need to come up with a creative solution." But his thoughts kept spinning off like little dust devils, driven by fear and confusion, in all directions.

Unfolding a canvas chair, he placed it where he could sit and keep an eye on her. "Why did you really come here?"

She turned her head toward his voice. "You invited me."

Oh, God, he did! First grabbing the old lady when she hadn't even recognized him, and then inviting this woman, just to show off his kiln and sell her one teapot. He leaned forward and called in to her. "I don't want to hurt you."

And he didn't. Catherine Running Wolf was one of the few people who really got it. He'd seen her bracelets, and she was a decent artist herself. Besides, she held his work in high regard. She was fascinated by the process of creating, just like he was. Not many of his customers thought much beyond getting a good deal and deciding whether or not the piece went with their living room furniture.

She wasn't like his mother, who refused to accept his chosen path and constantly harped at him to "to dress for success." Well, he'd seen firsthand that clothing guaranteed nothing. His father's tailored wardrobe hadn't changed overnight when his business went down the tubes, had it? Even after that, his mother continued to push him into the same business arena that had gobbled up their lives.

He'd tried for years to explain to her. His plans to be successful did not look anything like her plans for him. He just didn't have it in him to be part of that cut-throat world. Where would he be now if he had the money Dudley had pissed away, and a mother who valued his art? Not in the middle of this no-win disaster!

The more he considered his dismal options, the more the thought came to him: I'm not a killer. "I'm not a killer," he said out loud, and then repeated the words, louder this time. "I'm not a killer."

Her response was thick with sarcasm. "Thanks. I'm glad to hear it."

Maybe not so nice, after all. He felt a need to explain. "This is all just one big accident. I don't want to hurt you, but you don't leave me much choice." His voice cracked.

She was silent.

He got up and paced some more. "If I couldn't come up with the money, my landlord said he was going to have to evict me. He was counting on my rent to make his mortgage payment, and I couldn't pay the rent because some fat ass with more money than brains didn't pay me for the last job. Not like that's anything new."

The woman—Catherine—said something. He leaned over so he could see her face. She was sprawled on the ground, her lips were white with ash. "I didn't hear you," he said.

She coughed and a puff of ash blossomed under her raised head. "I'm sorry people treat you badly." This time she wasn't being sarcastic. "And I do believe you're not a killer."

He swallowed hard a few times to keep from crying.

"I think you want to do the right thing and let me go." He could tell she was trying to help him.

Even though he didn't mean to keep talking, the words spilled out anyway. "We had a great plan. I worked my ass off to pay for all this, and it was finally starting to pay off. My pottery is getting noticed. But these fucking, brainless, heartless assholes with money—they just don't care. Their lives are easy, they've always been easy, and it never occurs to them that the rest of us have to struggle. To them, paying me a few days late means nothing, but to me, it means my house, my car, my kiln, my shop, my whole fucking life." He slumped down into the chair and put his face in his hands.

"I understand. I really do."

Her voice was closer now.

He snapped his head up. She was crawling across the ground towards him! He jumped up. "Get back!" he yelled and brandished his pistol so she would know he meant business.

Her eyes got big and she backed up, still on her hands and knees.

Why had he ever trusted her? She was like everyone else, out for herself. Did she even consider how it would affect him if he let her out? She'd blab to the first person she saw.

Slowly, he stood and went to the woodpile. He had been saving the maple and alder for firing his biggest pot, but now it would have to serve another purpose. When he chucked an armload of wood in, she yelped like she'd been hit, even though they fell at least a foot away from her. He went back for more.

* * *

ROBIN SLOWED DOWN, coasting into the driveway. Cate's Range Rover was there, parked in the gravel patch near a trailer. Breathing a sigh of relief, she got out, looked in the windows of the SUV and checked the door. It was locked. Through the back window, Robin saw the pet cages Cate always had in the vehicle for transporting animals, and a fifty-pound sack of dog food.

While Robin knocked on the trailer door, Kiki rang the doorbell at the log A-frame. They shrugged at each other across the way, and then Robin watched as the girl slipped around the building. By the time Robin got there, Kiki had come around the other side to report she could see all the way through the house, and no one was home. The girl was holding herself tightly and her teeth chattered.

"I have a blanket in the car. You can wrap up in that." Robin was glad she was wearing her wool jacket.

Kiki didn't argue, and as soon as they were back in the car, she was eager to take the Faribault wool blanket Robin kept in her winter emergency kit.

Turning the key in the ignition, Robin drove forward on the bumpy dirt road. It led, she could now see, to a pole barn. Stopping only when she saw the "No Trespassing" sign strung between trees on either side, she backed the car up to a sheltered spot near a copse of trees.

"This place gives me the creeps," Kiki said, huddling under the blanket. She was still shivering.

When she'd seen the Range Rover, Robin had been relieved to see Cate had gotten here safely. But now Kiki's comment echoed her own sense of the place, and she was even more worried. That settled it. Although Kiki began to argue about having to stay in the car, she gave in when Robin said, "I don't know what I'm going to run into. I need you to be another pair of eyes and ears." Robin was about to tell her that if anyone should come, she should slide down onto the floor. About as effective as the duck and cover drills they had in grade school in preparation for a nuclear attack.

Just before Robin stepped out of the car, she reached for her phone.

"I set it on vibrate," Kiki told her.

Sticking the phone in her jacket pocket, she closed the door behind her with a *snick*. Led by instinct, she avoided going directly to the barn, instead she skirted a line of trees, trying to avoid getting snagged in the brambles or twisting an ankle. The flimsy shoes she wore for the tea party were hardly what she would have chosen for hiking over rubble and through prairie grass. She came to a small rise, and found it made a good observation post. Not too far from the pole barn was another structure, possibly a lean-to, but it was partially hidden by another stand of trees. Nord's studio, she reasoned, must be in that barn.

The wind had picked up, not much, but enough for her to feel the chill through her jacket. Scoping out the path she would have to take, she headed across the open space, stopping for a few seconds when she thought she heard someone talking. It might have been her imagination, because she didn't hear it again.

She could still remember how, as kids, she and her friends had enjoyed snooping around the neighborhood, which often involved some kind of trespassing. They took shortcuts through old Mrs. Shannon's yard, even though she'd told them not to. They stole apples from the Mallik's tree. They spied on Mr. Piper, who stripped down to his undershorts to hose down in the back yard after working in the garden. There was not much point to these adventures, except to take risks so they could savor the delicious thrill of almost getting caught. Holding their breath, their hearts thumping, they would keep going until someone gave the signal to run. Afterwards, they would squeal and huddle together as they relived their narrow escape.

So, here she was, trespassing once more, no longer a child but a ridiculous middle-aged woman, skulking about. Somehow it wasn't as fun as she remembered.

The dry prairie grasses swayed and brushed against each other, the sibilance menacing. A lower undertone came through, and this time she was more certain it was a man's voice. Her steps veered away from the path to the pole barn, as she was drawn now toward the lean-to and the structure beneath it.

She was only a few yards away when she caught movement. A male figure appeared, coming around the far end of the kiln, rounding the corner and stopping in front of the woodpile to load up his arms with wood. What had she been so worried about? Obviously this was Jon Nord, and he was putting wood in his wood-burning kiln. Now she really did feel foolish.

"Hello!" she called out. "Hello! Jon?"

He jerked his head up and froze.

Way to go, scare him half to death, she chided herself.

Then she heard a scream.

Waiting was a bore. Kiki watched Robin walk toward the building and then lost sight of her when the road dipped down. She wondered what was in the glove box. A packet of tissues, a nail file, an energy bar, some maps and a little zipper case with quarters and some small bills. She found a pack of gum and helped herself to a piece. Why did they call it a glove box, anyway, she wondered? Nobody ever kept gloves in there.

She checked her makeup in the mirror, brushed away a flake of mascara and wondered if Erik was going to come even though Robin told him not to. She picked up the paper which had the address on it. It was one of those things they stuck in magazines. She liked the ones you opened up so you could smell the perfume. This one said AARP. What an ugly name! She flipped it over and stared. It was the number Robin had written down, the one Erik read to her from Jon Nord's business card.

Except it was a number she already knew. She opened the address book on her phone, just to make sure, and there was the exact same number, right under Derek's name. Her stomach did a familiar flip, but instead of doubling over in pain, she felt the tight feeling move up her chest and into her throat. Suddenly she had to get out of the car.

Looking back and forth between the house and the trailer, she tried to make sense of it all. She let all of her thoughts go, took a big gulp of air, and then she began to pick up everything she knew about Derek, but in a different order. For starters, she remembered him telling some guy at a party that Derek Farmer was a lousy name for an artist. Obviously he'd changed it to make a better impression. There were still a lot of pieces missing, but she knew enough to know she had to get help.

She pressed the numbers 9-1-1 and was staring at the SEND button, wondering if she should push it, when a car pulled up. There were two barking dogs inside. The man with silver hair at the wheel had to be Erik. Running over to the car, she threw the door open, pushing the black lab's muzzle so she could get in. "Hurry," she yelled to Erik. "I think they're in trouble. Down there." She pointed at the path, and he gunned the engine.

"Careful, there's a chain across the road," she said, and he jerked the wheel, steering his fancy car around it. They bumped and bounced over a mess of rocks, stopping in front of the barn. As soon as he opened the car door, the dogs bolted.

Half running, half walking, Kiki told Erik as much as she could. Following the dogs, they ran in the direction of a weird building that looked like a super long igloo made of bricks.

And then all hell broke loose.

The screams sounded like they came from inside the igloo, and Erik started yelling for his wife. "Cate! Cate!" The dogs barked louder than ever, and then a guy yelled. Oh, God, she knew that voice!

Even in all the racket, she heard the gunshot, loud and clear.

Hardly breaking his stride, Erik shoved her to the ground and yelled at her to stay down. When she heard the second shot, she was up and running again.

And there, in front of her, was Derek, his arms flailing. He was screaming as he fought off the black lab.

Kiki couldn't move. Twice she watched the dog leap at Derek, trying to pull him down. The third time, those teeth latched onto Derek's arm and didn't let go.

Her eyes lit on something dark in the grass right in front of her. Now, with no hesitation, Kiki dropped down, crawling on her elbows to the long-haired dog. The poor thing was whimpering and kicking like it was trying to stand up.

Tuning out everything else, Kiki let the dog sniff her hand, and then put a calming hand on its chest. It was breathing okay. That was a good sign. "Don't be afraid," she said, running her fingers down the spine and the shoulders and flanks, then up and down all four legs.

She found the bleeding place, high on the dog's front leg. It wasn't a huge amount of blood, and after pushing aside the heavy fur, Kiki's fingertips found the wound. It was not a bullet hole, as she'd feared, at least not the kind that goes all the way in. *Thank you, God!* It was more like a gouge. It wasn't spurting blood, and she could feel a strong pulse. "Good girl," she said, close to the dog's ear.

Reaching down, her hands sticky with blood, she ripped off the bottom ruffle of Ashley's skirt. The whole outfit was a loss anyway. She tore the fabric again along the seam to make a long strip, rolling up the first couple inches to pack into the wound before wrapping the rest of it around the leg, ending with a clumsy knot. When she was done, the dog licked her hand.

"Stay," she said to the dog as she tuned back in to the craziness around her. Edging toward the place where all the noise had come from, she noticed the screaming had stopped. She shivered and pressed her body into the side of the brick igloo.

Very faintly, in the distance, a siren wailed. Carlton, the other dog, growled low in his throat. Kiki knew what that meant. You never wanted to mess with a dog that was giving you that message.

She moved her way down the length of the igloo until she saw Derek. He was on the ground, his legs twitching while the lab held onto his arm for dear life. Cate's husband, Erik, stood over him, his forehead bleeding and the knees of his pants torn out. A gun dangled from his hand. When the sirens were almost on top of them, he bent and laid the gun behind him on the ground.

Two policemen jumped out of their car, and ran right past her with their guns drawn, just like in the movies. She would never in her life have believed she'd be so happy to see the police, but right now she was ecstatic.

Erik and one of the cops talked while the other one holstered his gun and said something to Derek. Then Erik leaned over and stuck his arms into the igloo. A pair of hands grasped his and he pulled his wife out. Cate and Erik hugged, rocking from side to side, but then they let go and reached for Robin's hands. The first thing Robin asked was, "Where's Kiki?" She sounded frantic.

Erik looked up then, and saw her standing there. His smile looked like it might fall apart. "She's right here. She's okay."

Cate patted Kiki's shoulder as she brushed past her to tend to the injured dog.

When Robin pulled Kiki into her arms, they were both shaking. "I'm so sorry," they both said at the same time. Robin stroked the back of her head.

"Can you call your dog off?" one of the policemen called out.

Cate stood. She made her voice deeper. "Carlton, release." She only had to say it once.

Carlton let go of Derek's arm, but kept his head thrust forward and his entire body ready to spring into action again.

By the time they clicked the second cuff on Derek, all the fight had gone out of him. He stumbled a little when they lifted him to his feet and his head slumped forward. When they marched him to the police car, he would not even look at the girl he professed to love.

Still kneeling next to Mitsy, Cate looked up at Kiki with tears spilling down her face. Her lip was bleeding. Touching the dog's makeshift bandage, Cate asked, "Did you do this?"

Kiki nodded. "It was the best I could do." She knelt next to her. "Don't worry, the bullet didn't go all the way in. The bone isn't broken, I checked, but I'm pretty sure there's some soft tissue damage."

That seemed to make her feel better. Cate told Kiki she sounded like she knew a lot about veterinary medicine, and Kiki told her she watched a lot of programs on Animal Planet, especially the ones about first aid and surgery. "It's a really good sign that she's still alert," she added, stroking the dog's ears.

"Thank you," Cate said, and buried her face in the dog's fur.

The older policeman came over and told Cate he was calling the pet hospital to let them know a dog was coming in with a gunshot wound. "Just follow us. It's on the way to the station, maybe nine or ten miles from here."

"Let's just get her to the vet. We can come back for my car later," Cate said.

Erik, cradling Mitsy in his arms, didn't have to walk far to his car. Carlton plodded alongside them. After a long look at Derek, now slouched in the back seat of the police car, Cate got into her husband's car and Erik laid the dog on her lap. Carlton jumped up into the back seat. He could barely keep his eyes open.

The younger cop spent a few minutes making sure Robin and Kiki didn't need medical attention, and taking down their names and some other information. He turned to Kiki, and said, "You're the one that called 911."

She shook her head. "Not me. I was going to, but I never pushed send."

When he smiled, a dimple appeared on one cheek. "Well, you must have. Because as soon as they heard all the commotion from the dogs, and you said someone was in trouble, they started tracking you right away."

Well, she must have, then, but she still didn't remember doing it.

Watching the police take off with Derek or Jon, or whatever his real name was, Kiki shivered. She couldn't remember hating anyone so much. He had hurt everyone—Robin, Cate, Erik, the dogs, Great-Gran. . .

For the first time, she let herself think about what her body had been telling her all along. Her gut told her the only person who would have hurt her grampa was Derek.

Everyone who had been so good to her. Everyone that mattered. Harmed by a man she trusted.

"There's the white truck," Robin pointed to Derek's Tundra as they turned to leave. It was parked on the side of the barn where they wouldn't have seen it from the other direction.

Everyone looked exhausted, like a bunch of soldiers, Kiki thought.

Kiki grabbed her phone from the front seat of Robin's car.

"I think you need to call your great-grandmother," Robin said when they were underway. "Just to let her know we're fine and will be back in less than an hour. Oh, and make sure my mother gets the message too, okay?"

Robin saw she was shivering again and told her where the seat warmer button was. Kiki pressed the button and then covered herself with the blanket. As soon as her teeth stopped chattering, she made the call. Daisy answered the phone and said the police just left and Era was taking a little snooze.

She curled up in a ball and pulled the blanket over her head. She couldn't stop thinking about Derek and how he'd tricked her. But as much as she hated him, she hated herself. Not just for trusting him, but for lying to her grampa about him. None of this would've happened . . . She cried like she hadn't cried since she was a little kid.

* * *

VIVIAN ANSWERED THE DOOR to Era's apartment, and drew Robin to her. There were no tears or remonstrations. Era held Kiki's face in her hands. Wordlessly, their love was communicated.

Robin and Kiki told about the arrest of Derek Farmer, the man who had twice attempted to kidnap Era. There were still parts of the story they didn't know, and maybe they never would. There were also a few details she and Kiki kept to themselves. As a child, Robin had learned to edit the things she told her mother, who tended to worry obsessively ever since Robin's kidnapping. She could see Kiki was protecting her great-grandmother in the same way, and so together, they told the sanitized version, making it sound almost like an adventure.

Naturally, Wanda wanted to know all about Cate, and they assured her that her daughter was just fine, and would call her as soon as she got home from the animal hospital. That led to questions about how Mitsy had gotten hurt, and Robin simply said she'd hurt her leg and needed to be taken to the vet. When she praised Kiki's expert attention to the wounded animal, Era beamed at her great-granddaughter and nodded her approval.

Robin did not report, and probably never would, that she'd heard Cate's screams and found her friend lying on the floor of the kiln, her lips bruised and her fingernails torn and bleeding. Nor did she tell how Derek had threatened to shoot Robin if Cate tried anything stupid, or that he had shoved the gun in Robin's back and ordered her to throw more wood into the kiln. After that, he'd forced her to join her friend inside, where Cate had already begun to claw at the bricks around the little window to escape.

The thing Robin couldn't get out of her mind was that, despite the cruelty of his actions, his expression, in those last minutes, had not been anger, but sadness and regret. His last words to them, before the barking dogs announced their rescue, were, "You know I have to do this, don't you? But I'll shoot you first so you won't have to suffer."

In the retelling, Kiki slipped up when she said, "We got there just in time."

"What do you mean?" Era asked.

"I mean if we hadn't gotten there when we did, we—" She stopped herself in time. "He might have gotten away."

Nobody looked like they'd been fooled, but Kiki and Robin diverted other questions by saying there was still a big chunk of the drama that Cate would have to fill in.

Kiki told about seeing the identical phone number for both names, and figuring out Derek had been using a different name as an artist, even before Derek told it to the police. What Robin had not even told Kiki yet, was that the young man she'd been involved with had said enough to Cate to constitute a confession to murder. She would know soon enough, as would Era, but for tonight, this was enough for them to absorb.

Robin couldn't dissuade Kiki from telling the part of her story she'd kept hidden within her for too long. She told about meeting Derek and thinking it was love. She made no excuses. She said she'd sneaked around with him, and lied to her grandfather.

Sitting next to her on the couch, Era wrapped her arm around the girl and said, "You poor thing. You've had too much betrayal in your young life."

Kiki's reaction was a mixture of surprise and guilt, as if she didn't deserve kindness or understanding.

By the time Robin headed for home, it was dark. It wasn't until she neared her house that she remembered. Poor Brad had been waiting for hours for her, burdened with a message he would never have wanted to deliver.

Coming in through the kitchen, she heard the television and saw its flickering light in the porch. On the counter was her best crystal vase filled with white roses, the kind of arrangement she associated with funerals. A card propped against the vase had her name on it, in Brad's messy scrawl, but she didn't open it. The sympathy bouquet seemed a little premature.

"Robin?" Brad's voice was bleary, and she knew he'd fallen asleep waiting for her. The television went silent. When he stepped out of the room, the emotion showing on his face was almost more than she could bear. Overwhelmed with guilt at bringing so much pain into his life, she managed to say, "Hi, I'm so sorry I'm late. I didn't know—"

"It's okay, Robin. Erik already called to say you'd be back late. He also said you and Cate had quite a story to tell." He came to her because she couldn't seem to move. Giving her a quick kiss on the lips, he took her by the hand and led her to the porch. "Come tell me about your big day."

He sat on the extra wide chair and pulled her onto his lap.

"You first," she said, preparing herself.

Before he said a word, she was already numb.

After sleeping that night on Era's couch, Kiki woke from a strange dream to the sound of her great-grandmother's voice, so soft it was almost a whisper. Opening her eyes, she saw Era sitting at the table, two framed photographs in front of her on the table. She touched them lovingly as she spoke, moving back and forth between them. Kiki couldn't make out most of the words, but during the pauses Great-Gran would nod, as if she and the photos were having a conversation.

Kiki shut her eyes, not wanting to let on that she was awake. She had so much to work out in her head. In her dream, she had started to make sense of it all.

They were in an igloo that went back so far she couldn't see the end of it. She was sitting with Cate and Robin on one side, and facing them was her grampa. He sat on a big ice ledge. Even though the rest of them were dressed in normal clothes, he had a towel wrapped around him like people do when they're in a sauna. His eyes were closed. Suddenly, big pointy flames started shooting out of his head. The flames were beautiful, like they were made out of rainbows. The fire didn't seem to affect him. He opened his eyes, and his mouth turned up in a little smile when he saw her. She wanted to run to him. He didn't hate her after all. But as soon as she got up, he held up his hand, and suddenly her legs wouldn't move.

Now that she was awake, the dream pictures started to fall away until the only thing left was the heaviness of *knowing*. Knowing that what happened to her grampa would have to be a part of her forever.

"You're not fooling me."

She opened one eye to see Great-Gran standing only a couple of feet away, dressed in her fuzzy bathrobe and looking down at her with a mischievous smile.

"I know you're awake."

Kiki sat up and yawned.

"And I know you saw me talking to those pictures."

She felt like she'd done something wrong. "Yeah, but I didn't hear anything you said." On the floor next to her was a pile of clothes, and she remembered borrowing her great-gran's nightie last night, one of those high-necked things with short sleeves. "Were you talking to Grampa?"

She nodded slowly. "To him, and to his father," she said, and then she broke into a big grin. "Oh, I know they're just pictures, but it helps me to remember them when I see their faces. I sometimes think they help me get through the barrier between the worlds."

Kiki slid her eyes over to the pictures. "Do you think he can hear you?"

Era shrugged. "I can't prove it, but when I have a problem or a question, I talk it over with them and sometimes I get a very clear answer in my head."

She thought of a million things she wanted to ask. "What kind of problems?"

Era cocked her head and her eyes got misty. "I used to ask Gordon when I would be joining him, but I don't ask anymore. Time doesn't have the same meaning for him." She started to turn away.

But Great-Gran had said something about problems. "What problem were you talking about? Were you talking about me?"

She laughed. "Sweetie, you are not a problem. But we did have some conversation about you."

She waited. A picture came into her head of Derek seeing her in this old lady nightgown. He would laugh his butt off. She pressed her lips together to keep from crying.

"Let's get dressed and we'll talk about it over breakfast."

When she'd gotten dressed in Ashley's torn and dirty clothing, Kiki sat at the table and stared at her grandfather's picture. He was younger in the picture, but not so young that she didn't recognize him. He had the same look in his eyes that she remembered, gentle and intelligent. "I'm so sorry, Grampa," she whispered. "I was horrible to you." She listened for him to respond, but nothing magical happened. "You're not coming back, are you?"

Words didn't come into her head, but she could see something in his eyes that said he didn't hate her.

But even if he forgave her, she would always live knowing that their last words had been full of anger, and nothing she could do now would change what had happened afterwards.

That sadness, that knowing, would be almost impossible to live with, except for the other, brand new knowing that she was not just the unwanted daughter of parents who didn't know what to do with her. She was also the granddaughter and great-granddaughter of Winston Dudley and Era Dudley, two of the best people she'd ever known. And they would be a part of her forever.

While they made breakfast, Kiki wondered if Great-Gran had forgotten to tell her about the conversation. They set the table and sat down, and still she said nothing. By the time Kiki was about to remind her, Era said, "How do you feel about going back to school?"

"Is that what you and Grampa talked about?"

Era slathered butter and then marmalade on her toast. "One of the things."

Kiki had been thinking about that. School would mean giving up at least one of her jobs, and she would have to play catch-up with the other kids. Slowly, she nodded. "I do want to finish school. Even if I have to go to summer school, I want to graduate."

Era nodded. "And after high school?"

She had always assumed college was out of her reach. Get a job, get married, that's as far as she ever got when she pictured her future. But ever since her great-gran had hinted she might help her pay for college, she'd been thinking about what she wanted to study. "I want to work with animals," she said. "Maybe be a vet."

Era chewed on a piece of toast and took a sip of orange juice. "That is not an easy program. You'll have to take your studies very seriously, but you can do it. You're smarter than you give yourself credit for."

They talked over whether she should continue to work if she expected to finish her senior year of high school with the best grades possible. Kiki said she would quit her evening waitress job and talk to the coffee shop owner about cutting back to one shift on the weekend.

Era changed the subject. "How do you feel about living at your grandfather's house for now, at least until you graduate?"

That didn't feel right. "I don't know if I can do that. Not by myself, anyway."

Era pursed her lips together.

"Would you come live with me, Great-Gran? Please?"

She didn't answer right away, but then she said, "You don't want to be saddled with this old thing. No, sweetie. That house has too many stairs, and I have friends here—good friends. Besides, you need to start your own life with people your own age."

Kiki hung her head.

"Can you keep staying at your friend's apartment for now?"

She'd forgotten all about Ashley telling her she'd have to find another place to stay. Kiki blurted out, "Ashley's pregnant, and they're getting married. She just found out—" She stopped, trying to remember. Was that only two days ago?

* * *

WHILE ERIK WAS GIVING HIS STATEMENT to the police, Cate and Robin walked in a big circle on the well-kept grounds of the station.

Robin had been waiting for the right time to talk to Cate, and there was no better time. "I feel terrible I've been avoiding you, and I know I mishandled it. You were having such a tough time when you found out you have a brother, and I didn't want to throw anything else at you. It was a bad call and I'm sorry. I just wanted to wait until I knew for sure."

Cate stopped in her tracks.

She began to tell her about how hip pain had led her to call the doctor, which led her to having her hip ex-rayed, and when that test was inconclusive, they sent her for another, and then another.

Other than rapidly blinking her eyes, Cate's face showed no emotion.

"I'm fine!" Robin interrupted herself. "After all the tests, it wasn't cancer after all."

Cate took a deep breath. Her eyes shone.

"Every x-ray and scan showed some anomaly that had to be checked out. The hip turned out to be arthritis, but something else showed up on my spine. That turned out to be nothing, but then they found a hot spot on my collarbone. Two nights ago when I got home, Brad met me with a bottle of champagne and told me. They finally decided the spot on my collarbone was an injury, maybe a small fracture. When I asked Brad to show me the exact spot, he put his finger right here and I remembered how my shoulder hurt for weeks from the gun's recoil, you know, during our last—" She groped for the right word. "Adventure? Caper?"

"That would do it." Cate saw Erik beckoning them from the door. She hooked her arm through Robin's, and they followed him into the station.

"How did Brad get your test results before you did?" Cate turned to ask just before she went in for her interview.

Robin grinned. "He said if he told me, he'd have to kill me."

"That's not funny."

"That's what I said."

Cate's statement took the longest of the three. In retelling events to the policeman, she had to relive it. After Derek Farmer, aka Jon Nord, had forced her into the kiln at gunpoint, he had sat outside and rambled about how he hadn't killed "the old man," and that Winston had died all on his own. "He kept trying to convince me he wasn't a violent person, even while he was throwing wood into the kiln in preparation for its next firing," she said.

She got a chill, remembering her terror. She'd known immediately when she picked up the tooth exactly how Derek had disposed of Winston's body. She had time to picture it while she waited for Robin to pick up her distress signal.

She told the policeman it must have taken days to turn Era's son into nothing more than ash and a few pieces of bone and teeth. From what she'd learned about wood fire kilns, a potter would normally have plenty of help to load, fire and unload the pots. In his overblown artist statement, Nord had referred to "the hallucinogenic nights stoking a ravenous fire." If he had truly stayed up for three days and nights to stoke the fire all by himself, as he'd told her over the phone, he may very well have hallucinated.

With statements from Erik, Cate, Robin, Kiki and Era, the police were quick to extract a detailed confession from Derek Jon Farmer. His crimes were inept, but impressive in number and variety, including the murder of Winston Dudley, two attempted abductions of Winston's mother, extortion, several instances of theft, holding Cate and Robin against their will and threatening to kill them. Even so, he'd insisted he was nonviolent.

Derek didn't disclose what he'd done with Winston's car until the police broke the padlock on the far side of the pole barn and found the missing Cadillac. Derek filled in the blanks, then. In order to avoid suspicion, he'd left his own truck at a nearby auto mechanic, walked the two miles or so to get the Caddy and then drove it back to hide it in the barn. The next day he'd cadged a ride back to the shop with his landlord, Bob Gavin.

By then, Bob Gavin had already been deposed. He reported that he and Derek had clicked right away when Derek had answered an ad about renting the trailer. As soon as he found out his landlord was a painter, Derek had proposed the idea of an upscale artist community that would rent studio space and offer expensive retreats and workshops. They planned to build a gallery and be very selective about the other artists they would bring in. It was an exciting concept, and their big plans got even bigger. They borrowed money and went to work on the barn and the kiln, but it didn't take Gavin long to suggest the plan needed to be scaled back. Derek wouldn't hear of it. They continued to work long hours at their day jobs, finding little time and energy to create their art. Somehow they never got around to making a marketing plan to attract other artists to buy into the concept.

Soon the two artists realized if they couldn't come up with the cash, they would lose their entire dream—the land, the buildings, their tools and their vehicles. Derek, in particular, worked a lot of angles to come up with the money, Gavin said, but nothing panned out.

When Gavin told his partner he was going to look into foreclosure, he argued that he could paint just about anywhere, and suggested Derek could take his wheel and throw pots in a heated garage. Derek refused to discuss it. It would not be easy to find enough affordable land in a place that allowed unrestricted burning. And besides, the kiln was not moveable.

In the trailer, police found plenty of incriminating evidence, including several valuable Japanese carvings and Winston Dudley's computer, which was in plain sight on the coffee table. Forensics concluded Derek had been unsuccessful hacking into it.

* * *

BEST LAID PLANS," Wanda muttered when she arrived at Erik and Cate's door. She had bags under her eyes and her hair color was too dark. Her new down jacket, made for colder weather than today's, was too bulky.

When Cate asked if she was okay, she said, "I know I look like hell. I didn't sleep at all last night."

"You think you look like hell?" Cate's face was covered in abrasions no makeup could conceal, and she had a very purple bruise that went from chin to cheekbone.

Wanda opened her mouth for a retort, but instead, they both broke out in laughter when Cate held up her hands, showing several bandaged fingers and said, "We're the walking wounded here."

Mitsy whined. Her shoulder was shaved and swathed in gauze and tape, and circling her head was the Elizabethan collar she had to wear until her gunshot wound healed.

She and her mother were still laughing when the doorbell rang. Erik went to the door, and by the time they were all seated in the living room, the awkwardness was gone.

Ricky was tall, well over six feet, and when he sat on the low foot stool, his knees came to shoulder height, looking like a daddy long-legs spider. Carlton and Mitsy crowded in for attention.

Bunny was middle-aged cute, with a sweet smile, but she was nothing like the timid thing her name conjured. Her voice was deep and resonant, and her laugh came from the belly. Cate liked her instantly.

If Cate and Wanda had worried about how to break the ice in their first face to face meeting, they needn't have worried. There was nothing like bruises and bandages and dogs to get right to the good stories. Cate began to explain her appearance, and soon her mother and husband joined in.

"Good grief," Bunny blurted out when Cate got particularly animated. She gave her husband's shoulder a shove. "It's like listening to you!" Turning back to Cate, she said, "He talks with his hands just like you do, and just the way you tell a story—well, you'll see."

Ricky, petting a dog with each hand, looked back and forth between his mother and his sister. A small smile began at the corners of his mouth and spread.

35

May was Era's favorite month. As a child, she had gone out into the fields to pick wildflowers. Pasque flowers, buttercups, pussy-toes—she knew all their names. She used to get brown as a berry, and her hair was like corn silk. Two of her four best friends from those days had died long ago, one as an infantryman in the War, and one from the flu. The other two she'd lost track of, until she got a Christmas card from Bea's daughter saying Bea had died in a nursing home after a long bout with Alzheimer's.

May was her birthday month. She was too old for surprise parties, so she was glad when colorful invitations to her ninety-seventh birthday party were posted on the walls of Meadowpoint Manor. She hadn't needed or wanted presents in years, but Kiki had already told her about the two presents from her, and they didn't even have to be wrapped up.

Despite missing a month of school, Kiki had caught up and would be graduating on time, just a little over two weeks from now. The diploma with her great-granddaughter's name on it would be gift enough, but this morning, Kiki handed her a letter of admission into the University of Minnesota. She would live on campus, which would work out well, since her friend Ashley and her boyfriend had gotten married and had rented a townhouse—none too soon, with the baby due next week.

Era had been excited about this day ever since the invitation was posted. It was going to be a splendid birthday. She had bought a smart new dress and matching jacket, mauve with white piping, and had just come from the beauty shop.

Kiki, who had been downstairs helping with the preparations, came into the apartment carrying a plastic carton from which she took a most unusual corsage of white and purple flowers. "Pasque flowers and pussy toes," Kiki said, pinning it on her chest. She pirouetted in her pale pink party dress. "I clean up pretty good, don't I, Great-Gran?"

Era took her by both hands. "You're a treasure."

Walking into the party room and seeing the linens and china and flowers, Era thought back on the tea party she had never been allowed to finish. It had been such a lovely party, too. She held onto the loveliness of that day and this day, and so many days in between.

Whenever she began to feel despondent about all the things that happened last September, most especially the death of her only son, she would remind herself she was going to be graduating soon herself, and then she and Winston and his father, Gordon, would have eternity to laugh about both of her daring escapes.

The stories had already made her something of a celebrity at the Manor.

Robin and Cate, the two junior detectives, were all dressed up today. As the tables began to fill up, Era saw that they were all there, all the residents of the third floor—even the men—plus all five of the book club women. She'd gotten to know them all.

Ever since the tea party at her shop, Louise had taken to dropping by for a visit now and then. Foxy had offered to come to Meadowpoint Manor once a month to give free massages, and was so much in demand by the residents that she brought in two more volunteers. And Grace, what a blessing she had been for Kiki, who would someday be managing a great deal of money! Most of Winston's estate had been put in a trust for Kiki, as was Era's, and Grace had agreed to teach her the basics of money management. Besides setting aside money for school, Kiki asked if some of the money could be donated to Cate's animal shelter.

The lunch was catered, with two choices, chicken or Era's favorite, seafood Newburg on toast points. There were three layer cakes on pedestals. For as long as she could remember, Era had had Lady Baltimore cake every year for her birthday. Once the dinner plates had been cleared and cake and beverages had been served, Mary Gumm asked everyone to turn their chairs around for a special surprise.

Robin pressed a button on her laptop computer to start the slide show. There were photos, some beautiful, artistic shots of every resident, some candid and some posed. Music from the big band era playing in the background was soon drowned out by reactions from the crowd. Laughter exploded when they saw the black and white shot of half a dozen walkers lined up against the wall on movie night.

Murmurs at a close-up of several old hands reaching out to touch Carlton and Mitsy. Friendly teasing when the camera caught Frannie leaning ever so slightly to eavesdrop on the people at the next table. Frannie knitting. Virgil doffing his hat, with Iris coyly smiling up at him. Virgil in the atrium, looking like he and a squirrel were having a conversation. Daisy's cat curled up with her dolls, and one of Daisy looking directly into the camera with a dazzling smile. Vivian and Wanda playing cribbage. Wanda's sexy kitten heels. Vivian wearing a bathrobe and a red feather boa. Sparky waving at the camera, a cigarette in her hand. The couple who pretended not to be a couple, sitting on a bench outside, each with a long-stemmed rose in their teeth.

It went on for at least ten minutes before pictures of Era appeared on the screen. Robin had scanned several old photos from Era's albums, going all the way back to childhood. There were murmurs of remembering from the crowd. Then a couple of people let out a whoop when they recognized the music had shifted to "Ain't

Misbehavin'" and pretty soon they were all laughing and clapping. Her pictures took several more minutes, Era chugging down the hall, or checking herself in the hall mirror, or rubbing an aching knee. Era, her mouth open in song during an old-fashioned sing-along. The music changed to Fred Astaire singing "The Way You Look Tonight."

One of Era, seemingly asleep in the chair, stayed on the screen long enough for Era to notice the peculiar mist hanging just over her shoulder in the picture. Kiki leaned forward, staring. Then Kiki's picture was on the screen, rubbing Era's hands. In the last slide, Era, surrounded by half a dozen people, was throwing her head back in laughter, as if life had never been so good.

When the screen went blank, the room was silent. And then they erupted in applause once more. Before the program was officially over, Robin presented Era with an advance copy of the book they'd all been a part of. "The rest of you will have to wait until fall for the official release," she said.

Era made a show of handing the book back to her and saying, loud enough for everyone to hear, "I can wait. I plan to be around then, you know."

But after getting her laugh line, Era took the book back and held it to her chest.

The guests began to disperse. Era's five newest friends, the ones who called themselves No Ordinary Women, stayed to clean up. Robin suggested Era might want to rest after the festivities, and so Kiki went back to the apartment with her.

When Era was settled in her favorite chair, Kiki bent to tuck the afghan around her. Suddenly Kiki raised her head, a look of wonder in her eyes, and said, "Great-Gran, do you smell Old Spice?"

And just at that moment, Era felt the sensation of something brushing against her cheek, like a fleeting kiss.

-THE END-